THE PHILOSOPHER STONE

This is book one of the Stone series in which M. Locke Stone, Ph.D., sets out to fulfill his dream of applying the lessons of classic philosophy to modern day life.

Also by Philip Rushlow

Silent Night, the second in the Stone series

Sunny's Tale: The Watchbird

Wars, Women & Other Arguments

THE PHILOSOPHER STONE

Philip Rushlow

Writer's Showcase
San Jose, New York, Lincoln, Shanghai

The Philosopher Stone

Published by Writer's Showcase,
an imprint of iUniverse.com, Inc.

For information address:
iUniverse.com, Inc.
620 North 48th Street
Suite 201
Lincoln, NE 68504-3467
www.iuniverse.com

ISBN: 0-595-00080-0

For The Kid

What ever you do, you'll regret it.
Robert Heinlein

Foreword

Ron Carlson, recipient of the Ploughshares Cohen prize for fiction, whose Plan B for The Middle Class was selected as one of the five best books of 1992 by The New York Times, Director of Creative Writing at Arizona State University, says, "It is a tour de force, Rushlow writes with great authority."

Acknowledgements

Albert Iosue, M.D., a remarkable student of the mind who was the inspiration and my co-founding associate for The Institute of Applied Philosophy.

Mortimer Adler, Author and Philosopher, a man who is capable of releasing one's mind from its limitations.

Bonnie Rushlow, who thinks I am just being nice when I point out that she is God's favorite angel.

And dozens more but three's the limit. My high school Dramatics coach insisted on it.

Introduction

We are God's fiction. There is no other explanation. I offer my own case as an example; until a couple of years ago I considered my academic degrees and the years of study which both preceded and followed their attainment, an indulgence, a practical waste of time. There are few jobs for philosophers, even in teaching where there are more Ph.D's than interested students. And yet philosophy is the chief good among all pursuits, to study and ponder the thoughts of history's greatest thinkers is its own reward. With that in mind I decided study and thought must be considered a personal pleasure while making a living was something apart. Further, I decided were I to do a good job of the latter I might find more opportunities to indulge myself with the former. And so it came to pass. In time I was able to become the world's first practicing paid philosopher.

Just as an attorney has his law library in order to search out precedents and reach conclusive answers so too did I assemble a wonderful library of thought for use in developing solutions for every conceivable problem brought to my door, the handsome oak door bearing the polished brass nameplate; M. Locke Stone P.A. Counselor at Philosophy.

Having achieved sufficient financial success to ensure my modest needs I felt confident that I would rarely be disturbed in my primary pursuit of continuing study. My shingle was hung, which I felt showed proof of my being part of the modern commercial world. However, I couldn't imagine anyone would be interested in paying an hourly fee to obtain uncertain solutions to everyday problems. But I did feel confident that after more than twenty years of intense study I would be able to distill the thoughts of the great thinkers into common-sense suggestions should anyone actually venture to my door.

My only concerns were personal in nature. I wasn't certain of the source of my own idiosyncrasies and despite my years of study I suffered a shade of uncertainty. Could my suggestions be relied upon to benefit others? In fact, had my interest been in psychology rather than philosophy I could have been my own case study. No matter, damned few clients would likely show up to disturb my continuing studies. But, as an authentic business, I would at least be able to deduct related expenses in the unlikely event I developed additional income.

Earlier, having decided it would be necessary to earn and accumulate money in order to support my desired lifestyle, I discovered I was good at it. After completing an extended apprenticeship with a Boston agency I was convinced the advertising agency business could be run in a better way. I began to research other markets reasoning that some places would provide greater economic opportunities than others. Even old Socrates knew better than to make speeches in an empty cave.

"South Florida, Locke, that's where the expansion is. Everything from Palm Beach to Miami is growing faster than the federal government."

Steven Walinsky was a narrowly brilliant CPA and financial specialist who had become a friend and sometimes advisor during my years with the Boston firm. He was a straight-talking, hard-headed financial genius who held advanced degrees in law and accounting while retaining a love of philosophical debates.

"I don't know, Steven, I'm not a beach kind of guy. All that sunshine and jiggling flesh is intimidating. Oak paneling and fireplaces are more to my taste."

"I remind you, Locke, you said you wanted to make enough to afford the luxury of an early-out, what crude types call fuck-you money. You also indicated you wished to gather such goodies while you were still relatively young. If you mean it you better forget all things that dilute and divert. Understand ?"

"I suspect I need help, pray say on, maestro."

"Okay, one time special, I'll give you a million dollars worth of advice, you buy lunch."

"I don't know, Steven, your modesty is exceeded only by your appetite."

"Success, young turd, comes from a combination of talent, presentation, environment and purpose. Talent and presentation come from God, environment and purpose are options that control the amount and speed of success. You're a good looking guy who speaks well and you are the best client-growth man I've ever seen. God's been nice to you.

"There are four or five reasons to go into business: power, fame and money are the biggies. I watch this stuff like a hawk and my most successful clients share only one trait. They all know which of those they want and they never get off track. The dime-a-dozen guys want one thing today then something else tomorrow and they all wind up paddling around in circles. But, when you know your purpose, every decision, even the smallest one, gets made in accordance, instead of in conflict, with it. Do you know what I'm saying here?"

Steven was used to being smarter and faster than everyone around him from the time he was a kid. He spoke in a verbal shorthand style and constantly had to remind himself to slow down, that not everyone's brain whirred at his speed. Although he had to buy sex and he couldn't run forty yards to save his life, in matters of assets he was a star.

"I hate saying this but the point you make is totally logical and crystal clear."

"Jeez, Locke, I must have blown a battery or something. If a Philosophy major can keep up, I'm really slipping. But anyway, none of this means much in the desert, I've been watching my clients liquidate and take all their money to Florida for twenty years now. There's a fifty mile stretch of sand that borders a fifty mile ribbon of gold down there."

"I'd forgotten you have a Florida office. I figured it was mostly a vacation write-off."

"I didn't hear that. Two things, you open up down there and I can still run your money and taxes plus I guarantee you'll find a ton of clients."

"Sounds too easy."

"Nothing's easy. But you're good, I work with a lot of agency people and I know. But good doesn't count without money, you need the kind of backing that permits fast, impressive growth. When your clients are ordering forty, fifty million in media, you have to front the buys. What did I say a minute ago? People selling out and taking their money to Florida? They put it in banks when they get there with the result that Florida is *the* deposit surplus state. When banks have more interest-earning money coming in than they can place as interest-earning loans the resulting eagerness to lend creates fuel for the flames of growth. That's nice. When the streams are running over their banks it isn't hard to get wet."

After verifying everything with Steven, I decided on Fort Lauderdale, right in the middle of his "fifty-mile ribbon of gold."

It didn't take long to locate and develop my bread and butter client. I found a newly formed bank holding company whose principals were impressed with my big city credentials and flattered by my interest. In the environment of the times these people would be forced to grow steadily and rapidly and thus we were perfect for each other. I made their city, my city. I would open my agency in their town and, in return for their business, I would dedicate myself to their growth. It all worked exactly as a carefully constructed plan should. My business grew in all directions even as that of my primary client's grew in assets and offices. By the time they were ready to sell out at an incredible profit, so was I, and we all walked away feeling happy, wealthy and secretly smug.

Prologue

His mother sold him to the same men who bought her. Small as he was the only hiding place was behind the little Lizard God she kept on the old trunk in the corner. But she would quickly find him and he knew the fire would come, the terrible pain, the bad smelling, heavy, pushing, fire. If he cried the man might go away but then she would make the terrible noises, she would kick him and scream of her pain. When he bled he knew the pushing would soon stop and just the fire would stay inside. On his knees he would stare at the Lizard God who never made a sound. No one could hurt the Lizard God, he was silent and he made everyone afraid. If the screaming got too loud the Lizard God would open his eyes then they would all be dead.

When he kept his eyes closed he could become the Lizard God. The Lizard God did not cry and he would not cry. Sometimes he would peek to watch the Lizard God, waiting to see his eyes open and kill everyone except him. He would not kill him because when he grew up he would have stripes too, he would be the Lizard God, and he would always open his eyes. One day the Lizard God would stop the screaming and the pushing. He would make everyone's blood run into the dirt floor like the piss of the dogs who came to lick at the droppings.

I have always been a physical man despite my sedentary pursuits. Habit wakes me early and pushes me hard at the beginning of each day. It drives me as if I owe a desperate debt to the morning and if each installment isn't met the day will go badly every time. And so I pay with swimming, stress and weight workouts along with some short bursts of all-out running. Once done, once the payment is safely deposited in the bank of self approval, I can do as I wish. I can slouch around, read books, watch people, track butterflies, remember women or wonder how roads and buildings get completed when I can never catch anyone actually working at the site of such projects.

It isn't as if a practitioner of philosophy needs physical conditioning so it must be concluded, at least in my case, that it has to be something demanded by the inner man. It also helps in the matter of women.

The role of women in a man's life is often underestimated. My studies have convinced me that everything we males do, including the most remote and unlikely actions, relates to our ability to believe we can posses a female. That's a crude way of expressing it but, deep inside, that's how we men feel about it. She is *my* woman. Oh sure, I've *had* her. Like you to meet *my* wife. *I'm* gonna do her. *I* did her. It goes on, and it is expressed in such terms every day of the world. So I can only conclude that my daily workouts are rooted, at least in part, by a desire to look as attractive as possible to women. Regardless of all else, we are driven to attract and reproduce, or at least to attract.

My former business was advertising and since ad agencies have long been lopsided with female employees I was blessed, during those days, with endless opportunities to share countless pleasant times with women. But nothing is truly endless or comes without a price. Being with many women was a happy indulgence but it failed to turn up a soul mate. It left me without a special woman and the joys I imagined could only come from commitment. My strange lifestyle threatened to lead toward old bachelor status. Such thoughts, carrying their fragrance of failure, have lately begun to creep into my quiet moments.

My mid-life circumstance is that of a man with a passion for a remote calling who has opened an unlikely business. I may well be the first person in history to offer philosophical counseling to a disinterested world and to do so in a peculiar market. Fort Lauderdale is known for its beaches, beautiful women and every sort of vice. It's a nervous town which has suffered incredible growth from a laid back sandy strip to a giant, rich, metropolis, without any idea of whether to wear a tie or a skimpy bathing suit. And so I found myself in an unusual locale, open for business in a practice which was unlikely to generate much activity, and simultaneously open for new and improved female relationships, twenty or so years after the usual time for such searches.

I don't know whether or not I was prepared to meet Donna Delgado…but I sure as hell wasn't ready. Or perhaps I was too ready.

Despite the fact that little or no business was expected, I spent a good deal of time and money furnishing and decorating the reception area of my peculiar offices. I had located and purchased a small free standing corner building. The basic idea was to house my extensive library in a spacious and comfortable reading, study and meeting area which would occupy a section of approximately 1600 square feet. Alongside, I planned my personal office, with sufficient room for all my artifacts, in an adjacent space of approximately 800 square feet. Finally, the rest of the place, nearest the front door, would become a handsome reception and sitting area. The building itself was attractive with a brick exterior resulting in a pseudo federal style appearance. It was located just at the edge of the downtown business and financial area which, in turn, was edged by the swank streets which led past expensive homes and on toward the beach.

In all, a nice set-up, although a more practical person might have found it a foolish indulgence to have a whole, though smallish, building set up as an unreal business fronting nothing more than a place for one man to sit and read books. But in my case that was exactly the point, I liked it.

There was no secretary or receptionist seated in the front area because I didn't expect anyone to come calling just yet. Eventually someone would be needed if only to fill the space, help me keep things orderly and clean and smile when the postman arrived each day. In the meantime one of those little push-bells we all associate with hotel desks would do just fine.

Late on a Tuesday afternoon I was called out of a Reuben Velasois essay by an unexpected ping which, after a moment, registered as my little push-bell on the reception desk. Donna had arrived.

Feeling somewhat like Mr. Rogers peering out of his neighborhood, I held the door to the reception area open, staring at my surprising visitor. Her back was toward me as she faced the front door looking as if she was preparing to leave, as if she had changed her mind. Her skirt was smooth, tight, fluorescent pink, very short and showed the most attractive long legs and firm behind I could recall ever seeing. Her stockings were a strange open, net-like pattern and she wore silver spiked heels. A small black vest worn with a flimsy, lilac-colored, see-through blouse over no bra, and lots of cheap looking jewelry, completed the picture. The whole effect as she turned to face me was bizarre and yet she was beautiful, despite the make-up. She was young, my best guess was that she was somewhere between eighteen and thirty, give or take a few years.

Her soft voice didn't match the outfit, "I know I'm in the wrong place but I work around here. I've been watching this office come together and your sign outside is puzzling. If you are Stone, and it's okay, I would like to ask a couple of questions. If you're too busy, it can wait, it's probably not important, not really."

She was moving almost imperceptibly from side to side, as if she was unsure whether to stay or bolt. The impression she conveyed was that of one who was cautious by nature, deer-like, even shy, despite the gaudy clothing. The picture was definitely out of focus, her appearance didn't match the message of her eyes and the result made her look like an angel in drag.

"As the sign says, M. Locke Stone, at your service. Please come in and sit down. Apart from delivery people you're my first visitor, in honor of which you are granted three free questions."

My attempt at humor failed.

"Pardon my saying so," she said with a slight tilt of her long, green-blonde hair, " but you seem a little strange. Who are you, I mean, what do you do here?"

"Didn't take you long to use up your questions." I smiled, trying to be friendly. "First, I *am* Locke Stone and a little strange is probably accurate, but I'm in good health mentally and physically and I *am* a practicing philosopher. That means—"

"I know what that means. I mean, I know what philosophy is."

"Good, then you will understand when I say that just as people visit an attorney for advice and guidance concerning legal matters they can come to me for advice and guidance on living matters."

She looked at me with a controlled, flat gaze. Then, as if she had reached some decision, "I have a couple more questions if that's okay. Do you still want me to sit down?"

"Please," trying to pull my thoughts away from wondering how she was going to do that. The skirt, in fact her whole outfit, didn't seem to permit sitting. But she did so with remarkable grace as she kept her knees together and simply leaned those long legs to one side.

"Can you give me a for instance?"

"Sure, at least I'll try. Life doesn't come with directions and yet we often need them. How should we deal with the things which occur, countless things, endless challenges and difficulties? My role is to suggest the best way to proceed, to deal with events. Sometimes to lay out the options and point out the advantages and disadvantages."

"Like a priest."

"In a sense. But priests are somewhat like attorneys, one is limited to law the other to religion. Although I find both attorneys and priests often spread their advice far beyond their area of actual expertise."

"More like a Psychologist?" she asked.

"A Psychologist deals with problems of self whereas philosophy offers a choice of ways to deal with society and the resulting external problems. It's only a shade of difference but then most problems are only shades of perception."

"I understand. But you've opened this place right on the edge of downtown and everything west of here is bad news. I'm curious whether you expect uptown trade or street people for customers. Some places around here try for both."

"Truth is I don't expect much of either, I'm not sure anybody wants to talk to a Philosopher.

"Suppose some man had a problem like exposing himself to little kids and he came to see you about it?"

I hesitated at this point because I felt we were getting too specific but I wanted her to stay so I elected to keep going.

"Just the fact he came to see me would indicate he was on the right track and, sure, I could make some suggestions but I'd likely try to convince him to get professional psychological or psychiatric help."

"What kind of suggestions would you give the guy."

"Offhand I can't say, but without getting too far into it I'd probably point out how life is basically an endless succession of choices. With every step and every breath we are faced with choices. Each has its price, some choices are beneficial and worth the price, while others can be a poor bargain and actually destructive. The choices we make each moment are only of real importance in order to judge how we see and measure ourselves and therefore how we feel about ourselves and how we wind up behaving. The man you're talking about is making a lot of wrong choices. Once he understands, he might begin to make better ones. Do you understand?"

"How much do you charge?"

"Well, as far as I know this hasn't been done before so I'm not too sure about rates. Most likely I'll wind up charging something between the hourly rates of a priest and an attorney."

My humor failed again. She was so wonderfully attractive and yet odd, because of her costume, I didn't want her to leave. I wanted her to smile and stay a while.

"Like how much?" She was persistent.

"I don't know…it may depend on the person's ability to pay. If the man you're talking about came in here and he was just a regular working guy, I'd maybe charge him fifty dollars an hour."

"That isn't too much. Even I make more than that."

"And what do you do miss…you haven't given me your name."

"It's Donna. I'm a whore."

Same flat tone as if she said, Nurse, Stock Broker, Astronaut or Attorney, I didn't want Donna to be a whore. It didn't fit. That is, it fitted her clothing, but it didn't fit her. I waited for her to smile and say, "kidding." But she just looked at me with a level gaze.

Her look seemed to say, "And you, still another self-anointed, morally superior ass, one who is certain that your kind of whoring, whatever it is, is better than mine?" I actually fancied I could hear the words.

I said nothing as I walked over to look through one of the stained glass side-lights alongside the front door. The view was distorted by the passage of light through the altered translucency, but it was satisfying. It provided a different sense of the outside world.

"Most people around here won't trust you, you know, they've learned not to trust whatever they don't understand. And Philosophy? You can probably forget it."

"That's okay, there's no hurry. I guess I'll meet a few people in time."

"You keep staring out that window, is something wrong?" she asked as she stood up and faced me.

"I don't want to say anything that sounds judgmental."

"Maybe you just don't like speaking to whores. On second thought you're probably one of those bozos who likes to brag how he never bought it in his life. Maybe you're queer. But then, who cares? Anyway, I'm out of here. Sorry to just walk in on you," she headed for the door.

She sounded like someone trying to sound hard, it somehow sounded artificial. The possibility of some sort of prank flashed through my head so I asked, "How much, Donna?"

"Forget it Mr. Stone."

"I told you my price, we're just business people here, tell me yours. I'm not trying to insult you."

"You already have. Perhaps that's a way to make yourself feel superior, Mr. Stone, if so, you're welcome. Thank you for the information and good night."

To her credit she didn't slam the door as she left, instead she made a tiny almost-bow and flashed a head-tossing smile that deserved a standing ovation.

I had been out-debated and slam-dunked by a goddam tart and on top of everything else I felt like a real klutz.

II

For the next few days I found myself hoping it was Donna whenever I heard the stupid ping sound of the front desk bell. I wanted a rematch. But it was always the postman, or someone making a delivery, and once it was an actual client, of sorts.

"My name is Raymond, I'm a friend of Donna Delgado."

Now I knew her last name. Apart from his eyes nothing appeared wrong with Raymond. He stood about five nine, slightly receding hairline, soft features, cheap cut tan slacks and lifeless blazer. No raincoat. I always imagined flashers wearing raincoats or at least an overcoat, something they could sweep open with their back to the camera. It was the eyes that told me he was the man Donna had asked about, they were pulled down at the corners and they told his story as clearly as a print-out.

"Locke Stone, Raymond, how can I help you?" I was vamping because I couldn't imagine why Donna had sent him after leaving here in anger the other day. I wondered whether she might be getting even.

"Donna said I should come see you, she wants me to talk with you about stuff. And, oh yeah, she said to tell you she would settle up with you, for the bill, you know. Like I didn't want to come but she said I should. She's a good person and I'm okay. I never hurt anybody or nothin, just fooling around. I been arrested a few times, you know—"

"What else did Donna tell you, Raymond?"

"She said you would ask if I was one of her customers and I should tell you it's none of your business."

"Okay, c'mon back to the library. I've just made a fresh pot of coffee and we can talk a little."

He hesitated then followed me out of the reception room through the open area then into the conference room where all four walls were composed of floor to ceiling book shelves.

"You got any beer?" he asked.

"Sorry, maybe I should keep some on hand, you don't drink coffee?"

"Yeah, sure, it's just a beer might make me less nervous. Jesus, you read all these books?"

"I've read most of them, some two or three times but a lot of them are for reference and research. Do you read much, Raymond?"

"Nah, I got no time."

"Well then, what do you think about most often?"

"I don't think much, I don't like it, it's kinda like reading. I mean I keep books, so I use my eyes and I kinda have to think all day, but I worry about a few things."

"What do you worry about, Raymond?"

"Christ, I got plenty to worry about. I keep books for a warehouse company, we must be one of the last places in the country that's not on computer. How long is that gonna last? Then what? I don't know nothing about computers."

"Sounds like you're sitting in the back seat of a moving car with no driver. You want sugar? Cream?"

"Both, double sugar. What the hell does that mean anyway?"

"It means you let circumstances control your life, you let other people and things push you around. That's probably why you do a little flashing. Maybe it gets you a little bit even with things. I don't know. What do you think?"

"That's bullshit. I don't do that stuff, I just got arrested for taking a leak."

"Okay, Raymond. It doesn't matter. Besides, it's just a symptom, it's not the basic problem. You need to understand that I'm not a psychiatrist or a priest. I can't analyze you or prescribe any medication. I sure as hell can't absolve you of any sins or tell you whether anything is right or wrong. In fact, all I can do is talk to you like a man. By talking about what the great thinkers tell us we might be able to get a better idea of your capabilities. We can explore options, look into other ways to handle your life. Sometimes after developing an objective point of view you can begin to feel better about yourself and maybe take charge."

"My life? My life has been crap from the word go. I was born on the world's shit list and I never got off."

"Well perhaps that's what you want, Raymond. A lot of people prefer to blame somebody else for their problems, it takes away the need to take charge of themselves. I'll wager you know people who are always saying, hey, it's not my fault, I'm just unlucky. Understand, I'm not putting anyone down, Raymond. It's just a matter of choices, it's all choices. We all get to pick the life we want. Some people don't vote, some people don't want to make their own choices about life. Life can seem tough but it's all pretty simple. We're not born with problems or enemies but we often create both as we move along."

Raymond was a quiet man who was content to sit and talk for the next hour. I suspected he seldom had anyone to speak with and regardless of whether he understood or believed anything that was said, he listened well. For my part, I just spoke about the cumulative wisdom of the great philosophers from ancient times through the contemporary thinkers. Some of these men suffered great personal behavioral problems themselves and spent their lives trying to understand what makes people tick, themselves included. I wanted Raymond to accept the credentials of philosophy. My reasoning followed the line that if Raymond could be convinced of the value of thousands of years of careful thought, he might decide to believe in values and ethics. Perhaps, in time, he would come to believe in himself.

After an hour and a quarter I said, "Raymond, chances are pretty good you'll find yourself thinking about what we've said here today. When you come back we can talk about whatever interested you the most."

"I didn't understand a lot of stuff…I'm not sure what to think about."

"Think of our talks as water when you take a shower. Most of it may miss and wind up going down the drain but you'll use what you need to clean yourself. The big difference is we're trying to clean up your thinking instead of your body. Whatever sticks with you, whatever you think about is what we'll talk about next time. Don't worry about it and don't push it."

"Okay. But what do you think—"

"Raymond, my thinking doesn't matter, this is not some kind of test. There is only one person that actually matters to you and we'll talk about that next time. Let's set you up for twice a week. Thursday, same time, all right with you?"

"How long will this take, Doc?"

Hearing myself called "Doc" was unexpected, kind of nice. It didn't sound right for Raymond to call me, Locke, and Mr. Stone sounded wrong and, what the hell, I do have a doctorate.

"Don't know, Raymond. Like I said, this is new, no one's done it before. At some point you will either feel you got the message and don't need anymore talks or else you'll decide this isn't going anywhere and you're tired of it."

"What about Donna? I told her I'd stick it out."

"Stick it out? Is this some sort of penance? Sure, Raymond, you can stick it out, but not forever. When you're done, you're done, we don't need to spend her money foolishly. For right now let's knock it off or we'll have another hour to add to the bill. About Donna, how do you know her? I mean how—"

"She said to tell you it's none of your business, Doc."

"See you Thursday about ten, Raymond."

He stood, and for a moment I sensed he wanted to continue. As I walked ahead to show him out the door, it occurred to me that Raymond was a very lonely man. That we might have something in common was an unwelcome thought which was quickly brushed aside. Closing the outer door after Raymond left, I turned and sat in the nearby large winged back chair and heard myself muttering aloud, "I can't call her and I have no idea where she might be found or why I keep seeing her standing where she's not…and hearing her voice."

I understood that my intrusive thoughts of Donna were simply due to the novelty of it all. She's a beautiful woman who uses her beauty to make money. Lots of women do that, some marry wealthy men, others model or go on the stage, plenty of ways for good looking women to go. Still, I'd felt an instant physical attraction to her and when she told me what she does I acted like a schoolboy. I said everything wrong. Old "smooth Stone" had screwed up royally. My confusion could only have come from the fact that she was a puzzle. When I met her, I liked her. Probably wanted her as a friend, maybe a girl friend, but instead she was a whore. Big deal, I met a good looking woman who turns out to be a whore, so what. Sure, I didn't want her to be a whore, I don't deal with whores, maybe that's it, maybe I'm bothered because she brushed me off before I could dump her. It's not supposed to go that way, nothing fits. Her being a whore can't be ignored and yet there's something phony about it. On the other hand she's what she is, a rose is a rose is a rose. I can't be friends with a whore. Christ, I've never even spoken to a whore before, at least not knowingly. Damn!

Time to take up a new interest. There have been plenty of women in my life, so who needs Donna Delgado? Secretly, I've always felt pretty comfortable and confident around women. My nickname, Smooth Stone, was well deserved in my mind. Women never intimidated me and I've always been in control of every relationship. Just as it should be. Women want a man who can handle whatever comes along, they may always try to dominate and run things, but that's just a test. Well, Donna is no exception, I thought, I'll just ignore her and if she wants to know me better she'll just have to work at it. But look at this, instead of thinking about boats I'm permitting that silly woman to intrude again.

I hadn't been to a boat show for years, never to one where there were boats in the water. Walking through the packed and noisy admission tent at the Bahia Mar marina amazed me. The size of the crowd was over-whelming as were the number of displays and the prices; somehow, in a setting like this a million bucks became peanuts. I was interested in some sort of run-about, big enough to trust on the ocean yet small enough for one man to handle. Probably something with outboard power, good for running up and down the canals, inlets and rivers which lace Fort Lauderdale. My apartment includes dock space so I should get a boat. Never mind that, apart from riding in someone else's once in a while, my knowledge of boats and boating amounted to almost nothing.

Wandering through the dry-land exhibit areas where the smallest water craft and sport stuff was displayed, my attention was repeatedly pulled outside, toward the outrageous luxury boats that were priced beyond the reach of ordinary millionaires. One was especially impressive, it was large enough to carry a helicopter strapped to its own landing pad.

At that moment the crowd's attention was caught by a small knot of people coming from the main salon onto the deck of this spectacular ves-sel. Two photographers, along with three or four of their assistants, were backing in front of the actor-models taking shots with fill-in flashes. It was a small, high-action, event in progress with people shouting directions and waving their arms as if to stress their special importance. The photo-ses-sion subjects were trying to respond to all these directions while appearing not to do so.

In the middle of it all Donna Delgado smiled and turned toward her escort in a typical advertising pose. She looked incredibly good. No fan-tastic, hokey, tacky, street-working clothes this afternoon: hair, nails, make-up and sports clothes were all perfect. She was a page right out of Vogue. Having run countless photo shoots with dozens of models I was able to recognize that Donna was good, extremely good. I quickly turned away after watching for a moment. A sting of embarrassment caught me by surprise. Guilt rose in my chest, almost as if I followed her here hoping to see her again. A wagon full of Psychologists, never mind Philosophers, wouldn't be able to explain the confusion swirling around me as I quickly walked away.

"Nobody's supposed to stroll around a boat show in sunny Florida looking so mean."

The voice was full of music as Sharon Stern, a friend from my ad agency days took my arm and began to walk alongside.

"Lord, Stone, it's been too long. And I think about you every day."

"Sharon, talk about surprise, you're looking as spectacular as ever. Is Ben working this show? Are you still living in Atlanta?"

"Ben's hoping to sign up a couple of new outlets here and in Miami. I came along exactly because I was determined to look you up."

Her smile conveyed a special combination of warmth and welcome.

"And surprise, here you are, at a boat show no less. I'll pretend you came here looking for me. Don't answer that, instead, tell me everything that's happened after you sold out. Remember, I haven't seen you since New York and that's no way to treat a sensuous, loving, old friend."

"You've heard it all before and now I've finally done it. My library is gathered in one place and there's a shingle out front in case anyone wants to debate angels on pin-heads, or just pin-heads for that matter."

"Back up, please. When we got together in the city last year you had just sold out. I assumed the world's best ad man would just move on to bigger things."

"Sharon, I was never really an ad man, I'm a Philosopher, you know that. I went into business to make enough money to quit, to do what I've always wanted to do."

"You're serious aren't you? None of us ever actually believed you when you talked about sitting by the side of the road acting as a friend to mankind."

"Yep. Well, I meant it. I bought a little building to house all my books and the sign out front says "Philosopher For Hire at Reasonable Rates."

"Are you doing any business?"

"No, it's too soon, and probably too weird. But there is this girl—"

"With you, there's always *this girl*…"

"Not like that. This one is really strange. She looks and speaks like a class act but she claims to be a common street whore and yet I know she's a model, a damn good one in fact."

"Doesn't sound like your style regardless of how well she speaks."

I don't know, it's just that nothing adds up, nothing makes sense. The little I can get on her makes her out to be some kind of local Saint, she sent my first customer in with instructions that she would pay the bill."

"Has she paid?"

"No. I'm thinking she's actually a successful model who only pretended to be a whore, but that makes no sense. And then she may turn out to be just another phony. Hey, where are you leading me?" I asked as she pulled me around a corner and headed away from the main display area. "Did I ever ask you that question the thousand times you led me astray?

Sharon had been a lover-pal for nearly ten years during my advertising agency days. Part of the fun was finding off-beat and unusual places, even unusual ways, to make love. She was a rare combination of gutsy and cautious: anything, anyplace, any way, all made for great fun and games. But Sharon would never, ever, take any chance of doing anything which might embarrass "Big Ben," her older, traveling-man husband. Our mutual pleasure was enhanced by our understanding that we could never be in love, regardless of how much we were deeply in like. Now here she was, like a pop-up memory. I suspected she brought exactly the sort of perspective that was needed in my life, and not a minute too soon.

"Nope, you never asked. Bless you for that and bless you for right now. Let's go."

Sharon had been setting up a hospitality suite for the evening's activities scheduled to begin about six. That provided us with two or three hours to fill with talking, sharing and sweet, good-friends loving. Having nothing to prove and knowing precisely how to ring each other's chimes enabled us to create a sensational afternoon. It was highlighted with every shade of relaxed total vulnerability; that rare combination only possible with old and trusted friends.

After making plans to see each other during the few days while she would be in town, I returned from the hotel, which was situated adjacent to the boat show area, intending to resume boat-shopping.

"I'm not up to it," I said to a large, potted, tropical plant alongside the show entrance. The oversize orange flower just nodded wisely in the flow of artificially cooled air blowing across it's face.

I decided to head for the office to pick up some light reading before going to my favorite bar where the blackened Grouper sandwiches were perfect and the beer was so cold it brought on palate-chill. The western sky was working it's pink and mauve sunset light show against a pillow-pile of clouds forming out over the everglades as I angled the car into a spot in front of my office. I tend to be alert in this part of downtown as daylight fades. So the tall, slender, young man standing alongside a parade of newspaper vending machines just off the corner caught my attention. He was looking in my direction and while there was no specific reason to do so I kept my eye on him while putting my key into the lock and step-ping inside. Stopping for a moment, I glanced through the vertical blinds of the reception area to see that he was still there, still watching.

After using the front bathroom, washing my hands and splashing cold water on my face, I walked to the library to pick up the nearly finished Will and Ariel Durant biography. After scattering the day's mail around in case something worthwhile arrived, I decided to check the answering serv-ice. Nothing which couldn't wait until tomorrow. Putting out the light in the library darkened the whole place. Damn. I had forgotten there was no light on in the reception area and by now it had grown so dark that the room was pitch black. Carefully, I felt my way to the reception room where I saw a shadow cast from a street light cross the window moving toward the front door. Motionlessly, I waited for a knock or a ring but everything was soft silence. The place was still dark as I began to shuffle my way toward the rear door. I wanted to gain the advantage of approaching whoever was at the front door from an angle of my choosing.

Slipping outside, my neck hairs went on alert. There was an odd chill somewhere in my bowels. The rear door quietly closed and automatically locked behind me. I tried to walk Indian-quiet along the sidewalk leading toward the front entrance.

The same young man was peering in my front window.

"Can I help you?" Spoken in the most authoritative voice I could summon.

"Jesus, man, you scared the crap outta me."

"Why were you peering into my front window?"

"Is this your place? Are you Stone?"

"Yes. Now why were you peering in my window?"

"I saw you go in but it's dark and I wondered if you were still inside."

No street talk, no slurring or obscure words from this young man. He actually spoke clearly and well which made me feel a touch more at ease, as I said, "What can I do for you?"

"Donna Delgado's pushin' my baby sister to come see you and I wanted to check you out before I tell her it's okay. You got a problem with that?"

"Just one. I don't want to talk with your baby sister. Not unless you or some other adult is willing to come with her. Then you can ask questions and check me out all you want. But it has to be during office hours."

"You ain't showing no office hours."

"I didn't expect such crowds, I'll have to post them. In the meantime it's ten to four, Monday through Friday. When do you and your sister want to come in?"

"Shit, man, I ain't comin' with her. She's thirteen, I ain't nobody's Momma."

"Then I won't see her. That's the deal. Perhaps you wouldn't have to come every time. What's your sister's name?"

She's Aleena Wakins. Donna told her to come tomorrow morning."

"Well, you'll have to tell her to forget it, unless you decide to come along."

"Forget it? She's fucked up and I want to keep her from doing the wrong thing, that's all."

"What's the wrong thing?"

"Having the kid is the wrong thing, and don't be givin me no righteous shit. It's wrong for her and that's it."

"Well, now I really don't want to see her, with or without you. Please tell her to just forget it, I'm no physician, certainly not an obstetrician."

"It ain't her belly that's fucked up, man, it's her head. That's why Donna's sending her to you."

"And you want her to abort the baby, right?"

"Yeah. She's thirteen, black, not sure who's kid it is and neither one's gonna have a chance. She's gotta do school, get herself together and get a decent life started with a righteous man before she should have any kids. You know what I'm saying's true. She's too damn young to know anything. Stupid little bitch thinks it'll be nice to have a child to love. She'll have a dozen and they'll all be trash."

Maybe it was the body language, or the voice but whatever it was he made me feel his frustration. It added a tight quality to his voice. I guessed he had to be feeling like he was wall-bumping, wasting his time, wallowing in the sort of nightmare we all want to turn away from. And I felt it, as if years of frustration were shaping his voice. It's a lot easier to screw up your own life, I thought, than it is to watch someone you love do it to themselves.

"What's your name?"

"Why you wanna know?"

"Look fella, I don't think I can do you or your sister any good and I don't know why Donna thinks so. She doesn't even know me, but if you want to talk about this we'll go have coffee instead of standing here and I need to know what to call you."

"Coffee? I don't want no damn coffee."

"Fair enough. I don't want no damn coffee either. This is actually better because we can both forget it and be on our way."

Turning, I began walking toward my car.

Before closing the car door, I glanced back, but he hadn't moved. Feeling slightly depressed, I drove away. I didn't understand what Donna was doing or why she was sending these people to see me. It was clear that Raymond, and now this young man's sister, needed help but did they need philosophy? It was obvious that Donna was plugged into this community, but I wasn't. I wasn't making any connections with these people. So, what the hell was I doing anyway? I just wanted to read my damn books and now I felt like a phony, just another over-educated dilettante playing stupid games. What could I tell some thirteen-year old girl about having a baby ? Perhaps she needed to have something out of a life that was giving her nothing. But she has a brother who cares, she's got someone who loves her and that's more than a lot of people have. Hell, it's more than I have.

"Dammit!"

Hitting the brakes, I made a U-turn and drove back toward my office. My headlights washed the corner and illuminated the front entrance. The floor level of the building interior is a couple of feet higher than the street so the front door opens onto a chatahooche-rock, set-back which is under the roof. From there two steps lead down to the sidewalk on both sides with a single wooden post at the corner. He was sitting on the stone surface leaning against the support post.

He's smiling for Christ's sake, what is that about?

Angling in I stopped the car and got out facing him.

"Evening, Philosopher Stone. You came back faster than I expected."

"Yeah and I'm sure to regret it. This whole business about Donna, your sister, and whatever else is going on bothers me. If you don't want coffee, okay. But I'm hungry, so c'mon along while I get something to eat. If you care enough about your sister's problems to check me out we can at least talk about it. Who knows, maybe we can do each other some good."

He regarded me curiously for a moment then cocked his head to one side and flashed a five hundred watt smile, "M'name is James and I *will* let you buy me dinner because *my* time is dee-vine and because you had guts enough to come back."

The guy had a great smile, but I made myself a bet that he was tougher than toenails. He appeared to be full of smarts, giving me the feeling he was a straight up kind of guy. I was bucking all the odds here: I'm at least twice his age and staring across a racial gap handicapped with environmental, traditional, genetic, religious and educational canyons. It would probably be easier to raise Plato's ghost than to communicate with this man. But I knew I had to try, for my sake if not his. Anyway, I had nothing to lose by trying, except maybe dinner.

James wore an ecru color, knit shirt under a black, lightweight warm up Jacket, brown slacks and actual tie-up leather shoes. He was obviously different. As we turned onto the seventeenth street causeway he looked across at me with a flat stare, "I don't guess we be finding any soul food over here."

"James, how about you forget the color thing for an hour?" I said. "It's going to be tough enough for us to communicate across our age barrier."

"All right, it was a cheap shot," he grinned. "Besides, it'd be bad shit, fightin' on our first date."

III

The lounge was low of ceiling and high on TV. Eight overhead sets were spaced so at least one could be seen from every seat and each was showing a different type of sporting event. The waitresses were all nice looking women. Most of them had graduated from being nubile sex pots to efficient, heard-it-all, no nonsense, thirty or so year-old types. Most had a child or two at home, usually a husband or a live-in who, too often, was living off of her wages and tips. Laurie led James and me to my regular booth along the back wall with a quiet, "How they hanging, Smooth?"

After we ordered our beer, James said, "I heard that. *Smooth*, what is that? You doin that woman?"

"Smooth is a nick-name," I replied. "It has hung on since football days in high school and on through college in Boston."

"You any good?"

"Not like you mean. Just good enough to have fun but never good enough to even think about big time."

"You from Boston?"

"No. But after graduating I needed something practical, some way to make some money so I went to work in advertising, joined an agency in Boston and learned the trade."

Laurie brought an ice coated pitcher of beer with a floating plastic bag of cubes to keep it right.

"How about a bowl of steamed shrimp for us to chew a while? " I asked.

James kept prying me open with questions, which was fine with me. He seemed as eager to learn about me as I was to know about him. Best to let him dig first. He might acquire a bit of trust in me, failing that our relationship would never get off the blocks.

"Football, advertising, how come you hanging a Philosopher sign?"

"A couple of big questions bugged me all my life. Such as, what the hell is going on, what are we doing and why are we here?"

"Those questions bother a lot of folks."

"That's true. In my case I decided to go for answers." I was trying to decide how far to go with James. He was obviously smart. I quickly decided to stick with one of my basic rules, to speak at your own level, if your listener doesn't understand that's his problem. But never speak down.

"After reading and studying everything I could find in school and on my own, I wound up with a degree in Philosophy, no money and no way to get any."

"So okay, you're a Philosopher and—"

"Wrong. Studying Philosophy doesn't make anyone a Philosopher. Knowing what a hundred other guys, who were real philosophers, thought about life doesn't give anyone the capability of adding to the cumulative knowledge. In fact the bartender or the guy picking up aluminum cans outside may be more of a true philosopher. A college degree is a badge of discipline, not a source of wisdom."

I felt the sort of pleasure a teacher must occasionally feel when I looked into James' eyes. This young product of the neighborhood, clearly understood every word I'd said.

"Like I was saying, before the interruption," spoken with a slit-eyed smile, "you got a sign says you got something to tell people. Now everybody around here's waiting to see what kind of humbug you goin' be runnin."

The bowl of cold, spiced shrimp arrived and James excused himself to wash up before hand-peeling the appetizer. When I returned after doing my own ablutions he was popping shrimp with a vengeance.

"I've been thinking about what you said, James. You know, about folks waiting to see what's happening. The truth is I am too. Do you want to hear about this stuff?"

"Better than watching wrestling, maybe, I'll let you know. You're really asking; can I understand? Go ahead, I'll let you know if the words get too big."

"Good. I don't think this has ever been done before. But, what the hell, it seems right to me. I mean a physician studies to learn how to help heal sick people, a philosopher also studies and he should be able to help people think better and feel a little better. That makes sense, don't you think?"

"Shit, man, you *are* a fool if you ask me. Everybody's fucked up, but the only ones who admit it are already too far gone. All the rest are flopping around like fish outta water trying to hide it. Lots'a messed up people around, some sick, some stupid, some scared. And you don't know Jack-shit about these people, let alone how to help 'em."

"You're right. But, who else is helping?"

Like a pair of sparring beetles the two of us slowly and cautiously backed away from the main event and dipped into sports and boat show talk while we worked through our blackened Grouper sandwiches and the rest of the beer. After I ordered coffee, James wiped his lips and stood.

"I gotta go. Thanks for dinner."

"Wait'll we're paid up so I can run you back."

"Don't need it, I got some business here on the strip."

I stuck out my hand, "Will you be bringing your sister in?"

He stared at my outstretched hand for a moment, then shook it, "We'll be there at ten…maybe just one time."

"Good. Perhaps we'll all learn something, James."

Aleena Wakins eyes were those of a thirty year-old and they looked everywhere except at me. Obviously, she was having no part of visual contact. On the other hand, I was trying to keep from guessing whether her skinny thirteen year-old body was showing signs of pregnancy. I was as uncomfortable as she and her brother looked. I didn't want to be here, neither did they. I wanted to say, *This is a mistake. Donna is trying to get us together in order to help a child make an adult decision and I don't have a goddam clue. I can't help you people, I can't speak to a pregnant girl who doesn't even want to be here. This is stupid, let's forget the whole thing.* The speech sounded good in my head but I didn't have the courage to deliver it.

Instead, I looked toward Aleena with an attempted poker face and said, "Please tell me why you're here, Aleena?"

"I told Donna about what James wanted me to do."

"And what happened?"

"She said to come here because you could maybe tell me how to think about things."

"You mean like help you decide?" This was like pulling teeth.

"I guess so. But" she looked up, "I already know how to think."

"Lena, honey," James voice sounded full of love even as it verbally punched at her, "if you knew how to think you wouldn't be knocked up. You'd know better than to let them boys at you all the time. They don't think nothin about you, they just struttin an ruttin."

"It ain't the boys I care about, James, it's my baby that—"

I stood up to gain attention, "Let's stop right here before we get too far down a bad road. If we're going to accomplish anything it's important we speak in basic, exact terms. It will help if we can avoid word pictures which emphasize things we imagine. Aleena, physically you're an adult female, your body produces eggs and one of those eggs has become fertilized. *That's* the issue you're dealing with at this moment.

"If you start thinking and talking about a sweet, walking, talking, little child then we're wasting our time. I don't want to sound harsh but it's a difficult decision and we should try to speak as factually as possible. The fertilized egg you carry should not be diminished or enhanced, it's exactly what it is. No more, no less. One day, you'll be a grown woman and perhaps that fertilized egg you carry *might* have become a person. But all those things are in the future. It's important that we concentrate only on right *now* stuff."

We were seated in the reception area. James crossed his legs and I could see that the bottom of his shoe looked new. The sole was scuffed but the raised section toward the heel was shiny and unmarked. Glancing at Aleena, I saw that she looked exactly as young as her thirteen years. She was sitting in a large overstuffed chair with her hands folded in her lap as she looked at me for the first time. "You got any soda?"

To myself; *Soda? She doesn't understand or give a damn about anything that was just said.*

"Through that door and you'll see a refrigerator. In fact c'mon, James let's all walk back there. I could use some coffee. I don't think I'm making any sense."

"Not much so far, Stone."

We settled around the small circular table placed among the random assortment of filing cabinets, unpacked boxes, a microwave oven, a refrigerator and an unused desk.

"You charge the same price for talkin in the junk room as you do up front?"

"Being here makes you an insider, James, not everyone gets to see the back room. Aleena, are you comfortable here?"

"No matter."

Pouty little bimbo. "Well, probably no one is comfortable anywhere around here in the first place. The only reason we're here is because of Donna, and I don't know why she thinks we can accomplish anything but we do know she thinks a lot of you two. For her sake we ought to decide whether or not we can get anything done or whether we should just forget the whole thing and save her some money."

"Bullshit, Stone. You been trying to duck this thing from the beginning. It's not me an Lena that hafta decide. We showed our ass, we're here, you're the one who has to step up and stand tall. My sister needs some help in deciding what to do. She's sure not gonna listen to me but Donna thinks she might listen to you. So, deal the cards, let's see what you got."

Leaning forward, I rested my head on my hand savoring a favorite small fantasy in which I am standing at a lectern in a walnut paneled conference area with deep green leather chairs, extolling my principle beliefs. The distillation of intelligence gathered over the years is being explained to a small select uptown clientele of well dressed professionals and their indulged women. Nice. Probably never.

Looking up, I caught Aleena's eye, " I don't have the foggiest idea of what to tell you, Aleena. When it comes to advising a girl your age, I'm lost. So let's just try to forget who we are and put aside the thousands of reasons we can't communicate. We'll discuss all the things that might apply and may help you make your decision. The only possible way for any decision to be right for you is when it has been made by you. Are you with me? Do you want to try this?"

"Yes."

"We'll just jump in and start rambling around until we hit stuff that's interesting, you should ask questions or make comments whenever you feel like it. Okay, we are born without any instructions about how to live this life we've chosen. I say chosen as an expression of one of many different theories available. According to the particular one I'm thinking of, we choose to be born and we do so with a special learning experience in mind. Following that scenario you are a black female because you have chosen to be born as such. You came this time to learn something and that's the way you can best learn it."

Aleena's eyes rolled upward.

"Chose to be black, and pregnant?" James sputtered. "What kinda shit you layin' down, Stone? Aleena, I know Donna loves you, but she done sent you to a crazy man."

"That makes it even, James, Aleena's got a crazy advisor and a weird brother. There are lot's of theories about life and unless you can tell me you know which is the right one, I choose to respect them all. Choosing to learn and coming back to do it is part of one particular theory. Those folks are satisfied that most of us, perhaps all of us, live a lot of lifetimes, just as we live a lot of days during any particular lifetime.

"None of this matters unless it provides thoughts and information that may help you understand your personal situation. The point is there are numerous theories and each is usually based on interesting patterns of logic. The trick is to find the one that feels right to you and then use it to help you create a good life.

"Anyway, regardless of how we get here, it's as I said, we sure don't come with instructions. Life would be a lot easier if you had a rule book explaining everything so whenever you had a question, like the one you have now, you could just look it up and read the right answer. Some people believe the bible does that job, other people find their answers in booze or tarot cards. Some guys, like me, read everything they can about what the smartest men in history have said about living a good life. In the end none of us *knows* what is right. Not even you, James. We all have to make up our own mind and that includes you, Aleena.

"Since we're here, the first thing to decide is whether you believe these sessions can help you in some way. You don't have a lot of time before you make up your mind. So talk to me, Aleena, is this making any sense to you?"

"I think so."

"Well, all right, tell me."

"Like, I need to make my decision fast and…" she shuffled her feet back and forth, leaned over and stared at the floor, "it needs to fit something, some ideas maybe. Maybe some things that will keep helping me, right?"

"Good start, you're surprising me. That's nice. Mostly we'll talk about the kind of life you want to live. Not just right now but for the future too. Sometimes the best way to correct today things is to make a good plan for the future. Future plans can often correct today's actions. But we'll talk about your whole life and we'll try to make a picture of how you want things to turn out. If we can do that, if we can make a good, clear, strong picture for you to hold in your head then I can promise you it will come true. No matter how unbelievable your picture turns out to be."

After a moment during which everyone was quiet, James got up, walked over to Aleena and put his arm around her shoulder.

"Baby sister, you know I love you and you know what I want you to do. I'm not satisfied this guy can help you with anything. I think maybe he's nuts. But it's all up to you, we can forget all this and just talk it out ourselves or you can come here for a while. It's whatever you what."

Aleena crossed her ankles, put her hands together as she squeezed them between her knees and looked down at her feet, "I'd like to come, maybe for just a little bit."

Well, I thought, *somebody's about to learn something. Most likely it's the guy holding my coffee cup.*

Not knowing what else to do I continued telling Aleena the theory of life according to Stone. Searching for a viable connection, a foundation upon which to build I talked about religion. Explaining, for example, that some people felt God was unknown and unknowable. That these people were Agnostics who might feel overwhelmed with spiritual awe yet feel certain all attempts to explain, define and thereby limit God, were merely efforts to elevate one particular collection of myths over all others.

I told how Atheists rejected the concept of God, preferring in some cases, to believe life is a random chemical accident. How that doesn't make them lost souls because they also have an assortment of theories about how to live life in a manner that helps and pleasures them.

I went on to explain that most people wanted to belong and feel needed and certain in their faith. I was careful to explain that while organized religion might sometimes become overbearing, it was nevertheless composed in the main of people who could be skilled at comforting and supporting each other. That they formed important sub-communities of good efforts. That it didn't matter whether the group was conservative or liberal, Christian, Jewish or one of the Eastern faiths, the idea was still to locate the one which made the most sense to you.

If Aleena was to respect herself, I said, then she must first be able to respect the beliefs and efforts of all others. In our first session it was important to make a start toward helping her feel her own importance. Including her perfect place in society, the benefits of confusion and despair and, finally, the possible cumulative value of learning.

Rambling, at times feeling too extended, too vulnerable. Then I would deliberately force such feelings aside sensing that if I shielded myself, she and James would do the same. Knowing *they* would know, feeling that at the first lie, the first shard of hypocrisy, I would lose them both. It was exhausting and difficult and after an hour I was drained. But they listened and they knew that, regardless of whether my tale made any sense or not, it was genuine.

When I finally refilled my cup and sat down without speaking, James looked at his sister and smiled, "Honey, I told you he was nuts."

Then he turned the smile on me and said, "Same time tomorrow?"

For the first time, I felt I might have made some progress.

The envelope had been pushed through the mail slot in the front door and it was covered with the scattered pieces of a later mail delivery. The only address was "Not so smooth Stone" and five one hundred dollar bills appeared when I tore the end open. The money was wrapped in cream color note paper bearing a single word followed by a single initial; "Thanks, D."

The use of the nick-name alerted me that Donna must have been speaking with James Wakins, the only person who knew about it. That bothered me. I felt like a total outsider and worse yet, as if I were being manipulated. I pulled open the top drawer of the reception desk and tossed the money, still in the envelope, inside. This had to be the end of the whole damn scene. I didn't like it. It wasn't amusing and I didn't need to spend my time being aggravated by an increasingly strange cast. I would tell James, his sister, even Raymond the flasher, the game was over; no more consultations.

They'll have to tell Donna to come get her money back because I want no part of it. Screw this stuff, life is just too short and too goddam scary with this group. I'll stay with my books. Abstract thought is better than reality and I can just think along with Kuhn and Montesquieu or debate Spinoza and Pascal. Somebody once said, "Philosophy bakes no bread." Well it doesn't have to break any eggs or try to solve real problems either, but this philosopher needs to have a drink and get laid and so I shall.

At certain times of the year the light over south Florida is as alive with ethereal beauty as the fabled painter's light of Firenze. As day exits stage-west and before night falls, the peach-colored sky along the horizon forms a background for clouds of soft pale blue with bright pink intermingled puffs ranging to hot reds Schiaparelli could never match. In some magical way the light reflects back and forth between gulf and ocean, building an extravagant proof that we are part of something more glorious than we can imagine. It stops me every time.

The voice startled me. It sounded as part of the diminishing light, to come from everywhere, until she spoke the second time.

"Nice…isn't it? Full moon tonight, the shrimp will be running at the inlet. Want to go shrimping?"

"Sure. Where the hell have you been, Donna?"

"Is something bothering you, Stone?"

"You're damn right. You're sending me these messed up people without asking. You're dumping money in my mail chute like I'm a goddam street musician. And we haven't talked about any of this stuff."

She was wearing jeans and a cut-off sweat shirt. Her hair was pulled back into a ponytail and I was hit with a surprising and preposterous urge; I wanted to take her in my arms so badly I nearly doubled over with a strange pulling agony.

"I told you about, Raymond, the flasher."

"Does everyone call him that? Every time someone calls him that it seems more natural. I can't help somebody like that and I sure as hell can't help a knocked-up thirteen-year old kid."

"You don't know it but you *are* helping Raymond. He told me he's thinking about things he never thought about before. We'll talk about everything while we're shrimping. Do you have any shorts, any sneakers and old clothes in your office?"

"Donna, what are you talking about, what shrimping, where?"

After a quick stop and change at my apartment, Donna drove her odd little hatchback up the coastal highway to a small isolated residential area where she parked near a gated enclosure.

"Grab the nets, there's a pair of extensions we might need, I'll bring the big pail and the light."

I couldn't even guess at what was going on. I'd never heard shrimping used as a verb. I didn't know this woman with whom I had shared only one brief, bitter moment, and she was acting as if we were old pals. I was in a strange neighborhood, with a prostitute, about to do something that until an hour ago I had never heard of, and I was feeling okay, uncertain, but okay. Donna hoisted a Santa-size sack over her shoulder, kicked a five-gallon pail toward me and headed for the locked gate with a key in hand. I followed her through the gate along a walled walkway then out onto the beach which looked for all the world like an Italian water carnival.

Too many boats to count, every size and shape, each with blazing lamps aimed over the side, in addition to their running and cabin lights. All packed in between the shore and the nearest reef, a distance of no more than a couple of hundred yards. Spaced among the boats in the shallow water were people: men, women and children, wading around, waving and dipping short handled nets. Other people hung over the gunwales of the boats with extension handles on their nets and everyone was chattering and shouting. I expected someone to step out of the crowd on shore and break into a lusty song. The water was calm and flat, the moon was full, low and huge and the scene was enough to move a chronic depression victim to laughter.

Donna selected a site where she dumped our stuff before sticking an extension pole into the sand as sort of a marker. She pulled off her jeans, beneath which she wore a swim suit. Handing me a huge lantern she said, "Let's go."

The water was surprisingly cold as we waded in to her hip depth.

"Hold the lantern so it shines straight down into the water, I'll do the dipping, then we'll trade off."

"What are we looking for?"

"Their eyes reflect the light as they're coming in to nip your thighs," she laughed.

And sure enough, aiming the light directly down into the water I was delighted to see tiny bright spots all around us.

"Hey," excited now, "I don't believe this, are they always here?"

"Just a few nights of the year."

Donna knew how to handle the net and after each trip ashore to empty it we traded off. The trick was to move the net through the water in such a way to keep the earlier catches held inside while you swooped up more. In just over an hour our pail was full and we flopped down on the blanket Donna pulled from her sack and spread on the sand. The moon was higher now and the crowd had thinned some and a depth of wonder beyond definition took charge of my senses. It was welcome. As I sat with my arms locked around my knees, saying nothing, just looking, Donna turned to face me.

"I know you're going to help these people, Stone. I can't tell you how I know, I just do."

"I don't feel that way. In fact I feel like a phony. Who the hell knows what to tell a knocked-up thirteen year old, never mind an introverted flasher. Mostly I don't like taking your money."

"Stone, there's no one to help these people, you must know how screwed up the social system is. Perhaps you're right, maybe you can't help, but you sure can't hurt and I have such a strong feeling about this. It's the first time I've felt hopeful in a long time. As far as the money, you know how I earn it, let me take something away from the way I spend it."

"Understood. But good for you is bad for me. I'll have to work it out. And, besides, there's no way to ever find you."

Straight, deep into my eyes, "What do you want me for, Stone?"

"If we're gonna do something, we're gonna do it together or not at all. The first and last time we spoke I pissed you off and you told *me* off. Now here we are sitting on the beach like a couple of lovers. The whole thing is crazy, but if you want to play then we'll play together. That's the deal. Period."

"That's fine with me, Stone, I'll give you my number and we'll talk anytime you want and as much as you want." Face tilted down now, with an impish grin as she raised her eyes to mine, "besides, you're the perfect date, that's why I invited you tonight."

"Don't stop. Apart from my masculine beauty, why am I your perfect date?"

"You're such a hard-ass you wouldn't touch a whore for all the tea in China. I can be as relaxed, playful and sexy as I care to be and you won't lay a glove on me."

Catching her off guard I grabbed her long hair, pulled her down on her back, reached across her and with my face close to hers said, "You are dead right, you are also the most incredibly appealing woman I've met. You are obviously educated, you carry yourself with class, nothing about you makes any sense. But you're a mystery I intend to solve. As far as being a whore, I don't want that to be true, didn't from the first moment I met you, it offends me, it poisons me, it makes me impotent and madder than hell. But I also believe that among the great miracles is that which enables a woman to be born each day as a virgin. The past is nothing more than an impulse. And whether you call it Nature, God, the great Is or just The Source, I know *It* wipes the slate clean every day, for every one of us, so don't count on my being a perfect date...ever."

She was silent, her eyes stayed closed for an eternity. She finally looked up at me with no expression.

"Were you sleeping?" I asked in my best sarcastic mode.

"Praying…time to go home, Stone."

We spoke little as we carried the stuff back to her car. The pail, well over half full of live shrimp and sea water, weighed a ton as I lifted it into the back of the car and clamped down the lid. Still in near silence she drove back to my apartment. I got out then stopped and leaned into the open passenger-side window, "Donna, I have no idea of what's going on, just a sense something *is* going on and that somehow it matters. Thanks for this evening, I had fun."

"So did I, Stone, maybe you're a good guy after all."

"You okay?"

She pulled the gear lever into drive, "I'm a little scared, but then I'm always a little scared," and she was gone.

Sharon Stern left town before there was a chance for us to get together again. Business pressures forced her to leave immediately following the boat show and my whimsical, off and on desire to buy a boat was too flimsy to return me to the show before it ended. She left several unanswered messages on my machine but that was okay, she was a good friend and we never had to exchange excuses. Now I was wishing she was still in town. It wasn't merely that Donna had aroused me tonight, it was due more to loneliness, there was no one around with whom I could speak openly.

"Who does a talker talk to?" I asked the Herman Miller clock in the reception area. All it gave me in reply was a half-hour single bong.

Back at my office I pulled a never-fail yellow legal pad from my desk and began to write out the basic aspects of my muddled thinking. Under the headings of Pro and Con I wrote everything that came to mind regarding the current situation. In twenty minutes an answer showed itself. It felt right. Two minutes later I was pulling the front door shut on my way to my favorite bar. Suddenly I was dog-hungry.

"Some date," I muttered, "she didn't even fix me any shrimp."

Laurie phoned her sister from the bar to make sure her kids were okay, to leave my number where she could be reached and to explain she would be a couple of hours late. It was a casual and irregular routine with us and she never failed to soothe my anxious libido with consummate skill and shared pleasure. She was a wounded bird and a thoroughly nice person who deserved more than life was dealing her. While our compatibility never got past the physical stage we were always pleased to re-discover each other. Later, when she whispered, "sweet dreams," rolled off of me, then off the bed to begin dressing, I slid into a deep and righteous sleep. I didn't hear her leave.

In the morning I awoke hungry, wondering how Donna handled the heavy pail of shrimp after she arrived home. A short time later I was walking into the downtown diner where I knew the cook could do a great omelet and there stood James Wakins. He was waiting to be shown to a table.

"Hey, James, how about I join you?"

"No way, Stone, I see too damn much of you as it is. But then I hate to see a Honky trying to deal with rejection, so c'mon."

"You're not too pretty this morning, James, looks like you been up all night. Everything okay?"

"Stay outta my face, Stone. You ain't my daddy. 'Cause like the song says, "*My daddy can't be ugly so, look away, Momma look a boo boo dey,*" the last sung in a high whiny soprano accompanied by frantic air guitar.

"If you're gonna sing any more, I'm sitting somewhere else."

"Say what, Poppa? Not coming to the back'o de bus wit yo boy?"

"Now you've done your comedy and pathos bits, can we just have breakfast, please? I have something to tell you."

"Tell away, Father O'Malley," in a remarkable imitation of Barry Fitzgerald, "tell me how you been bumping them nuns in they little buns."

"As pathetic as it sounds, the fact is you're the only person I can talk to about certain things. I'm acquainted with people all over the western world but not one has any idea of what I'm doing or what I've gotten myself into. How could I tell them when I don't understand it myself? So, James, you're the guy I can bounce things—"

"No I'm not. I'm not about to become your Jazzbo."

"Jazzbo? You talking about Craig Price, about *Poor No More*, Jazzbo?" My voice raised an octave at this remarkable prospect.

"You ain't the only one who can read, Smooth."

"Yeah, but that's a pretty damned obscure reference, James."

"I guess not so very, you caught it."

"Well, that sure as hell settles one thing, you're the right guy to speak with."

"Man, Stone, talking to you is like talkin to my Aunt Rose. So okay, go ahead, what's your big problem?"

"You already know there's no guarantee I can help your sister or anyone else Donna sends to me. All I can do is talk about my own conclusions regarding a good life. Whether that can help anyone is just a guess. But at the same time I realize there is nowhere else for these folks to go, at best, everyone they talk to will have an ax to grind. If anyone will bother to see them at all it will generally be to use the problem to further their own cause, to get more money or just a bigger power base. The system is a joke. Help, if it ever comes, is too little, the wrong kind and too late to boot."

"Instead of wastin your speeches, Stone, why don't you run for office."

"Up yours, James. So, because it's uncertain about how much good I can do I hate having Donna pay—"

"Everbody gotta right to do right and feel good, Stone."

"I'm going to set up one regular time for Donna's people and no matter how many she sends along, within reason, I will only let her pay one hourly rate."

"You saying that, let's say she's sends you six people, you will talk to all of them at once, at the same time, like a classroom?"

"More like a seminar, everyone will have a chance to talk. But my basic message is the same for everyone. Don't you see? I can't advise about abortion or drug use or perversions, but I can talk about stuff such as self respect which, in turn, is what everyone needs in order to make the best decisions."

"Sort of one size cures all, Stone?"

"More like shared experiences, I'm just looking for an answer."

"For you?"

"For everyone, James."

"Sounds like bullshit to me, but then everything about you is humbug as far as I can see. You been sobbing about having exactly what you *claim* you set out to do and all I hear from you is how tough it is to *hear* about all this shit. Man, you should have to *live* this shit sometime. Somebody been either wipin or kissin your shiny white ass since the day you born. I just wish you would either shut up and do something or take down that stuck-up, asshole sign that don't even tell nothin."

"That's good, James, now we know how you measure me. Now tell me how we're supposed to measure you. I admit I don't know whether what I'm doing is right or wrong. Nobody's been down this road that I know about. But I'm goddam doing it, and as far as I can tell all you do is bitch and whine. Lots of people believe that black people should put up and shut up, like all the immigrants before and after them. That they should work hard and control their children, like everyone else does. And stop cry-babying with their hands stuck out for every freebie that comes along, then most of their problems would have gone away long ago. So where do you stand? Tell me about how you are doing more for people than I am."

James turned full face toward me, leaned across the table and hooded his eyes, "I ain't putting out no goddam signs, Stone." Following a long silent pause, "D'you believe the shit you just said?"

"Nah. I'm a miscegenationist. I believe in intermixing, spreading the gene pool as far as it will go. If everyone followed Lincoln's personal beliefs we'd all be cafe au lait color by now and we could be picking on the Portugese, or maybe the Albanians."

"You are one weird cat, Stone. Really weird."

"And so far I have no idea of what kind of cat you are, James."

IV

My big idea was a flop. Nobody wanted to show up when anyone else was there. But I salvaged the one-payment idea and extracted a promise from Donna that there would be no more money until I said so. I felt a little better by then even though two more characters had entered my life.

Randall Preston was a tall, thin man of 65 years who loved to spout whimsical philosophy and doggerel. Obviously possessed of a fair education, he survived by virtue of a trust fund which paid him enough to live a work-free life or remain drunk. Randall chose to live among a group of transient associates in refrigerator and television cartons, situated among scrub growth alongside the railroad bridge. There to embrace his one true friend; sour mash whiskey.

The bridge was important to Randall and his friends because it provided shelter during tropical storms. And being a man of high resolve, Randall regularly tithed, although good churchgoing folk might say his method of doing so was irregular. But, on the ninth day of each month Randall would visit the bank and cash sixty percent of his monthly receipt. Fifty percent was to keep him in a comfortable state of mind for two weeks and ten percent was to nourish his soul. His soul took its nourishment from Donna Delgado, his "Girl of the golden locks, dear friend of a thousand cocks."

Donna loved Randall dearly and while he was always "temporarily unable to quite raise a proper erection" he was content to bask in the "luscious and consoling warmth" of his girl of the golden locks. He also knew when the remaining forty percent had been spent before the next ninth, Donna would provide. She was more than his love, she also served as his insurance, right up to the day she threatened to cut him off unless he agreed to visit my office.

Randall railed about the value and importance of the free, unfettered and independent life. He swore he would lie across the railroad tracks to be sliced into three equal and precious parts before he would submit to discussions with a "half-baked junior philosopher from Boston, for God's sake." But Donna prevailed and on the morning of the tenth, a mostly sober, Randall Comsworth Preston, late of Philadelphia, Don of the railroad bridge society, pinged my bell promptly at eleven.

Donna had set the appointment and, as usual, gave me little more than the basic facts about Randall's background. I gathered the preceding information only after a number of visits. But on that first day I knew nothing beyond his name and his dependency. We stood and took the measure of each other. I finally extended my hand and said, "Locke Stone, Mr. Preston, I was expecting you."

"Of course you were, you hedgehog. It is my understanding that you exist for the sheer pleasure of living a vicarious life. I want you to understand that while the splendid Miss Delgado has some special arrangement for paying you, she is doing so with my own money. I am a renown swordsman who remains the only man able to competently serve Miss Delgado who, as a result, is my absolute love slave. She begs to pay me for my unmatched talents beneath the counterpane, but she alone, of all the women who worship at my godhead, deserves my best, without the tarnish of gold. That said, I will speak of her no more but will instead attend to your puny preachments concerning my preference for the creature over that of mountebanks such as yourself. Do you provide a place to sit?"

"Certainly, Mr. Preston, let's go back to my office. I have much to learn from you. Were you a drunk in college, perhaps even in high school?"

"In the womb, Stone. The sperm that crashed the maternal egg was spunk-drunk on bathtub gin."

Malka Yelick was as silent as a rustle when she appeared. As I was preparing to leave after meeting Randall in the morning and having turned Aleena away after lunch, Malka materialized in the reception room. I hadn't heard the door but I was deeply engrossed in reassuring myself that sending Aleena away had been the right thing to do. She had arrived for her appointment alone. I turned her around at the door and said, "I'm sorry Aleena but I cannot, *will not* meet with you alone. I've explained that to James a couple of times. Now you'll have to come back when he is with you."

"He couldn't make it today, he's the one tole me to come ahead, he don't worry about you."

"I understand sometimes he can't make it and I'm willing to meet with you two anytime, even in the evenings. But I can *not* be alone here with an underage girl."

"I ain't gonna do nothin, Stone."

"I know, honey, but the world is chock full of people who can only believe bad stuff. So we're not about to give them a chance. Tell James I said anytime is okay but he has to be here. Now scram, little pal."

"I am Malka Yelick, are you Mr. Stone, please?"

Her voice was so soft and yet it was a perfect match for her demeanor. Fifteen pounds overweight, cheap clothing-too small, hair carrot-color stringy, but eyes that were as big and soft as Bambi's. You knew she had to be a nice person.

"Yes, Miss Yelick, I'm Stone, won't you come in?"

Donna told me Malka was suicidal because she was too sex-obsessed to create any sort of rational life. She also suggested Malka should decide whatever else I should know and that she had advised her to tell me everything. I immediately knew I didn't want to hear "everything."

"Do I understand that you wish to set up a schedule for some discussion periods?"

"I came to know Miss Donna when she would see me on the street all the time. She is very nice and she says talking to you will help me. I have never been able to tell anyone about my —"

"Excuse me, Malka, may I call you Malka?"

"Please."

"It is very important you understand I am nothing more than a Philosopher, one who studies the theories of life. I cannot tell you what to do, I cannot prescribe medication. I can only offer suggestions about how to create a better feeling about yourself. You may be much better off seeing a different sort of counselor such as a psychologist, a psychiatrist or perhaps a priest."

"If you do not wish to see me, I understand. I am a pitiful person, not someone a man like you would find attractive, I know that. I told Donna."

"Donna told me you often feel depressed, that's all. If we can speak about ways to offset depression then a meeting or two may be worthwhile. Do you think you want to try?"

"Mr. Stone, I am on the street all the time because I —"

"Please think about what you believe to be the cause of your bad feelings, think about it carefully then come to see me tomorrow. What is a good time for you, Malka?"

"Mr. Stone, I have no one I can tell everything to, no one wants to hear, if I can not tell you then it would be a waste of your time, mine too. Can you be so strong, Mr. Stone?"

"I don't know, it might be too hard."

"It will be hard for me because I will want to love you, I already know that. I will even beg you, I beg lots of men."

"That will not happen, Malka. Let's set tomorrow at four, can you make that time? If it goes badly, we'll stop, that's it, no harm will be done. Just try to relax, okay?"

"I will be here. Please be patient, I think maybe I'm crazy."

As I watched Malka Yelick walk away I thought it might be time to remove my sign, lock my door and shut this rapidly expanding nightmare out of my life. I hoped Laurie could get away early tonight. That thought was immediately followed by a clear warning sound in my head, a buzzing that sounded like an alarm, a warning that a pattern was developing which was all wrong.

Whenever I phoned Donna I reached her service. Her handling of phone calls was purely responsive. She spoke to whomever *she* wanted to, whenever *she* wanted to, period. Most times she never called back, which pissed me off so much I never called her unless it was important and said so. In that event she always responded quickly regardless of whether she was auditing her calls or her service beeped her. When we did speak it was increasingly in person. I began to convince myself she enjoyed being with her "perfect date."

We never said so but I became aware that our times together were becoming her sessions. She slowly and cautiously released minuscule bits about herself while she exhibited an unrelenting interest in my life. She wanted to know everything, from the time I was a child. She queried me with a near hunger, it was as if she was totally unfamiliar with the concept of an orderly life. She would say nothing about her past beyond recent times. She limited her talk to her modeling jobs, the people whose lives we shared and a rare comment about our strange relationship.

For my part I came to know I liked this woman as much as anyone I had ever known. The beach became our hangout and that somehow felt right, the immensity of the ocean forced a perspective that might have to be struggled for elsewhere. The smaller hotels with their piano bar lounges, sometimes their pool bars, other times their casual dining spots, all served to give us a sense of isolation, perhaps of freedom that comes from brushing the depth of the Florida night which was just barely held at bay by the neon of the strip. We might walk barefoot in the soft, lapping surf or sit and talk with our backs against a coconut palm. We never touched. The agreement was unspoken yet as perfectly understood as "step on a crack and break your mother's back."

On one such night she told me Raymond Casper told her he hadn't done any flashing since he began meeting with me. He felt, she said, as though he entered into some sort of contract he didn't want to break.

"Does he mean a contract with me?" I asked, feeling rather proud and certain that was what he meant.

"No, he feels he has some obligation to me for as long as he continues seeing you."

"Great. Why wouldn't he tell me? Did he say his actual feelings were different?"

"He said you were giving him a new way to look at things."

"I'll settle for that. I wish Aleena Wakins would give me as much feedback, although she and James are surprisingly bright."

"Don't tell me the great Stone stereotypes people. James and Aleena were raised by their Aunt Rose who is a retired middle school Principal. James graduated Valedictorian at sixteen, did a hitch in the army and came out as a master sergeant. These are bright people, my friend. James, especially, plays with language, they both do. They have to live in two worlds and they do so very well. The only reason James hasn't gone to college is because he supports the family."

Aleena Wakins seldom gave me a clue, the kid was a half-pint, walking stonewall. But, after reading a copy of Richard Bach's *Illusions* I had given her as a must read, she finally gave me a grain of response.

"Those creatures from the river were like people, right?"

"Did you think they were like people?" I asked.

"Sure, everybody just hanging on, afraid of everything, even afraid of taking a chance, even after they saw somebody else makin it. There's some stuff I don't understand but mostly I do and, man, I like the stuff that handbook says."

"Have you read the part about the movie yet, where they go in to see *Butch Cassidy and the Sundance Kid?*"

"No, they just had the sky full of loud music and stuff."

"Well the movie thing is coming up and I'd like for you to read it a couple of times, read it until you understand how it fits your life, right now. Once you do that I think we can really get down to whatever you decide to do and what it will mean for the rest of your life."

"James says what I want to do will spoil my whole life."

James put down the magazine he had been reading, "Being black and being a woman is all the problem anyone needs in life. You having this baby is like loading your pockets with heavy rocks just before you're about to swim across a big, deep river."

With that Aleena looked toward me, "Is that right, Stone?"

"Sure. You know a baby will make everything harder. I guess neither James nor I can possibly know how a woman, or just a girl, might feel about it, but, like everything else in the world, there *is* a price to pay. What you want to do is figure how big the price will be and whether it is best to pay it now or at some later time. James wants you to have children but he wants you to do it later on, when you are better able to deal with it and when you can give the baby a better chance."

I immediately knew I made a mistake when I said, "the baby." I had allowed the zygote to become something more.

Aleena struck like a snake, "*This* baby only got one time and that's right now. Maybe *I* can do it later, but *she* can't." I glanced at James who, I felt certain, shared my feelings that once words such as *baby* and *she* were out in the open, they could never be made to disappear.

I tried to move away from the quicksand, "Anyway, the movie part is really important because it shows us a way to think objectively."

"Even for *just a girl?*" She echoed what was said a moment before. Anyway, what does thinking objectively mean."

"It means backing off and being able to make a decision without letting your feelings get in the way. It's kind of like making a decision for someone else instead of yourself."

"Say some girl, like me, my age and all, got pregnant and I had to decide what she should do?"

"I couldn't have said it better."

"But you could have taken longer to say it." James countered.

"Sure, James, and you could have said it smart-ass."

I found I enjoyed the little thrust and parry games James played so well. I turned my chair back to face Aleena.

"There's one more thing about this, Aleena, I feel absolutely certain we always know the right thing to do. I believe we have an infallible inner compass which never fails to point out the right way to go and it is never that which fails us. You know what I'm saying here? We always *know*, sometimes deep down, the right thing to do. But we are born with free will, which means we can ignore our compass, we can choose to do the wrong thing.

"You probably know people who do the wrong thing most of the time, in school, in the neighborhood, in their families. Don't you sometimes just look at someone and think, "What's the matter with that fool, anybody can see that's a stupid thing to do?"

"Sure, see it all the time."

"Right, you know they know, they have to, but they *deliberately* choose to do the dumb thing, the wrong thing. Now maybe that's how we learn, I don't know. Perhaps we're programmed to learn by doing, so even when we know it's wrong we feel like we have to try it. But there is something wrong with that, something you have to be careful about, can you tell me what it is?"

"Sometimes you get into really bad trouble."

"Yes. Good. But bigger, let's think bigger. Worse than just bad. Some things can't be undone, some things change your life forever. You go out and get AIDS and there is no way you can undo it. You damage your body and brain with drugs and you will live with that forever. And maybe the biggest one of all is getting pregnant because then you are messing with two lives…forever. The good thing is that unlike some other things, you have a chance to make a change. You can undo fertilization for a while, for as long as that is all it is, lots of people argue about it, but that doesn't matter. The law says you have a while, just a little while, to make up your mind about your life and the life of the person who may result. The reason I asked you not to think about a cuddly baby is because that is not the problem. Cuddly babies very quickly become cranky children, bitchin teenagers, miserable grown ups then troublesome old people. And James is sure you are not ready for all *that*, and *that's* what you have to decide, and soon."

"How soon?"

"Very soon. Most young girls try to run from the problem until it's too late. Most people feel once a fertilized egg develops a heartbeat it is no longer yours and you'll know it. Remember what we said about the right thing? The right thing is to decide, then act quickly and move along with your life, or with your lives, whichever you choose. That way you'll never have to look back and suffer any regrets. I think I can promise that."

"You promised we would talk about the kind of life I want. When we gonna do that, Stone?"

"Thursday, little buddy. We'll do that on Thursday, I can hardly wait to see how tall an order we'll have to handle.

Discovering anything about Donna was next to impossible because nothing made sense: she was a street hooker, no, she was strictly a high-class referral. I heard she was selective, careful and fussy about her Johns. I even heard she was a lesbian, that she charged more to rich guys and gave freebies to poor guys who were in need. All nonsense. The point is she had become a local legend and like all legends, people made up Donna tales. The little I learned amounted to almost nothing helpful. Donna had shown up about three years ago with a story that she was from Canada. She said she arrived in south Florida to appear in a TV commercial for a flashy day-cruise ship which went broke and left the film production company unpaid. She was forced to turn a few tricks to survive.

That story didn't wash. She was too pretty, she could have grabbed a legitimate job in a heartbeat. The stories I *could* believe had to deal with her being a soft touch with a double sawbuck for anyone who asked. That she never drank or used, that she carried her own condoms without which no one ever touched her, and she would stand up to anyone, *for* anyone and she was absolutely fearless.

I had been planning for weeks to ask her to work for me when she unexpectedly called one afternoon.

"How about coffee? I asked. "I have something I want to say."

"Important?"

"To me."

"It's three forty, will five thirty be okay with you?"

"See you then."

I was into some research on notes I had taken a few years ago during an Aspen Institute seminar. An hour would have been just right to finish the project except my eyes kept going out of focus. I would read a line or two then find myself rehearsing my Donna pitch. My gaze would wander to a point three feet west of the copy machine or maybe center on the little red light on the coffee maker. I gave it up and checked the answering service before calling the barber shop for an appointment. I walked into the bathroom to wash my hands and brush my hair, *maybe I should shave. Cut it out, you're not some kid on a date.* I finally punched on the tape recorder to review my first session with Malka which I felt needed editing before I had it typed.

"My brother was older than me by seven years and he was like a god to me. I thought it was wonderful to have sex with him. From the time I was very small I would suck him everyday, sometimes more, sometimes he—"

"Malka, I want you to be able to talk about the things you feel are important but please don't feel it is necessary to tell any more than you are comfortable with. Understand that I am not a medical person, not even a trained counselor. I am just a student of Philosophy. I am also a man and hearing sexual details from a woman makes me feel embarrassed. Do you understand what I mean?"

"Not exactly. I was raised in a very small village and these things were understood. As a child I watched the farm animals fuck and then have babies, I heard my parents fuck every night and I never had embarrassment. I knew, because my brother told me, I could not fuck until I was married, that I had to remain a virgin or I could never get married."

"But your brother also told you that sex with him was okay?"

"Yes. He told me I was helping him to become a man and he was teaching me how to pleasure a man and keep a man very happy. For later, when I would be married."

"Did he tell you to keep it a secret."

"Oh yes, he said people would not believe we would not fuck and they would be angry. Even when I was older and he also began taking me from the back I knew two things: I had to remain a virgin and I must never tell anyone."

"This was a regular thing from the time you were a little girl until when, Malka?"

"Until I was seventeen and married, then my brother stopped for a while. My father stopped forever, he was a religious man."

"Malka, it's break time. Let's have coffee, maybe you would prefer a soda."

"Coffee is good. I like it with sugar, lots of sugar and no milk, may I please serve you? Are you being embarrassed, Stone?"

"Yes. But it's just a difference in cultures and backgrounds, Malka. It is nothing against you, or me, for that matter."

"Good, I am sure you are not a woman-man, Donna must love you so much because you fuck so good with her. Someday I will find a man who can satisfy me and I will stop fucking with everyone. I know it's not good. I want very much to fuck with you right now and you are just trying to help me. I know these things."

Every word after ..."love you so much," was a garbled sound in my head. Listening to the tape was, in a way, the first time I actually heard much of the remainder of Malka's remarkable story. I had decided to just sit back and let her spin out whatever she felt she needed to say.

With repetition, we can become immune to almost anything. But Malka's tale was outside of reality to the point I wondered whether she was fantasizing. Now, listening to her recount how her father and brother had sodomized her daily for more than five years, after her brother used her for fellatio, even longer, seemed more like bad fiction than real life.

On the other hand I knew that if I had learned anything during my life, it was that any extreme of action which could be imagined can always be surpassed by reality. When human actions are objectively evaluated against that of all other animals the only reasonable conclusion is that we are essentially insane. Perhaps that is our highest achievement as well as our terminal curse.

Malka caused her own downfall by convincing her brother to continue their sexual relationship after she was married. She wanted more, she wanted what she had. The result was so bad she was forced to leave her home and her native land, but her obsessions traveled well and forcefully. She believed her sexual desires were insatiable. I believed she was being her own puppet. Booze, food, sex were all self-inflicted grown up versions of "I'll eat worms and die," in my opinion. But my opinion was meaningless, *in* my opinion, because in *my* opinion, self-opinion was the *only* opinion that mattered. And, goddam it, it's five thirty, where the hell is Donna?

I called her number and let the busy signal irritate me while I held the phone and thought about how she was always on time. I hesitated, somehow being connected to her phone, knowing she was apparently at the other end of this thing in my hand, raised a peculiar feeling. I couldn't place it but something didn't feel right. I didn't know where Donna lived. I cursed myself for not knowing, then I cursed myself for being such a nervous Nelly. *She'll call as soon as she can, she's on the phone with someone, she's running late, she'll call.*

Another forty minutes and I began to feel as if I were in a desert. I didn't know whether Donna lived around the corner or across town, I should have troubled to find out but she was always so secretive that I avoided asking. I also kept my distance from her friends. I couldn't even call James, he probably knew where she lived, but I didn't have his number. I decided everyone knew where she lived except me. I wanted to go and find her, to satisfy myself that everything was fine but I had no idea of where to begin. I thought about going out and finding other girls who worked the streets and asking them about her, where she lived. There were always girls on the causeway strip or working around the flashier clubs on Federal highway, if I paid them I might be able to find out something.

That's not only stupid but I'm better off here, I thought, waiting for her call. Regardless of what's happening I will eventually hear from her.

Another hour and I was becoming a jangled nerve-end. I decided it was time to do something, anything, rather than pace around here. I went to my telephone answering device and changed the message and the timing so a caller would be answered on the first ring and would receive my cellular phone number. I was uneasy about doing that but I had to bail out and I had to know Donna could reach me. I headed out to Calahan's for a couple of stiff drinks, dinner and some loud television. Perhaps there was a Basketball game on tonight.

At a few minutes before nine I was trying to settle in at the bar when my phone rang and I felt incredibly happy for half a minute. It was an unfamiliar and disappointing male voice, "Stone?"

"Speaking."

"This is Mark Todd. You don't know me but I'm Donna's lawyer and friend. I will be at Broward General Emergency Admitting in five minutes, meet me there, fast. It's bad."

He promptly hung up following which I could only move the phone from my face and stare at it for a moment. Then I signaled Laurie, threw money on the table and quickly walked the twenty yards to the front door where I paused and turned to look back, feeling as though I was being watched. No one appeared to even notice me except Laurie who wore a questioning look.

I drove the short distance to the hospital in a few minutes The emergency entrance was clearly marked and I pulled into a handicap spot near the door. When I heard myself mutter, "I'll pay the five hundred," I knew my head was up my ass. It didn't matter. I just wanted this to be something other than what I knew it had to be.

I was met by a well dressed man in his early thirties who looked as if he might play pulling guard for the Dolphins, "I'm Mark Todd."

"Locke Stone. What's up, where's Donna?"

"I'm trying to get us in to see her for a minute. I have to pull some strings because they may be losing her and the cops have her guarded. I'm waiting for an okay."

"Losing her? What the hell happened, Todd?" "I can't be sure but, believe me, I'll find out. In the meantime she's hurt so badly she may not make it."

"What was it?," I sputtered, "a car, an accident, what happened."

"Somebody caught her at home and busted her up real bad. If a nosy neighbor hadn't seen the bastards leaving, she would have laid there and died."

"Someone saw who did it? Christ, I've got a million questions, how did you know to call me? Who the hell are you? Do you have any idea who did this? Can we—"

"Stone, let's just try to see Donna. Let's find out about her chances. Then we'll sit down and I'll tell you everything I know, and I know more than anybody else. Okay?"

The uniformed cop waved us toward him after answering a call, "Just for a minute, and I mean it."

From the relatively small parts of her we could see, Donna was a badly battered mess. Her eyes were swollen and her face was a patchwork of massive bruises, abrasions and blood. All her front teeth appeared to be gone and her lips were puffy and torn. The attending physician was telling Mark that the internal damage was what we really had to worry about, it was capable of killing her.

"She's all busted up inside, we think she was repeatedly kicked and battered with some sort of club, like a baseball bat. It'll take a while to work up an accurate diagnosis but somebody went nuts here. A young body can take a lot of punishment but this is insane. You her husband?"

"I'm her lawyer…and we're both friends."

"What time did they bring her in?" I asked.

"Around six fifteen, they can give you the exact time at the desk. Why?"

"She was supposed to meet me at five thirty."

"I think she was in big trouble by then, her shirt was torn, her panties were gone, semen was all over the place, that stuff and the beating took a while," The doctor started to say more, thought better of it then turned back to his work.

"C'mon, Stone, nothin we can do here and we need to talk."

"We sure as hell do," I said.

As I said it, I was overcome by an intensive hatred for this bastard and everyone else who knew Donna. How could they let this happen? With tubes stuck everywhere she looked like a little kid laying there. If I was an insider, one of those people who knew her better, I would never let this happen. Sonsabitches. I would never let this happen. Nobody should. *I feel like I want to kill somebody. Who? Please God, just let me know who.*

Mark Todd was three inches shorter than me and about forty pounds heavier.

He carried himself with the air of one used to being in charge and I was battling an unsettling and totally unreasonable urge to smack him in the mouth.

"They say the next few hours will tell whether Donna's gonna live." He said, "I'm not going anywhere. How about you?"

"You said you know more than anyone, Todd, I want to hear it, every goddam bit of it. We've got time and I'm sick of not knowing what's going on."

"I've been working on this case…oh man, I don't mean *case*, for Christ's sake. Wait a second, Stone, I need to pull it together, that kid means so much to me."

Walking over to the water cooler, he cupped his hand to catch some water which he rubbed on his face before wiping it dry with a clean, initialed, handkerchief. Then he walked to the beige vinyl couch which formed a corner v-shape with my chair. He pressed his thumb and forefinger to the bridge of his nose for a moment then sat back and said, I'll have to start at the top."

"Please do," the urge to hit him having subsided into abject sympathy.

"Ten years ago I was a cop. A good one, too good, for political purposes. After trying me on everything from motorcycles to boats, the Chief, actually a pretty nice guy, told me I was building up a lot of bad news. The writing was on the wall as far as police work was concerned and I was rea-

sonably close to taking the bar. The point is that while I was making enemies I was also making some valuable friends. So blah, blah, blah and I
finally hung out my shingle.

"I met Donna when she was busted for prostitution shortly after she
arrived in town. I knew damn well she wasn't a common street whore. I
mean, she was, but it didn't fit, she was a ratty-hair, toothless mess, but something about her was all wrong. I helped her get straightened out, cleaned up,
teeth fixed and like freakin' magic, she was beautiful. So beautiful."

"She didn't get her teeth knocked out today?"

"No. All her front teeth had been knocked out long before, years ago."

"So, what're you saying? She's been through this before?"

"Worse. I'll get to it. But I couldn't get her to give up hooking. Between
that and her modeling she made as much money as she wanted, worked
when she wanted and had plenty of money for helping street people. She
wants to do that, she owes it, she says, and she even tries to repay what I've
spent on her She's like some goddam misplaced angel. You're a big deal to
her by the way, she believes in you, Stone."

"You've known about me then?"

"From the beginning. Let me explain something: Donna is special, you
know that. Hell, everyone knows it the minute they meet her, but she's
like a toy you'd find at the dump, she's all broken up. Her guts, her soul
and her sense of personal worth have been wiped out. She thinks of herself
as some kind of rotten, spoiled flesh. Too low, she says, to be anything but
gutter trash. Says she'll never be able to open up to anyone. I can tell you
that after years of trying, she trusts me just so far and believe me, I've had
to earn every inch of *that*. She does tell me about a few things and you're
one of them. She's big on you. But, try to understand something, Donna
believes she died when she was seventeen. She died and was taken to hell
and she believes she can never return.

"I've been digging and researching and piecing her story together, bit
by tiny bit, until this happened. And I *know* who did it. Now, she may be

dying in there and I don't want to deal with this alone. So, here goes, Stone, like I said, from the top:

"The first trace of a man called Saint Jake comes from El Paso, where he beat a street whore to death for holding out on him. She died for the sin of putting a couple of bucks up *her* nose instead of his. He was her pimp though she was nineteen years older. She was thirty-eight when she died. He took two of his other girls and left Texas.

"Three years later he was arrested in Santa Fe, for a limp manslaughter beef. He rammed a woman through a garage wall with his pop-top van. He claimed he panicked and didn't realize it as he spun his wheels back and forth over her body.

"Like some bloated fungus buried in shit, our man began to ripen to his full potential once he was in prison. That's where he acquired the name, Saint Jake. He started out as Santa Fe Jake, but his reputation spread as he forced more of his victims to kneel in front of him and pray to let them live. The praying routine brought on the name and he liked it. I'm told his favorite line was, "Pray, motherfucker, pray you can make me come, pray Saint Jake is satisfied, and maybe he won't send your torn-up ass to hell."

"So this man is psychotic. What's his connection to Donna?"

"You have to get the whole story in order to understand. I'll get to it. Jake stands six foot four inches tall, weighs around three hundred pounds and he can toss a Chevrolet over a wall. He's milk chocolate color and if that isn't enough to make him stand out, he's striped."

"Striped?" You saying he has stripes? What the hell does that mean? What kind of stripes?"

"Saint Jake has broad white stripes tattooed like rings around each arm from armpit to wrist. He also has a single stripe around his forehead which looks like a sweat band, and more stripes circling his chest and belly right down to his cock."

"How have you managed to get this information, Mark, how accurate is it?"

"Most of what I make has gone into this obsession. Private Investigators, informants, tips, sometimes lies, but after the bullshit falls away a mainline story develops. Jake is nuts all right, but he's also cunning and deadly."

"So far he doesn't sound too smart, just a crazy black guy with muscles and hate."

"Jake's not really a black guy. The reports indicate he's the result of some genetic stew. Apparently a mixture of Indian, white, Mexican, black and Polynesian. Truth is there's no way of checking, his origins are totally unknown and he claims to be some reincarnated Central American demon. He sometimes rambles on with a lot of gibberish about spirits and shit. Usually just before he busts somebody up with his weapon of choice."

"How does a guy have a weapon of choice in prison?"

"Jake's favorite weapon is as cute as he is. One of our reports describes it as a wooden piston. Supposedly he heard about some deranged con who bit his tormentor's dick in half after which Jake decided to avoid the chance of ever being called "Stubby." To protect himself he began knocking out the upper and lower incisors of his whimpering victims. Sometimes he thoughtfully left them intact from the cuspids back, which enabled the guys to chew their food.

But it was clumsy work. He used the edge of his hand, sometimes a piece of pipe, whatever he could think of, but it was hard. Teeth would break off leaving jagged edges, not a good thing for Jake's delicate pecker. Mouths would get all busted up. It was sloppy until some talented wood carver devised this wooden piston thing as a favor to Jake, maybe to save his own life. I've never seen it of course but it's described as a wooden shaft, like a dowel, about an inch and a half across, maybe six inches long. The shaft is cut from a broken shovel handle, scraped or sanded smooth. It fits inside a wooden collar so if you hold the collar you can slide the shaft back and forth like a piston. Fit the collar against the front teeth, bang the shaft with the butt of your hand and you've got eight presents for the tooth fairy."

"Aw, for God's sake, Mark, not Donna. Please man, tell me not Donna. I can't handle that. I'm gonna be sick from the thoughts *that* puts into my head. I can't. But I am, I need some water.

"Don't just stare at me, Mark. I know there are things in this world that are beyond understanding. You said "claims to be a demon?" That sonofabitch *is* a demon, unborn, puked out on a rock by some slimy other-world aberration. Society can't handle creatures like him, he's got to be destroyed some other way. Jesus, Mark, I'm sorry to rave like this, but how the hell can you just sit there?"

"Sit here? Just sit here, you pompous prick? I've been where you're just beginning to go. I've crawled through sewers you can't even imagine to gather this information. You think I don't know this monster? Let me tell you his stench has been in my nostrils for years. I want his ass so bad the bile in my throat never goes away. And now this nightmare sonofabitch has come into *my* town, into *my* face and shoved it right up *my* ass. The woman I love with all my soul, is dying in the next room. I don't need your theatrics, you over-educated asshole, I need help."

I put my forearms across the bottom of the up-ended water jug that supplied the cooler and rested my chin. I was suddenly so tired, so alone and so frightened of my own rushing mortality. Suppose, I wondered, this is all there is. Suppose all my artfully constructed spirituality is humbug, no cumulative, unending, learning existence. No goal, just pointless, brief, miserable awareness, of creatures who suck the righteousness out of the world and into a black hole of rotten reality.

I looked at Mark Todd, who was quiet now. He didn't want to talk any more and I didn't want to hear any more.

"Sorry, Mark, sometimes I fill my own universe. Of course you're hurting, you've been her friend for a long time. You've probably saved her life in the past and somehow I feel you're not going to lose her this time. Please go on, I need to know this stuff and it helps with the waiting."

He sighed, smacked his palms against the top of his knees then got up and walked over to lean against the window.

"Not much to tell about that phase except Jake had several models of his new toy made, he quickly discovered he had a hell of a weapon. The thing looked like a toy, couldn't be picked up on a metal detector and it could break ribs, other bones, even kill, depending where and how it was placed. Can you imagine such a thing held against the side of somebody's head, say over the ear opening, with the head against a wall or on the floor?"

I didn't answer but I imagined the feeling, all too easily.

"Mark, what about the police?"

"What about them?"

"Can't they do something?" Even as I asked the question I knew the answer. The familiar quotation, "Ask the question correctly and you will already have the answer," came to mind as I said, "Never mind, silly question."

"Jake came out of prison with a big idea. Saint Jake should have his own following, pious believers who would do his bidding and be his absolute slaves. He would start with a woman. He boasted to his pals how his perfect woman would become the core of his new army, one which would gather all other social victims together under one banner. His queen would be young and pure before he took her and taught her how to believe the real truth. He told how it would take a long time. In fact, he would tell how he might have to go through any number of young women before he found the right one. But his armed religion would have it all, confessions, snake handling, whippings, circumcision, forceful fucking, singing, and white stripe tattoos for all, maybe around the neck. Jake would be the only one to be completely striped and it would take years for him to finish, to be fully encircled. It had already taken years of pain and patience."

"Mark," I said, rather softly, "I hope telling all this is doing you some good, helping you to get through the night maybe. But I have to tell you,

I've got a pretty clear picture of this guy, now tell me why you think he's the one, tell me about his connection with Donna. I'm afraid to ask because I have this lousy, rotten feeling about her being a victim before tonight. I'm feeling so goddam torn up. I have to hear it, I don't want to hear it. God, it's been like that from the first minute, I didn't want her to be a whore, I don't want Saint fucking Jake to be her tormentor and now I don't want her to die. Give me something, Mark, I need something to shine through this stinking muck. Please."

"She's all brains and heart, Stone. She's smarter than Jake and she's better than the rest of us. Because despite everything, she can forgive the world for being a shit-ball. She can give everything she has to help everyone she touches, including you and me. The only filth she recognizes is herself. She talks about surviving her purgatory, about the things she has to do and how she is too soiled to ever go back."

"Go back to what, where?"

"I can't be totally sure. There's a lot of weak spots in my information, but I *think* she's from somewhere around Santa Barbara. I think Jake grabbed her when she was sixteen or seventeen."

I heard myself making a strange guttural noise which Mark took as a signal to continue.

"We suspect—"

"Mark, you keep saying *we*, who's the *we?*"

"After a while a network developed among some of the people I hired, a PI here, a cop somewhere else, informants, clerks, paralegals. Some of them began to care and kept in touch. We'd sometimes talk back and forth. I just began to think *we* instead of *me*, I didn't feel so hopeless.

"Anyway, we think there were a few failures before Jake got to Donna. There was the body of a young social worker found buried in a shallow grave in Monument Valley with her front teeth busted out. There was no autopsy so there's no way to be sure. Then there was the clueless disappearance of a young nun, actually a novitiate, in Portland that fits into the time pattern, but again, we can't be sure.

"In the Santa Barbara case, the one we think of as Donna, a sixteen-year old girl was forcefully pulled into a ratty looking van outside a girls school and was never heard from again. The girl was universally described as attractive, smart, socially popular and a leader in a flock of activities. Her name was not Donna, but I suspect Donna's name is not Donna either.

"I've tried to talk to her, to get her to open up, but she stonewalls me. She claims she ran away from an orphan's home in Canada, says she has no family. Says she worked the streets as a whore from the time she was sixteen. No trace of a Canadian accent though, and besides, when was the last time you heard of an actual orphanage. Without specific details we can't disprove what she says and we probably shouldn't try. I don't think she needs confrontation. I'm convinced she's ashamed, maybe totally traumatized and doesn't want to admit, or even know about her time before Jake. When you read about people surviving crazy stuff, sometimes their mind wants to erase it, shove it in a corner and deny it."

"Has she ever admitted she was kidnapped by Jake, any form of recognition or admission?"

"None, nothing, not a word, never. But once, when I was trying to convince her to get off the streets, to live with me and let me take care of her, she said something that might have been a clue. She said she had to do what she promised the angels. She said she had to use her bad self to do some good. It's frustrating as hell. I can't be sure of anything. But I know goddam well it was Jake, it all fits."

"Is there any chance you're pushing the circumstances, making it all fit the profile you've created. Any chance she did run away and she's telling the truth?"

He walked slowly and ominously across the small room to stand over me. I could feel the waves of frustration emanating from his whole body. Dislike for me, I wondered, or for Saint Jake? I half expected him to punch me, but Mark Todd was a controlled and patient man.

"When I first saw her, her front teeth, upper and lower, were busted out, busted out! The dentist who worked on her said several of the teeth had been broken and healed over. She had busted ribs, severe gonorrhea, anal and vaginal infections, badly bitten nipples and too many bruises and old injuries to count.

I have witnesses who can place Jake in Tampa just a few days before she first showed up here and a few days before he was arrested there. Now I know he's still on the loose.

"Donna's dying across the hall with a body that's been beaten to a pulp.

So tell me Mr. Philosopher, tell me about a better theory and while you're mentally masturbating, Saint Jake is out there, cruising the streets of Fort Lauderdale. He's waiting for her to get healed enough so he can do what he did to her for years. Are you hearing me, Stone? For years. I'm convinced Donna somehow survived Jake and his pals for years"

"Okay, Mark. You're right, too many pieces fit too well. Still, we have to try to be objective about this thing. I understand how you feel about Donna but—"

We both turned as the attending physician walked in and stood watching us. No one wanted to speak. Mark stared at the young doctor, I looked at Mark, *he loves Donna, really loves her, maybe more than I do.* It was an unsought, renegade thought. I brushed it aside and guessed at what we were about to hear. I was wrong.

"Miss Delgado is still unconscious but she is somewhat stabilized. The next few hours will be critical. If she makes it, she has a fighting chance. There is nothing you gentleman can do here, I suggest you go home and check back in the morning."

"I suggest you stick to your job and we'll stick to ours. I want someone by her side until we know. I don't care about costs or staff problems. I'm her attorney and I'm insisting on maximum care. Who do I have to see, doctor?"

"No one. It's being done, trust me, we don't want to lose her. She's in good hands."

"Has she regained consciousness at all?" I asked.

"No."

"Isn't that unusual? Is she comatose?"

"Sure, but it's too soon to worry about that. Right now I just want to keep her alive and as comfortable as possible. I take it you both are staying put?"

"We'll be right here," Mark said.

"Okay," he smiled, "We need all the positive vibes we can get around here, I'll keep you posted."

"Can we see her?" I asked.

He turned back before leaving, "No, not yet. I'll let you know." He started away then turned back again, "I'm going down for a coffee break, you guys want to join me?"

Mark turned to me, "Go ahead, Stone, I'll just wait here."

"C'mon, Mark, let the room clear out. You've put so much smoke in here you can't even see the No Smoking sign anymore. Let's go pump the doctor for a few minutes instead of each other."

VI

Marilee Cutter was four and a bit, when she decided she could wait no longer, it was time for school. She gathered a worn *Bible* which belonged to her Grandma Logan, *Travels Around The World* by A. Boy, and a dog-eared version of *The Cadaver Of Gideon Wick*. She tested their combined size and weight, found them to be too heavy and swapped the Gideon Wick for the smaller, *The Ink Bottle Babies*.

Feeling well prepared she tucked the books under one arm while she held the banister with the other. Down the six front steps to the sidewalk. From there around the corner alongside the small frame house for the short walk to the building which served as both church and school for the Saint Thomas parish.

This walk was familiar to her because on most days she watched for young Father Wood, who her thought processes turned into his being her "wooden father," to take his meditation walk, an event she was sure required her presence. She would scramble to reach his side where he would silently and absent-mindedly take her hand. She knew she mustn't talk no matter how hard it was to stay quiet because her wooden father was praying.

Past the church/school, past the large empty lot which was the planned location for the new church building. Marilee would walk a few steps then hop or run a few to keep up until they finally returned to the side walkway which would take the priest inside. Father Wood would kneel down, tell her she was an especially good girl, give her a pat and send her toward home. As she skipped away, he would watch her safely around her corner before going about his duties. He looked forward to her companionship to the point that his meditations felt incomplete on those rare days she missed. She had that effect on everyone in her small world.

Saint Thomas continued to be the centerpiece of her life. Her seamstress-mother made uniforms for most of the neighborhood girls and her family participated in every church and school fund raising event. The Nuns were Marilee's extended family. Her father's cousin, a teaching Nun at a larger, nearby Detroit parish kept in touch with the Saint Thomas group in a combined effort to ensure that Marilee would find her way into one of the teaching orders at the proper time. Sister Loyola, the cousin, was convinced Marilee was a special child, perfect in so many ways that she must surely be one of God's chosen few. She felt the rare combination of physical, mental and emotional perfection made that clear to anyone wise enough to recognize the signs.

As Marilee approached her teen years she was visited with increasing frequency by Sister Loyola and one or more of her cohorts. Loyola was progressing upward in the hierarchy of her Immaculate Heart of Mary, the strong IHM order, and her increasing influence would be helpful in getting Marilee onto the right path. The IHM Monroe facility was only twenty five miles from Marilee's Lincoln Park home and it housed Saint Mary's Academy, a boarding school which provided easy access to the convent.

Marilee's mother, a quiet southern Baptist lady by birth, had been a beautiful young woman who harbored a secret guilt. In order to escape her unhappy rural background she married an itinerant salesman when she was just sixteen. The marriage enabled her to break away and travel north to Chicago and eventually to Detroit, where she established herself with an independent career. In time, she was forced to shed the husband who had become an abusive and jealous drunk.

When she later met and fell in love with, then married the man who was to become Marilee's father, she unwittingly separated him from his beloved church. The rules of the times were such that a Catholic man married to a divorced woman could not receive the sacraments of the church. Marilee's mother carried that guilt. She was therefore the subtle driving force in her daughter's religious education. Should Marilee actually become a Nun, she reasoned, she would no longer feel the long standing pain. The money she made over the years of endless late nights cutting and sewing school uniforms along with other dresses for neighbor children and their mothers had been faithfully squirreled away. The contents of the tinny lock-box of precious possessions hidden in her lingerie drawer would help pay the way.

As so it came to pass that Marilee was sent off to Saint Mary's Academy to live and study until the time arrived for her to become the bride of God. Those qualities so remarkable in her as a child continued through her high school years. At seventeen, she was a beautiful young woman, possessed of self confidence, intelligence and a strong sense of logic; perfect qualifications for a Nun. Or a victim.

It came, as terror often does, from nowhere, unexpectedly and totally as a random twist on the endless ribbon of chance.

Jake Chimoro's quest for a young woman strong enough to become the perfect convert had gone badly so far. Three young women failed by dying before their soul could become his, before they could survive the degradation necessary to meet his needs. Not one survived Jake's soul-replacement ceremonies whereby their inner self would become his own.

The method of accomplishing this wondrous, demonic vision had come to Jake during a drug induced dream while he was in the prison hospital recovering from a drug overdose. His brilliant flash of pure understanding was focused on his maleness, the realization that his strength and his life purpose were all contained in his semen. By persistent, constant, inundation of every orifice, a female could, over time, be forced to become himself, she would become one with total understanding. She would become one who would far exceed the incomplete understanding he felt unable to articulate. But *she* would. She would become the core of his following, the holy mother, the bride of the Demon Saint.

Jake understood it might be some time until his recent victims were forgotten so he decided to abandon the West until things cooled off. Despite everything east of the Mississippi being strange territory for him he reasoned he could handle it. He figured it would be a lot more crowded, but his pal, Smother Tipton, had worked the east and he said there were a lot more places to hit.

Jake, Smother and Bushy Willis crossed the big river at Saint Louis then headed generally north. Their stolen, live-in van, after two months of housing three seldom washed males, smelled much like old sweat socks dipped in garlic then soaked in stale beer. After passing through Illinois and Indiana, Jake decided to head north toward Detroit where he thought he knew the whereabouts of some former prison buddies. The three men were running short of cash so they decided to rob a convenience store on the outskirts of Toledo. Because they weren't sure the beaten and stabbed clerk would survive, they decided crossing the state line as quickly as possible was a good idea.

The first Michigan town they entered was Monroe. Just past the center of town they spotted a large circular drive dividing an immense lawn fronting a group of impressive brick buildings. Jake had Smother pull into the drive. He wanted some time to look over his road map and plan their next moves.

He was awestruck when, a few minutes later he looked up from his map and saw Marilee Cutter, walking alone, across the soft green grass under the beautiful tall trees, right toward the van.

Marilee had no thoughts about the van parked on the drive right where she would pass. No reason to do so, visitors cars and service vehicles were often parked there, except they were usually closer to the buildings. This one was over a hundred yards from anything and it was partially shielded by the trees. As she drew alongside the vehicle, her arms wrapped around the books she held against her breast, she was engrossed in thought about this afternoon's debate. Suddenly, the large door of the van slammed sideways to reveal the most startling sight she had ever seen. A mountainous brown man with broad white stripes, naked to the waist, sat with his arms outstretched as if in welcome.

Her response was a sharp step, a stumble backwards, away from what her disbelieving eyes took in: he was covered with white stripes, each outlined in black, from his bulging biceps to his waist. Another stripe ran across his forehead above his eyebrows and below his bald head with it's single knot of long hair which hung like a ponytail alongside his face. He beamed a brown toothed smile of total satisfaction, much as if he knew he was ending a very long search, and he reached out for her.

Before she could scream, kick, think, run or even fully react, Marilee was struck from behind by one of two men who converged on her. Bushy Willis had been sent behind the van from where he emerged to strike her with the weighted fish-billy. Then Smother Tipton rushed from the front of the van. Together, they tossed her, along with her books, into Jake's waiting arms.

Smother, the one who had come around from the front side, darted back around the front and into the driver's seat. He headed the van out of the drive, down the short block to the main North-South highway. Within three minutes the men and their captive were on their way toward Detroit.

Bushy Willis jumped into the van, slammed the door shut and was clawing at Marilee's skirt before they were out of the drive.

"We got ourselves some sweet young pussy today, Jake. I sure as hell need some."

Jake was silently appraising his prize, "This is a good one," he muttered, "leave her alone for a minute. I want to get her fixed before she wakes up."

By the time they passed Marilee's home which fronted a vacant lot overlooking the North-South highway, some fifty minutes later, she was gagging on the blood draining from the sockets of her missing front teeth mixed with the first of Saint Jake's ministrations.

Father Wood, walking his daily walk, past the new church construction, while reading his office, stopped and looked heavenward. He felt a sudden pain in the left side of his head. He began to pray for something he wasn't sure he understood. As he prayed, he absently-mindedly reached down, as if for a little girl's upraised hand.

The closed, commercial van with nothing but foul smelling clothing, rags, blankets, empty bottles and food remnants, along with a dozen more just like it, stolen and later abandoned, became Marilee's prisons for more than three impossible, unimaginable, sustained-nightmare years.

Jake's personal torment during that time was trifling compared to hers but it was unbearable to him. Despite his mistreatment of her, the withholding of food and water, the continuous sexual depravity, the physical abuse, punching, biting, cutting, the endless stench, lying in her own wastes and worse, in that of others, Marilee somehow locked herself in a secret place which was beyond his reach.

She never spoke a single word.

Jake followed his plan of filling her with his own body fluids. He was endlessly torn between his need to possess her as his own and the conflicting need to keep his followers in line. He suffered tremendous frustration from his inability to force her to respond. He wanted her screams, he needed her tears. Bushy and Smother didn't give a damn about Marilee's reactions, their desires were limited to their own needs to abuse and violate her body. Jake, in turn, needed male supporters, he couldn't be alone, and yet he hated sharing Marilee.

He tried rules; for a while, his friends could only sodomize her. But that was less than they wanted. Bushy died when Jake returned one day and caught the hairy bastard fucking her. Jake's large, dirty knife almost severed Bushy's head because he swung it with such force. Marilee was soaked in Bushy's warm blood but her only feeling was relief. Later, she felt pleasure after Jake and Smother were forced to steal a clean van. They had poured gasoline over Bushy's body and all the bloody rags and blankets in an effort to burn everything beyond recognition.

Her life was spent chained to the same floor bolts which held the seat belts in place. The chain was long enough to permit Jake to move her into whatever position he wanted but otherwise, it was short-locked. Then it was not long enough for her to crawl into the front area or to reach a door. Once she managed to begin drumming her bare feet against the sides of the van when everyone was away. The only result was to have Jake demonstrate how his wooden toy could be used to painfully break an ankle bone.

"Try that again," he said, "and I'll bust the other one, or maybe a knee."

Marilee not only refused to speak, she also refused to see Jake. Regardless of what he might do, she would not permit her eyes to focus on him. It drove him to greater excesses. Still, she neither spoke nor looked. Jake didn't exist.

At times her strength of will drove him to a frenzy of hate, leaving her bleeding and unconscious. Other times he would display his power over her by granting those who were with him free use of Marilee, sometimes three at once. He frequently used her inability to resist as a quick source of cash. Despite the filth and stench, she was a beautiful woman and her helplessness most often incited her tormentors to every sort of excess.

Occasionally she would be alone for as long as two days with nothing but food scraps and insufficient water, hands tied in front, legs tied to prevent standing. During such times she knew screaming would bring on nothing more than a dirty rag stuffed into her mouth. But during those periods she allowed herself to feel the sweet joy of a temporary respite.

For three years Marilee dreamed and prayed and kept herself alive with her faith and her sense of logic. *If God exists, as I have been taught, then this is a test and I must prove my faith by survival. My body is not my eternal soul and my soul cannot be reached or damaged, it belongs to God and I will remain locked inside my soul until I return to my God or I prove myself worthy and I am set free.*

If God is an impersonal force as others believe, then earthly life is an extension of that force and my eternal self is part of such a God and cannot be reached or destroyed. I need only to await my release either through eternal knowledge returning to itself, through death, or through forces of life which I do not understand. But, I will survive, every line of logic leads to survival. This torture is for today only, only for today, tomorrow it will end, I will survive.

She imagined herself locked in step with Sisyphus, painfully pushing that huge and weighty rock up the mountain only to watch it roll back to the bottom each time they reached the crest. She became competent at removing herself, from herself, each time she was abused. When Jake peddled her flesh to a street gang in exchange for cocaine one night, each of the dozen or so abusers simply became another crashing rock to be rolled back up that eternal mountain.

Her joys were rare but no less significant: a glimpse of the outdoors through the windshield, a breath of fresh air through an open window, time to sleep, a rare moment of being alone. These were the events which, combined with her prayers and logical conclusions of survival, kept her alive, if not fully sane. She could no longer picture her mother or father, sometimes she didn't know her name or where she came from. She felt her brain was being eaten away by some terrible parasitic form of life. The crawling, consuming life Jake forced into her, over and endlessly, constantly, day and night, whether she was conscious, sleeping or trying to stifle even the silent screams.

If only he wouldn't tell her every time, wouldn't press his massive face to hers every time he came inside her. Tell her every time how he was coming, why he was coming, how he was pumping her body and her soul full of his powerful juices until one day she would be his, she would be him. Then her angels would come and lift her away while she, with every pulse of her heart, chanted to herself, *never, never, never.*

After Jake murdered Bushy, Smother Tipton ran away, afraid he might be next. But Jake's henchmen came and went in a steady stream. Most of them soon became frightened of Jake's delusions, threats and brutality. They all used Marilee as their perverted desires and Jake's whims permitted. To her they were nothing more than another bad smell, a new pain to endure, just one more test on her road to absolution and freedom. She was right. She and her angels were stronger than their combined evil.

Marilee awoke under a pile of stinking blankets alongside a snoring Jake one night. The van was parked in a wooded area, behind a shabby gas station, south of Tampa, Florida. He had passed out while on his knees over her upturned hips. Her chain was unlocked. Days before she had hidden a heavy, open-end wrench, under the carpet, beneath the driver's seat of this, the latest van. Now she moved as slowly and silently as a snake from under Jake's body.

She hardly dared to breathe as she concentrated on the fluid smoothness of her movements. She forced herself to match the slight rhythms of sex in an effort to keep from arousing him. She prayed that in his stupor he would relax in the belief that he was still fucking her. She feared her heart would burst from the incredible pounding that was sure to awaken Jake. She had to keep pulling her mind back from its eagerness to rush away, to lead the escape into the night. When her right hand finally closed around the wrench she paused and she began to tremble in fear.

She couldn't do it.

She knew if she failed to hit him just right it meant her death. Not necessarily by Jake's hands but because she knew there would never be another chance and that knowledge would surely kill her. Suddenly Jake raised his head and opened unfocused eyes. Feeling her there, he rolled slightly and dropped his head back to the hard floor. A moment later he realized he had failed to lock the chain and this time he came fully awake, just as the heavy wrench landed with all the force her depleted body could muster.

The first blow caught him on the temple and Marilee was up in an instant, up into a position where she could swing the heavy wrench with both hands. She landed repeated crushing blows to the skull. She had not spoken aloud during the past three years and now she heard a strange, hoarse voice repeating, "Never, never, never!"

Naked and barefoot, she leapt out of the van, only to fall to her knees as unused muscles rebelled. Reaching back into the van she tried to pull a foul blanket around her as she struggled to stand. Then looking around she was dismayed to see they were parked on the edge of swampland, full of tall, straight Jack Pines with no apparent escape possible. *Better to die in the swamps*, she thought, and as she turned she came face to face with a frightened young black man who had just walked out of the gas station.

Roland Pell had never seen such beauty and love expressed in his life as that which emanated from this toothless white woman with dirty-hair, a stinking body and bloody hands who reached out to him, smiled and quietly said, "Please save me," as she collapsed in his arms.

Pell's instincts rallied after glancing inside the van at Jake's huge form. He dragged and carried Marilee to his battered pick up truck parked only ten yards away. He was headed south to Naples with a load of turnips and he knew that regardless of the circumstances, this woman needed to be away from this place. He didn't stop to think how or why he knew it, he just knew it had to be. He also knew the people at the station knew where he was going and that worried him.

After driving less than ten miles Roland reached a fateful decision and turned onto a small road which he knew would eventually connect with the Interstate. He reasoned if he could get this girl across the state to Miami, or Fort Lauderdale, she could get help, get lost, and she would be safe. Somewhere he would have to get her some clothes. He only had eleven dollars but he had a tee shirt and a spare pair of old jeans she could use. Maybe he could buy her some cheap sandals and still have enough for gas to get back across Alligator Alley to his Uncle's place. He decided he had to do some careful thinking.

When he looked over at the sleeping Marilee, he knew he could do it. He had never seen so much radiance in anyone's face in his life. Not even in church.

VII

In the reflective surface behind the counter I caught a glimpse of three strange looking men going through the cafeteria line for coffee. Alan Barber, the ER attending physician, was in his greens with a stethoscope sticking out of his back pocket. Mark Todd looked sharp and crisp in a well cut, pin stripe suit and I was wearing jeans with an open collar and sport Jacket. Before we could pay up, sit down and start a conversation Barber was paged and had to settle for a quick sip of coffee. He excused himself and hustled away.

"What do we do next, Mark?"

"I can't say what you're going to do, Stone, but if Donna makes it I'm going to see that she has total, absolute protection. Then I'm going after Saint Jake."

"And if she doesn't?"

"Then I'm going after him sooner and harder."

"Sounds as if Jake is dead meat either way, or maybe you are, and you still have no real proof he's the man."

"I know he's the one. I don't care about your kind of proof, I'm not planning an arrest. And, don't forget the neighbor who saw them leaving Donna's place, if she saw Jake, she'll know it. And when I find that sonofabitch, he'll tell me, trust me. What about you, Stone, what do you plan to do?"

Nothing in my life made me feel as empty as that question. Not that the question was empty, I was. I felt as if I was staring into the center of the universe, like those film promo's on Star Trek, where everything is rushing past. I not only had no answer, I had nothing. I couldn't imagine *what* the hell to do now.

"Mark, you have to know I'm lost in a situation like this, you know my background. I'm taught to look at life from a thousand years away, this stuff is real. What *can* I do?"

"I know that, Stone, I just had to toss you the ball to see what you would say. Maybe you're a stand-up guy. Maybe you'd like to help, but I'm afraid you can't deal with this anymore than I could step in and do brain surgery."

"I want to help, I want to do something."

"I know, I understand. We'll think of something, don't worry about it."

With that he removed his suit jacket and laid it over the back of the couch, sat down, pulled off his tassel loafers and stretched out. I didn't comment on the shoulder holster and gun he wore, it spoke for itself. He threw an arm across his face and I took that as a signal for silence. I didn't want silence, he hadn't finished telling me what he knew about Saint Jake and while I didn't want to hear the rest, I had to. But I also had a ton of thinking to do. Donna Delgado, or whatever her name is, was not someone a thousand years removed. She had become an important part of my life.

I picked up a *People* magazine, thumbed it and saw nothing. I settled for staring at the window above the couch on which Mark Todd was pretending to be asleep.

I must have dozed off because when I looked up, young Doctor Barber was talking to Mark, who was standing. Barber looked happy, Mark looked serious then he turned to me, "Donna's stable, she's gonna beat this thing."

I looked at Barber.

"It's like he said, her vital signs have settled down and her chances look better then I would have expected. She's still out, but I think that's okay."

"How long will she have to be out before it's not okay," I asked.

"I expect her to come around before sundown, if not, then I'll begin to worry. But, and listen to me, none of us should worry until then, I mean it. You guys can see her for a minute, and I also mean for just a minute."

"You two go along," Mark bent for his shoes, "I'm going to check on her protection schedule, then I'll be there."

It was six AM, straight up, when Mark Todd and I walked out of the emergency room reception area.

"I want to hear whatever you have left about Jake. I'll buy breakfast, what do you say, Mark?

"My favorite meal."

We each drove our own cars and I followed him to a place that specializes in breakfast around the clock. Sliding into a booth he said, "While we were driving here I was thinking about the rest of the story and it's a bit strange."

"Strange, how?"

"There are years of information, well over a hundred reports and statements, but while each piece is important, it all fits into a repetitious pattern than can be easily summarized. It just seems wrong as hell to do it, you know, it's like trivializing a really terrible thing."

"Do you have all this stuff in writing somewhere?"

"Matter of fact, I do. I know better than to rely on memory so I keep every scrap of paper along with every note I make on phone calls. I've even taped some of the incoming calls and one-on-one conversations. Why?"

"That's good, Mark. I have an idea but first give me an overview. How would you categorize what you have, what sort of sources, how does it all add up in your mind?"

"I know someone who produces mailing lists for all kinds of businesses all over the country. This fellow has specialized computers and printers that run around the clock, turning out lists for every sort of manufacturer and mail order house you can think of. He worked up a print-out of every sheriff's office and police department in the country for me, at least every one he could find, and it looked to me as if he found them all."

"How did he get that information?"

"We may not have a very efficient network for spreading police information but it turns out that the mail order people who sell everything from pepper spray to bullet proof vests do. They don't send salesmen around anymore you know, now it's all mail order. Joe Telly, that's the computer guy I know, put together one hell of a list for me. I made up a form letter asking for information, any kind of information, on Jake. I described him and said he was known to have been holding a young woman captive in a series of stolen vans. That he was joined for varying periods of time by other scummy bums and was roaming the whole country. I repeated the basic message every couple of months because I realized some people would toss it out until something jogged their memory. Cops are pretty screwed up and hamstrung but on an individual basis there're a lot of good cops trying to do a job. I received hundreds of calls, notes, photocopies of reports, fax messages, you name it.

"Basically it adds up to a totally obscene situation. Jake kept Donna chained up like a dog, he abused her, he used her to get drugs and cash, his cronies also abused her and somehow she survived for as long as three years. We're pretty sure that a handful of other women failed to survive before he grabbed Donna. The details are pure puke, but the bottom line is an incredible story of survival. If you read the stuff you wouldn't believe it."

"That's exactly what I plan to do. I'm no good as a cop or an investigator but I know how to read and surmise. That material you have has to be full of answers. With your permission I want to do what I do best. I want to study every thing you have on Donna's case."

"I like it, Stone, it'll keep you out of trouble, bring you into the case and, who knows, you may save the day. In fact I love it, you've got carte blanche to my office, my secretary, my files, my computer system, whatever you need."

After breakfast and following a long night, I felt totally wrung out. I decided to head for the club where I did twenty minutes on the treadmill, half an hour of weights, then finished up with a tough twenty laps in the pool. After steam and a hot tub I stretched out on a padded bench and exercised my best snore-tunes for forty minutes.

I came up feeling pretty good and decided to head for my office to check my calendar and plan my attack on Mark Todd's files before looking in on Donna.

My head was full of plans as I pulled up at the office. I was excited with the prospect of searching out Saint Jake's weakness. I turned the key, swung the door and, as usual, prepared to push the mail away from under the opened door. The door contained a mail slot through which mail dropped on the floor inside. Whenever the door was opened some of the mail would catch under the door. I had no secretary or receptionist to pick up the mail before I arrived.

But today, the mail was already pushed back, out of the way. I froze. Next I backed out and closed the door, removed the key and started to leave. As I turned I found myself staring into the face of a raunchy, dangerous looking man holding a tire iron.

"Just go on inside, Buddy, somebody wants to see you."

As he stepped toward me he began to smack the palm of his other hand with the iron. I heard the door behind me being pulled open and I knew I had to do something. Just as the iron hit his hand again I lunged. I feinted a punch but as my weight shifted to my left foot I kicked with my right. It caught him full force in the balls. He folded. I ran.

My office building faced a small park covering a square block. By crossing the park diagonally I could reach a busy street and one short block further would put me at the busiest intersection in town. I was laying them down as fast as I ever ran in my life. I reasoned that if Jake weighed three hundred pounds, as advertised, he sure as hell wasn't going to catch me. The guy I left groveling on the ground was out of it and if there was somebody else involved, they'd have to be Olympic class to catch up.

Nobody tried.

I reached the busy intersection, stopped and bent with my hands on my knees sucking for oxygen. I was panting like a three-minute miler and breaking into a monster sweat at the same time. After catching my breath I realized I was at a stop when a bus hissed to the curb. It was heading toward the beach which struck me as the morning's best idea.

As the bus traveled East it backtracked past the corner from where I could see the length of one block to my building. I had just a brief look, but it was enough. Three men were headed toward the park's parking area where there were about a dozen cars, vans and pickups. During that brief look I couldn't tell about their exact destination or identify their vehicle. But I was sure the biggest one of the three was Jake. It had to be, his stripes were covered by a denim shirt, but he was huge. God, he was tall *and* broad. As the bus carried me past the view and before other buildings interfered, I swear he stopped and looked directly at me. My feeling was that he knew I was on this bus and he was deciding whether to follow it. I knew two things at that point: we would eventually come face to face and, I wasn't anxious for it to happen.

It was coming up noon when I climbed off the bus in the middle of the beach strip and a blue million tourists. There was no sign of Jake. If he had followed we couldn't have spotted each other. I wanted coffee, maybe a drink, a chance to think and access to a phone. But every place looked full. In a normal environment people eat and drink at predictable times which means you can walk into a bar or restaurant before or after those times and be seated. But in a resort area it's all different, basically all tourists do is eat, drink and shop. The result is that every place is crowded at all times. Mix in a mid-morning snack, a mid-afternoon wallop and, bingo, full seats at all hours. I settled for take out coffee and a seat along the wave wall in a rare patch of palm shade.

I knew I had to get back to my office but there were problems. First was security. Jake and his pals had broken in so I had to take steps for a better lock up system. I couldn't deal with those bums being able to catch me off guard or, worse yet, from inside. I was also feeling the strange sense of violation we all feel whenever someone has gotten inside our private places. I decided to call Mark Todd for advice on that one, he was a former cop and he would have some good ideas. Next problem was just going back in. What if Jake was lying in wait? I needed help going back in, maybe the police. But what could I tell them?

Finally I decided Jake wouldn't wait inside, at least not in daylight on the same day he had been spotted there. He wouldn't take the chance of my returning with cops. I decided to return. I didn't want to, but, if it was done quickly, it would be safe. I had to go back sometime.

And there was another problem, the biggest problem of all: until now I felt like an observer, not a player. I had nothing to do with Saint Jake, he didn't know I existed, or so I thought. I've never been one for direct involvement. I listen, I talk. I've made a lifetime habit of non-involvement. One of my standard jokes is repeating that my family motto is, "It's a strange and tortured world, for everyone but me."

Mark Todd was out when I called so I left a message.

"Tell him," I said, "The Game is afoot. Yes, that's all, and tell him I'll call back within a couple of hours."

In the bright full glare of early afternoon my confidence level began to rise. I hailed a taxi cruising the beach intending to take it back to my office. Then two disturbing thoughts crept out of a dark corner: if Jake was watching the office he might expect me to return by cab. That thought was immediately followed by an even darker one; there was stuff all around the office that informed Jake of my home address. But what the hell, I was in the phone book and he knows my name, so my home address is no secret anyway.

I changed my instructions and had the driver take me to an auto rental office. Playing my version of cloak and dagger, I asked for an inconspicuous model of car, preferably one with darkly tinted windows. No dark glass was available, auto rental places don't tint glass. But a run of the mill four door model seemed inconspicuous enough.

I drove to the parking area situated just a couple of hundred yards from my office front door. I cruised the lot slowly as if selecting a parking spot. I was actually peering into every vehicle in order to see whether Jake, or one of his henchmen, was watching my place. Except for a guy in a shirt and tie, filling out some papers and eating a sandwich, every car was empty. I chose a spot and parked. Now it was possible to look at all probable locations where a watching car might park. I was wishing for some binoculars when I saw a familiar car pull up near my front door and saw the even more welcome figure of James Wakins step out. I immediately started the car and raced toward the office at a speed most unusual for that quiet corner.

James looked apprehensive and crouched into a defensive turn as I approached.

"Damn, Stone, what the hell you doin, rammin up here like a chase movie."

I wanted to hug him. "I'm just glad to see you, James. I hurried because I didn't want you to get away."

"Bad words out on the street, Stone. I found out about Donna this morning so I went over to the hospital. She's in bad shape, man. She's not awake yet and I hear it's almost twenty four hours. I saw Todd there and he filled me in, he's hurtin worried."

"You know Mark Todd?"

"Course I know him, he's my lawyer. Donna took me to him when I had some trouble."

"I should have guessed. What's the latest word on Donna? I'm going over there as soon as you help me out here."

"Todd said she'll make it, but he's torn up that she hasn't come out of it. He's worried about an extended coma. Help you…how?"

I told him about this morning's problem and why, even though I was sure the coast was clear, I was glad he was here to go inside with me.

"You enjoy endangering my young ass, Stone? Remember I told you about bad words on the street? From what I hear the guy that did Donna makes the devil look like a pussy. Now you and me gonna just walk in cold, and worse yet, stay inside where we can be trapped? I don't think so. If I'm going in with you then I'm carrying, and you should be too."

"You mean a gun?"

"No, a condom. Of course a gun. You know how to handle one?"

"Of course, yourself. I held an expert rating in ROTC, rifle and side arms."

"Goody. A college rah, rah gun handler. Let's go. What're you driving?"

"I picked up a rental car to get back here. Go where, James?"

"Let's leave both our cars here. We'll take the rental in case anybody's watching. I'll drive while you call Todd. Got your phone?"

"I'll grab it out of my car. Why Todd?"

"It's a good idea to bring him up to speed and tell him we're picking up two hand guns. See what he says. He's one smart, tough guy, for a Honky."

As James drove I called and reached Todd this time. He wanted every ounce of detail I could tell him from the time we parted this morning. He said getting the guns was a good idea and he would meet James and me at my office in forty five minutes, with a locksmith in tow. Also, he ordered that we not go in to the building until he was there.

James angled into a spot directly in front of a small gun shop in an old, semi-hidden part of town.

"Even the cops buy guns here," he said.

It was a small shop with a glass showcase dividing the space into front and back halves. The back half contained a beat up overstuffed chair facing a TV set perched on a telephone cable drum. Two very large Dobermans raised their eyebrows but not their heads from their throw rug beds. An antique seven foot safe stood in one corner with its door ajar. A storage closet was built into the rest of the space not taken up by a small bathroom which also had an open door. The proprietor was a very large man who was wearing expensive looking casual clothes, a Rolex watch and several rings. When he turned to look at us I could see an enormous Italian horn on a heavy gold chain around his neck.

"Help you guys?"

"We're looking for hand guns," James said. "I do some work with Cal Brisboy who says you deal right."

"How long you runnin with Cal?"

"Three, coming up four, years."

"Since before his bad bust?"

"Right after. He says he never did do any junk."

"He never did. What're you looking for."

"Easy carry, probably a thirty eight revolver."

"Not planning any gun fights, eh? Anybody serious gettin Glocks and such."

"We not lookin to get in, we're looking to stay out. Hope we never have to pull down with nobody. Just carryin so some folks don't think wrong shit. You know?"

He motioned to the dogs and hauled himself out of the chair with an embarrassing amount of effort, "Old war wounds," he smiled.

I was beginning to feel as though my life was being overly affected by three-hundred pound males. Raising a box from the storage space under the display he opened it to show a white metal revolver. "This is as good as they get. It's a Ruger SR one o' one, three fifty seven magnum, stainless, nice piece, never rust. I can give you a good deal."

I still hadn't said a word when James asked, "You got a regular black one?"

"Sure, it's cheaper yet."

Turning to me with his "James, the man," kind of smile, he said, "What do you say, Smooth, a black one for me and a white one for you? You know, so we can tell them apart."

Turning to the shop owner he asked, "One stainless, one regular, a pair of belt holsters and two boxes of bullets, what's your best deal? And by the way, don't neither one of us know a fair deal, but Cal does."

"Fill out the gun purchase information forms, give me your driver's license information and walk away for five fifty. Pick em up in three days."

I decided to get into the act, "We'll pay the price, give you all the information you need but we have to take the guns out today, now."

"The law says you have to wait three days unless you have a permit to carry. Nothing I can do about that."

"Do what you have to do but we need the guns now."

Looking at James he asked, "What's your last name?"

"Wakins, James Wakins," James answered in a James Bond tone of voice.

"Come back in five minutes, Wakins. I'll see if I can help you."

I spoke up, "What do you mean come back…"

James took my arm, "C'mon, Stone, give the man a minute."

As we stepped outside I asked, "What the hell is that about?"

"The man got to call Cal to check my bona fide's"

Mark Todd was waiting when we returned to the office. He was out of his car before I was fully stopped and as he approached me he said, "I never figured on this thing spreading beyond me and Donna, Stone. I'm sorry as hell you've been dragged into it."

"I'm not. Let's just get the sonofabitch."

Following Todd's instructions I stood off to one side as I unlocked the front door. He swept a gun from somewhere, up into firing position and stepped inside before quickly swinging it in a half circle ending at the door to the back offices. He already told James and me that he agreed it was unlikely Jake had hung around and we should keep our new guns holstered to our belts. Even so, it was unnerving to watch him taking such precautions.

"James, cover this door while I check the rest of the front area. Stone, how many offices are up here?"

"Two, and a bathroom."

He was back quickly, "James, now cover this front door area while I sweep the rest of the place. I don't want anyone crawling up my ass. Stone, stay close behind and tell me where everything is, are there light switches near this door? It's pretty dim inside."

"Just inside the door, lights up the whole place. One room to the right, another to the left, one more bathroom, immediate left. It's all pretty open."

"Then let's go."

This time he swept from right to left then paused, "that archway?"

"To the back filing and storage area," I said as I stared at the opening.

Todd hesitated, then apparently making up his mind, "Slowly draw your gun and hold it on that rear opening while I check the bathroom."

I felt as if I had just won a merit badge. I held a two handed aim at the back opening while my eyes kept flicking toward the conference room on the right.

After a moment, "Move forward so I can pass behind you to check the other room."

Another moment, "Hold your aim on the left side of the opening and walk a little ahead. I'll cover the right."

Then it was over and I needed to sit down. I walked toward my desk then stopped short as I saw two large turds plopped dead center on some unopened mail. James had just called to Todd to announce that a lock-smith's van was pulling up in front.

"If it's a white van with nothing but Winkler Services on the door, bring him in."

"Todd, that rotten bastard climbed on my desk and took a shit. What the hell is that, what sort of crud does that?"

"Don't touch it," he said.

"I'll try to resist."

He walked over and stared at the offering.

"Phony Bastard," he said. "You saw the size of the man, he'd play hell perching on your desk. This is set up to scare you. I'm willing to bet it's dog crap."

I grabbed a dust pan into which I pushed the pile, mail and all. If it wasn't junk mail before, it was now.

Mark introduced James and me to August Winkler, an elderly gent with a German accent. They walked off together to size up the place while we walked back up front.

"Thanks, James, I appreciate your help in all this. I just hope Saint Jake isn't watching and drags you into this thing."

"Stone, you might be okay, I don't know yet, but anything I do will be done for Donna. You know that, she's everybody's special lady and that includes me. She helped me keep my shit together, way back."

"We found where they came in, Stone, the rear overhead door is a joke. Augie says this place is like a fortress though, small high windows and all, he'll have you fool-proof by tonight. Then I want him to check your apartment, he thinks he can be there by seven thirty or eight, does that work for you?"

"Yeah, sure, that's fine. How about James and his family?"

"I don't think Jake has made you yet, James, but let's make sure your place is tight."

A strange look crossed James' face. I had the feeling he wasn't used to having people care about him.

"This bum probably don't know, or care, about me and in my neighborhood everybody's got good locks, but I *would* feel better if I could have Mr. Winkler take a look. Maybe tomorrow. That be okay, Mr. Winkler?"

"Come to my place at one o'clock, we ride over and you show me. We take a look."

"It's too bad Mr. Winkler didn't work Donna's place over before this happened," I said.

Mark looked at Winkler, then at me. "We did that, Stone, long ago. She must have let him in."

As I stood alongside Donna's bed that afternoon I wondered what to do. At times such as this, personal beliefs are tested; you are forced to ponder all those things you accept as truth. The greatest wonder is not what we know, but what we don't know and yet we feel. I knew of no way to help Donna and yet I simultaneously knew there *was* a way to help her. A way I knew, or have known, which lies hidden in the mists of deeper knowledge.

I slid the fingers of my right hand into the palm of her left and gently closed the contact with my thumb on the back of her hand. Then, on an impulse, I reached across her to slide the fingers of my left hand into the palm of her right hand. I pictured myself as a power source, perhaps like a storage battery. I concentrated as hard as I possibly could on willing my strength into, through and on out of her body.

I pictured the two of us as a closed circuit, my strength flowing in one side, her weakness flowing out the other. My eyes were closed. I focused and pulled way down, deep inside myself, until I felt there was no more. Then I stopped and removed my hands.

Nothing.

I halfway expected Donna to respond. She didn't. I stared out her window and did the only thing I knew to do, I spoke to her.

"Donna, you've heard some of my beliefs, you know something of how I think, but what about you, what can I tell you that you already know and only need to be reminded of? Now that I know something of what you have suffered I have to believe you must have a remarkably strong faith. I don't necessarily mean religious beliefs, but certainly spiritual conviction. You have needed it before and you need it again, right now.

"It is obvious that life is a gift and it is interesting that the donor has chosen to remain anonymous. And in that anonymity there is logic, a logic that tells us that because we can't know, we must seek, and because the life gift is anonymous, it is also without strings and it is perfect. It is ours, ours to make or break, ours to enjoy or change, ours to direct, ours to begin anew each day and above all, ours to use to learn."

When I turned to look at her again her blue eyes were open and a tear was running down her cheek.

Donna's recovery signs energized everyone in different ways. Aleena Wakins prayed for her friend and now she decided that, regardless of the difficulties, she was going to keep her baby. She further decided she was going to do as her brother wanted, she would finish school then concentrate on getting into college and becoming a nurse. No more babies, she said, not until after she had her degree and a right husband. But now she was certain she was meant to keep the one she carried.

I gave James my cell phone with instructions to call with every scrap of information he picked up on the streets. Mark told me James was working numbers and horses and neither he nor Cal, the man he worked for, would touch anything outside those two relatively harmless pursuits. I reasoned James would be a good outside man.

When I replaced the phone I picked up two more. One went to Raymond the flasher with the same instructions to call me day or night. The other went to Malka Yelick who was still searching for love in every bar on the south side, every night of the week. I also kept my meeting schedule with these folks but more often than not we talked about Donna and watching for signs of Jake. Adding that focus to their lives seemed to do them more good than all my philosophical pronouncements.

I buried myself in studying every scrap of paper Mark collected during the past three and a half years and the portrait of a demon began to take shape. I came to believe it was time to turn the tables.

VIII

The broken-brain characters who served briefly in Saint Jake's unformed army were frequently under arrest as they bumped through their oddly reactive lives. During the inevitable interrogations they would often speak freely of their days with Jake. These characters were like "Tin Men;" they loved to tell their tales to anyone who would listen. Even when the listener was a cop. Sometimes the policemen would remember reading a Mark Todd memo and would pass along the stories they heard, adding another piece to the portrait of a madman.

The accumulation of notes, facsimiles, memos, phone call write-ups and photocopies of arrest reports, gathered for a period of just over forty months, accumulated like brush strokes on canvas. As the picture formed I began to realize Marilee Cutter / Donna Delgado more than survived Jake, she had beaten him. He was determined to totally dominate her, to capture her soul, to impregnate her, to brutalize her. He struggled to destroy her mind to the point that she would become his. His vision for her was in the fashion of Dracula's women in the old Bela Lugosi movies. But he knew she found some mysterious way to protect her inner self from his atrocities. He knew she prayed, even when he beat her senseless. He felt it when she crawled into herself during his pressing, pounding brutal attacks. Regardless of his ranting, his rabid insinuation of himself inside her, he never could, never would, reach the inner woman she denied him. Her ability to remove herself drove this madman deeper and deeper into his fetid dreams.

At times he would protect her from other men, refusing to let them touch her. Other times he would use her to demonstrate his domination by having other men watch while he used her viciously, sometimes choking her with his penis until she passed out. She was near death many times. Once from a terrible infection that resulted from his decision to mark her with Jake Stripes. He used the point of the large, dirty, knife he always carried to scrape deep scratches in her skin, his intention was to cause permanent scars reminiscent of his stripes. He began the procedure on her upper thigh and when, after a long feverish period, the infection had run its course, he lost interest.

She was an important part of his income because he sold her for uses no prostitute would ever tolerate. Most times for cash, sometimes for drugs, often for favors. The men who used her were usually as unclean as the women, but the women were sometimes more brutal; one nipple had been bitten so badly it remained forever mutilated.

And still she won. The final insult, her failure to kill him during her escape, drove him around the bend of reality. Now there was only her, nothing else could matter as long as he lived. He would possess her or destroy her.

When she stumbled out of Jake's van into the arms of Roland Pell, it was her look of absolute love and trust which moved him to do the right thing. With little more than a glance at the unconscious mound of striped flesh, Pell used the precious moment to save her sanity as well as her life.

Jake's pals left him, along with his stolen van, parked on the apron leading to the emergency room of a Fort Meyers hospital before disappearing, then reappearing on a New Orleans arrest report two days later.

Saint Jake survived and after serving thirty months as an indigent repeat offender, car thief and armed robber, he embarked on the search for *his* woman. But no longer could it be just any woman, his obsession was Marilee, she had to pay, to be his or he would forever be nothing.

IX

Our band of misfits began to score. On her way out of a four AM club, Malka spotted Jake making a drug buy in the club parking lot. We had carefully rehearsed such situations. She knew better than to get too close or arouse any suspicion. She also knew to get the make, model and plates before he drove away. When the police caught up with the stolen vehicle just before sunrise, they found his two cronies but Jake was elsewhere. Now, for at least a couple of days, he was alone, and I believed Jake couldn't stand being alone.

Three nights later, on my way into the hospital for a late visit with Donna, I noticed the security cop on duty smelled badly. Suspicious, I stopped, backed up and said, "Good evening, officer. Everything all right here?"

At close range the man's body odor was remarkable. He nodded, didn't meet my gaze, and quietly muttered, "Everyding's fine."

He held his upper lip down when he spoke but I could see he was missing most of the teeth on my side. That did it.

I stepped inside the room and waved hello to Donna. She was awake and smiling until I grabbed her phone. I surmised that if my suspicions were right we were ahead of Jake this time. I held Donna's hand and stood facing the door while I dialed James who picked up on the first ring.

"Yo."

"James, we have a cop with bad BO, missing teeth and pants that are too long, standing outside Donna's door."

"She okay?"

"She's fine."

"Got your piece?"

"Holster's unsnapped."

"On my way."

James showed up in less than ten minutes with two burly young friends.

"Evening officer, how you doin tonight," with his best James grin. "I'm the driver. You know, the chauffeur for Mr. Stone who is here visiting, Miss, you know, the lady inside there. These two gentlemen are Mr. Stone's bodyguards. You know, they like ride shotgun, you dig?"

The cop, sweating now, nodded his head, "Yeah, sure. Everyding's fine here."

James couldn't leave it alone, "Man, there's a terrible stink around here, you step in something?"

Then he cracked the door, "Everyding okay in there, Mr. Stone?"

"Everyding's fine, Mr. Wakins. I think our timing is especially good tonight."

"I'll be right outside, Mr. Stone, I'm waiting for some friends to show up. By the way, does it smell like shit in there? Say, where you going officer, aren't you on duty?"

The cop half turned, "Quick piss break, be right back."

"You're going the wrong way, it's down this way, toward the door there."

The phony guard hesitated, then saw Mark Todd bearing down on him leading two real cops. He spun and made a break for the entrance doors but James timed a kick at his ankles which sent him sprawling. Before he could get to his feet the real policemen had guns pressed to his head.

He quickly gave up everything: how Jake threatened him, how Jake was coming in to grab Donna, how Jake had popped the real cop, even a description of Jake's current van. The man was a bad smelling blabbermouth.

The police were suddenly in the game, up to their hips. They do not take kindly to those who abuse one of their own. The duty officer had gotten caught off guard by a second Jake follower dressed in hospital greens. He forced the officer out the nearby side door then into the parking lot and a skull fracture in Jake's van. Convinced that Jake would kill the officer in order to safely dispose of him, the Fort Lauderdale police moved with astonishing speed. They nailed Muff Thatcher in the van within the hour. The injured officer was still in the back but Jake, the demon, had vanished.

Mark and I agreed that without help, wheels or funds, Jake was bound to be confused and angry. We also believed he wasn't about to give up and we didn't have a clue about what to expect next.

From my reading I surmised Jake was a Pit Bull, one who would rather suffer death than humiliation. I believed him to be smart, maybe a brilliant psychotic, but a man frightened of real life and totally dangerous. And for the moment, he had disappeared.

Our little street team was listening and watching but getting nothing. Now the police also wanted him, every cop in town had his description. It was unimaginable to think that an extremely tall, three hundred pound man with a white stripe tattooed around a brown bald head, with a top knot shank of hair, could just vanish. Then Randall Comsworth Preston came knocking at my office door.

I was waiting for Aleena and James Wakins to show up when the new outside bell rang and Preston, who hadn't shown up for the past three weeks, opened up on me faster than I could open up for him.

"Well, professor asshole, had you included me among your Dead End Kids, this incredibly important information would have been more timely. I know things, you know. I could have helped."

It turned out that Randall hadn't learned about Donna's beating because of a clash of his and her happenings, she was attacked on the day he slipped into a prolonged drunk. Otherwise, he might have seen Jake hop aboard a north bound freight instead of wallowing, semi-conscious in his own private deep green fog. He wouldn't have believed a man so large could move so well.

One of Preston's cronies supplied James with a description of the events surrounding Jake's departure. The passing freight train slowed for the bridge but it was still moving when Jake came up from under the bridge. He trotted alongside for a moment, grabbed the hand ladder, swung one foot up to the lowest rung, pulled the rest of his huge bulk up and slipped around between two cars.

It was the second day before Randall was able to understand things well enough to realize what had happened. By then he also learned about, what some of his drinking buddies had begun to call, "Stone's Gang." Of course I apologized for his failure to show up for his appointments or to be sufficiently sober to take part in recent events.

"After all, Stone, everyone at the bridge knows my whereabouts. You know that girl is the most important person in my life. I want to help. Don't take it upon yourself to make me beg."

"I'm sorry, Randall, and I mean that. I should have tracked you down, should have given you a phone. We need all the help we can get and, who knows, we might have been able to nail Jake if I knew what the hell I was doing. I'm not very good at this stuff, and, yes, I do know how you feel about Donna."

It never occurred to me that non-confrontation could be more difficult than confrontation. How long can you keep your fist clenched? I knew for certain Jake would be back, his obsession for Donna eliminated all other possibilities. Mark Todd knew it too, as did Donna. That knowledge formed the root of the problem which began to develop. Jake had failed and he was forced to bail out without friends or money. But the longer he remained away, the safer it seemed and the harder it became to remain alert.

Life began its inexorable return toward normalcy. The actions necessary for existence produce a soothing balm, repetition and familiarity make it hard to stay alert. Meanwhile, my little building had been made into a fortress by August Winkler and Mark assured me there was no way Jake could break in unless I failed to lock up correctly. That fact prompted me to begin thinking about Donna's safety after she left the hospital.

I automatically stepped up my morning conditioning routine in response to my fear of Jake. Fear of the unknown, mixed with the uncertainty of timing, makes for a strong brew and I drank deeply. I also realigned my sessions with everyone. My avowed purpose was to keep everyone focused but I also realized it was necessary if we wanted to keep "Stone's Gang" at the ready. Jake would be back. We would all need each other, just as Donna would need us all.

Raymond Casper looked the same as always, "I brought your phone back, Doc, it has to be costing you a fortune with all those phone charges you're picking up. I wasn't much help anyway."

"Keep the phone, Raymond. It's important we hold our little network together. This thing isn't over yet and every pair of eyes will be important when the time comes. Have you signed up for that computer course yet?"

"Yeah, I really did, Doc," he said with an edge of surprise in his voice. "It's for two hours, Tuesday and Thursday nights, over at the old high school. I've already signed up. They've got a room full of computers over there and the instructor, I met the guy, says I can pick up a used computer, the same kind, pretty cheap."

"You sound rather high on this program, Raymond. I have a feeling you'll solve computers in no time. How are you feeling, what kind of plans do you have?"

"I'm not sure, Doc, but I'm a good bookkeeper and once I can handle a computer I know I'll have a lot more opportunities. It's just a tool, you know, and software programs are just another kind of ledger. Do you mean it, about all of us really making a difference in protecting Donna? She's one helluva woman you know, I'd do anything for her. She actually cared about what happened to me, all along."

"Raymond, sometimes I think strange thoughts, you know that. One such thought is that we, and I mean all forms of life, are a single creature.

It's hard to describe, but picture…no scratch that, it's too hard to picture. Instead, think about our being part of a blanket of life which covers the planet and extends from a few thousand feet above the surface to a few hundred feet below the surface. I'm not saying that is exactly how it is but it's one way to think about things. In this case it helps make my point. If we *are* connected to this blanket of life then one of the worst things that can happen to us is to be become disconnected, to feel as if we're apart, alone, that no one cares whether we live or die. My point is that a handful of us came together for a while to do a job, to work together and now we all know we have people who *do* care about us."

Raymond smiled for the first time since I met him. "I'm getting worried, Doc. I'm beginning to understand some of the weird stuff you talk about. I don't know whether I'm getting better or you're getting worse."

My days were carving out a short-term pattern. Morning workouts, with forty five minutes added for weights and bag, shower, breakfast and a look-in on Donna. An hour or two at Mark's office reading old or incoming new reports, sending out alert memos, looking for signs of Jake. Usually an afternoon meeting with one of the group followed by some reading time, an afternoon visit with Donna, then dinner, maybe a video and frequently a late visit from Laurie. Sometimes it changed a bit, I might visit Donna after dinner or have dinner with Mark, but the point is, the waiting was beginning to bug me badly.

"What else can we do, Mark?"

"We can wait, we know he's coming. This is always the toughest part, it's like being geared up for a battle. You're all charged up, scared and eager, mostly anxious to get it over with but you don't know when it's going down. We have no control, unfortunately, that part is up to Jake."

"I've never been in a battle."

"Did you play any football in college?"

"Yes."

"Same thing. Remember how you always felt like you had to go to the toilet, just before kick off? Same thing."

"I don't think so. How about when you were a cop?"

"Oh yeah, I had plenty of both, then. Lot's of waiting, cops will tell you the toughest part of their job is not the action. It's the waiting, the waiting and the paperwork."

"Were you a tough cop?"

"I was too goddam pushy to be a good cop. I'd lose it with the punks and start slapping them around. Some wise-ass would spit on me and next thing you knew, he'd fall on a curb and break a couple of ribs. Ribs hurt for a long time. I liked motorcycle duty but I hated radar guns, I always felt like some sneaky weasel hiding in the bushes. Chief Robbins tried, he finally transferred me to the boats. I grew up on the water so it was a natural, but riding around in a small boat all day gets really boring. How many water scooters can you chase away from the beach?"

"What about drugs? I've heard they used to bring the stuff in by boat."

"That's true. For a while you could set your watch, the go-fast boys would shoot out of the Hillsboro inlet at eleven o'clock most every night. But we couldn't do much. There were some heavy hitters involved and they were protected. Also lots of search and seizure stuff made it hard. We could spot somebody riding too low and we knew he was loaded but that didn't constitute cause. The bigger the bucks, the greater the spin."

"Mark, I want Donna to come to work for me. I need your help to convince her."

"Good luck with that. But tell me about it."

"She'll soon be released from the hospital but she'll have a lot of recuperation time ahead of her according to Alan Barber. He says she needs to be off her feet most of the time and she has to follow a program of recovery. She also has to go back in for regular professional therapy. Working for me is perfect. I need someone, I have for a long time, but it's light duty. She can sit at the reception desk, handle the phone and the mail, pay some bills, help me keep the place together, schedule appointments. And—"

"You have that many customers?"

"No. But with someone there I'll probably pick up some more. Anyway, you know that Winkler made the place into a fortress, so we'd both know she would be safe during the day. It's also totally private, she could take naps, do exercises, whatever. It's perfect, you know it's perfect."

"It's a great idea. I've had Winkler examine her apartment and it's in good shape too, but I'm going nuts trying to figure how to keep her safe. She's a rock-head, you know. I've been begging her to take an apartment in my building. Truth is I've been begging her to move in with me but she's full of nutty ideas about pay backs and such crap. She's convinced herself she's contaminated for life, she's certain the only thing she's good for is whoring. Stone, you know I love her. I'm afraid to ask, and I don't want to know, but I suspect you do too. I can't get through to her but as much as I love her, I would be willing to lose her to you if you could do it, if you could somehow turn her around."

I ignored the love talk. "I suffer from the lousy idea that no one or nothing will turn her back toward the light as long as Saint Jake is alive. It's a chilling thought but maybe he partially accomplished what he wanted, maybe some part of her soul does belong to him. Maybe that's why that sonofabitch has to die, so she might be able to live.

"I talk with her, Mark, you know that. She's tight, nothing much gets out. But she somehow stayed alive for more than three years and I think if we can begin to understand how she did that, we might develop the keys we need. Personally, I think she made a lot of serious promises during that time. You know how we all say, God, get me out of this one and I promise I'll …whatever. Well, when you consider the mess she was in…you get the idea. She may have made promises which enabled her to survive. If she did so, she won't walk away from them. Think about how and why she wants to help the people she sends to me."

"Long before you showed up she was paying for medical treatments, all kinds of special help, education, operations, legal fees. I'll tell you, Stone, she was a one woman Salvation Army. She worked, hooking and model-ing, around the clock, and she never spent anything on herself."

"I'm no Psychiatrist, Mark, but it sure seems to make sense, and when the premises are right, the conclusion can't be too far wrong. Let's go to work and convince her she has to work for me and live with you, at least until Jake comes back, then everything will be different. Regardless of the outcome."

Aleena brought her Aunt Rose when she showed up for her appoint-ment. I wondered whether everyone had an Aunt Rose. I decided every-one did, somewhere.

"James wouldn't come today, he's trying to make up his mind about how mad he should be with me. He also says ain't no damn sense in my seeing you anymore since you couldn't convince me to do the right thing. So, since I know how worried you are about people thinking you might be slippin something more than advice into my skinny little body, I brought my aunt Rose."

"You feeling cute today, half pint? That's the most you've spoken at one time since I've known you."

Then, turning to Aunt Rose, I asked, "Aunt Rose, does smart talk run in the family? This one's beginning to sound like James."

Aunt Rose looked as if she was sent directly from central casting. She wore a church-going hat, a print dress and her smile made me think of cook-ies and milk. She was obviously the source of James' big smile. "Mister Stone, you know there is no way to teach *real* manners to today's children."

"I'm afraid the whole world is pushing kids the wrong way, Aunt Rose. I'm not sure a youngster could find the right path even if he wanted to. I'm not sure, but I think you and I *wanted* to become good people. It might be harder to reach such a decision now. Won't you come back and sit with us? I have coffee, soda, perhaps tea."

"I think I'll sit right here, in this nice wing-back chair, if that's all right. It looks comfortable and I brought a magazine. Besides, Aleena will feel better talking with you alone. I know it's important, you've given her lots of new ideas she likes."

"That's fine. I'll leave the connecting door open so you can just walk back if you change your mind. I think I even have some cookies in the refrigerator. Another client brings cookies all the time so she can dunk them in her coffee."

Aleena went to the refrigerator for a soda before settling in her usual chair.

"I'm sorry to hear about James."

"Truth is, I think he's kinda happy about, umm, three things."

"Tell me."

"Well, I think he's happy about my plans. I'm doing everything he wants because I know he's right about education and marrying and stuff, and he knows I mean it. Then I think he's happy cause he figures I'm going to be through with you here and he won't have to babysit me no more. I even think he's glad the arguing is over about the baby. He lost, but not really, and I know he's glad I made my decision. He knew all along I couldn't abort my child, no matter what."

"Tell me about right and wrong, Aleena."

"You mean in my stuff?"

"Yes."

"Okay, James is right about everything he said. I know that, but nobody's wrong."

"Wow. Good answer. How about the abortion?"

"There ain't no right or wrong. Sure the baby will make it all harder but, it's like you said, it's a personal decision for me and I made it. If I couldn't make it then I didn't deserve no child. For some other girl abortion might be best, even for the baby. Excuse me, I should have said, for what would maybe become a baby."

"Aleena, you may be only thirteen—"

"I'm fourteen, I had a birthday."

"Why didn't you tell me? We could have gone to lunch and had a party. Anyway, I was about to say that though you're very young, I think maybe you're smarter than ninety percent of the people in this wacky country of ours."

"I hope so. Lot's of women have babies when they are fifteen and I'll be almost fifteen. Maybe we'll have a double party next year, we'll even invite James. Right now you all been too busy chasing that bad ass. James says he's coming back. You gotta get that guy, Stone. Donna's going to be my baby's Godmother, betcha didn't know that."

"Betcha I might have guessed."

X

Mark and I gained a split decision with Donna. She refused to discuss moving in with Mark or even into a separate apartment in his high security building. Her refusal was based on her right of privacy. There was absolutely no way, she said, that she would surrender her right to come and go as she wished. Later, however, she told me otherwise, "Can you imagine how Mark's neighbors and business associates would react to his living with a common, street whore?"

"Why do you feel it's necessary to describe yourself that way?"

"Stone, please don't start conning me or else we'll stop having honest communications. You know as well as I do, that is exactly how Mark's neighbors and friends would describe me. Some of them may even have known me, biblically."

She also insisted her apartment was perfectly safe and it was her own carelessness which enabled Jake to get at her. She opened the door, she said, never dreaming he would be standing there. She told Mark and me how she was expecting someone else at exactly the time Jake and his buddy rang her bell. She also told us she was flat paralyzed at the sight of him, almost as if she had passed out yet remained standing. The shock was something neither Mark nor I could fully appreciate. Thinking about it made me sick, literally and physically sick. She wouldn't, or perhaps couldn't, tell us anything about the terrors of the following hour. Hopefully the merciful roll-back aspect of our minds, that feature which renders us unable to recall the actual cutting, tearing, hurting events of an accident, for example, blocked out much of Jake's savage attack.

Mark believed Jake didn't carry Donna off because there was no chance he could have dragged her senseless body out of the building without being seen. It was either that or he believed she would quickly die.

She was reluctant to tell us who she had been expecting that evening and we didn't press the issue. We didn't know why she insisted on protecting someone who was partially responsible for her troubles, but she did and we left it alone.

Her employment was another matter because I had real leverage there; I pointed out that by working for me she could use part of her salary to enable her friends to continue their counseling.

"Would you cut them off, Stone?"

"No. You'd be the one doing it."

"You are one hard hearted male."

"It takes one."

"Okay, you have a deal. But it's temporary, only until Alan Barber, my other pseudo mother, says I'm okay. Understand, I won't work for the kind of chump change you'll pay me once I can get back to business. Okay, boss?"

"Sure, as long as you understand that if you can't make decent coffee, I may fire you before you're ready to hit the road."

"You know, I think I liked you better as a perfect boyfriend than I will as a nagging boss."

Donna was making wonderful physical progress, she still limped, especially when she was tired, and she had to rest frequently. But mostly I worried whether we would ever be able to bring her back to her pre-Jake self. I had a deep abiding conviction that if we failed to do so, her physical survival might be a sham.

A photocopy of a Savannah crime report arrived at Mark's office as I was leaving for the day. A young officer remembered our description of Jake and wondered whether a recent holdup man might be the same guy. The report contained details of an extremely large, dark skinned man, described as either black or Latin, wearing a turtle neck sweater, a dark blue watch cap and a white sweat band. The report also indicated a second man, possibly called Sutter, who had threatened to sodomize a young boy, age ten, who was in the store with his older brother. The large man used the second man's name when he ordered him to forget the boy and leave at once. The small grocery store robbery netted the men between six hundred and six hundred fifty dollars.

Phoning the Savannah police department, I was fortunate to reach the same young officer who had forwarded the information.

"Officer Yates, I want to thank you for sending the data, it's good heads-up work. We're almost certain the large man described in your report is Jacob Chimoro, also known as Saint Jake, the man we're interested in, but we need to be sure. Would it be possible to check back with witnesses in order to make certain about the headband? Our man has a tattooed white stripe around his head. We need to know if what your people saw was an actual headband instead of a tattoo. We would also like it if they could be more specific about the second man's name. Could you do that and let us know A-sap? And, of course, any additional information will be helpful."

After he had me repeat the details of the headband type tattoo, Officer Yates assured me he would be happy to help us. He promised he would reply as soon as he had something.

"The vehicle they were driving probably doesn't mean much because they keep stealing new ones, I mean different ones. And, most important, do you have any recent disappearances of young women? Our man has a record of grabbing women off the streets."

"This perp sounds like a real sweetheart, Mr. Stone, I'll check it all out."

"Thanks in advance for your help."

By noon the next day we had confirmation. One of the clerks had noticed that the large man wearing the white headband with thin blue stripes looked as if he had another sweat band painted underneath. He hadn't said anything about it because it sounded too silly. The second man's name sounded more like Summer than Sutter and most important of all, Alicia Bates, a seventeen-year old student was reported missing from the grounds of the downtown Savannah art school. Her books and papers were found scattered in a nearby park indicating force was used.

The news from Savannah threw me into one of the worst troughs of despair I had ever known. I felt drained, weak and incompetent.

"Christ, Mark, how do we handle stuff like this. I don't think I've ever felt more rotten or more frightened. What the hell do I do now?"

"Bad shit, Stone. You know too much. Mostly we shut out all the lousy things that happen to other people, but you can't. You've been burying yourself in the details of Donna's case and you can't get away from what you know is happening to this new girl. You're there, man, you're sharing her terror, you're not gonna sleep tonight, unless you get drunk, and that's not the worst part. First, we have to keep this away from Donna, and second, there is every chance this girl won't survive. If we hear that, your ass is gonna come right up through your throat and you're *still* gonna have to sit on the information.

"We have to fight for perspective here. A hundred and fifty people will die in the US of *unnatural* causes today, just today: murders, accidents, beatings, tortures, shootings, stabbings, snake bites, and every goddam one of them is a tragedy. Death is personal, Stone, personal and tragic to the victim. It doesn't become more tragic because you happen to know the victim or witness the death. Death is complete all by itself and it can't be more complete because more people die or because you know someone. Do you understand what I'm trying to tell you? Goddam it, Stone, you're the Philosopher here, you can't fold up now. We're locked in and, I don't know about you, but I'm not about to let that slimy sonofabitch do it to our Donna anymore. No fucking way, man, we're all that stands between him and her. Now, get the hell out of my office. Go do what you have to do to pull yourself together. Please."

I walked out of Mark's office feeling more alone than I thought possible.

I knew that every word he said was true. In fact, he rather surprised me, ordinarily I would have been expressing the thoughts he was shoving in my face. I also knew that I had to find some reserve of inner strength to regain perspective and resolve. I was sitting dead center in a genuine crises and I was being tested in a way I had never been before. I wasn't sure I could stand up to the job at hand. But, I had to.

Alicia. I wish I hadn't heard her name. I wish I could get her out of my head. It's been several days now, is she still alive? Maybe she's strong, like Donna, maybe Jake is being more careful. I kept seeing her as Aleena. Maybe she's hurting right now. If she's alive she has to be so frightened, so unbelievably frightened.

By the time I reached my car tears were running down my cheek. I couldn't help it. From the time I was a little kid my reaction to extreme distress was tears. Sometimes just a book or a movie could bring it on. Today it was a girl I didn't know, never would know. Just a girl named Alicia, an art student from Savannah. Maybe just one of today's crop of one hundred and fifty miserable, merciless deaths.

I drove to the beach and gave my car to the parking attendant at the Bahia Mar hotel. I wandered inside and wrapped myself around three scotches before deciding I didn't want to become stupid. I reminded myself that after a brief high, alcohol just creates more depression.

I paid up and remembered my last visit to this hotel. Sharon and I came here from the boat show about a lifetime ago. I must call her and Ben. I stepped outside and decided to walk to the overpass then down to the beach.

It was a scudsy day, too much wind, too many clouds, too much surf, too much bad news, just too fucking much everything.

"I plan to catch a few rays and become a man of greater color. Or perhaps I should say an even greater man of color. What do you think, Smooth?"

The last person I expected to encounter at the beach was James Wakins. I was as glad to hear his voice behind me as I had been glad to see him during the Jake break in.

Without turning I said, "James, I never thought I would hear myself say this but I am pleased to hear your raggedy voice. Come sit beside your ole daddy here."

"I do not put my delicate buns onto dirty old sand. There's a picnic table ten feet away. Let's go sit up straight and share our gum with the whole class."

We walked over to where a barbecue grill was encircled by several picnic tables. James sat on top of the table with his feet on the bench seat. "Do you have any idea how sand messes up a delicate pair of Bally's?"

"Just try getting some bunker-crude off some white Rockports. How did you find me?"

"Your cell phone is powered off so I called Mark Todd."

"Mark doesn't know where I am."

"No, but he knew how you were feeling and upon hearing that, I simply reasoned that since we Homo Sapiens are drawn to water, more especially to larger waters with breaking waves which create uplifting positive ions, you would no doubt drag your sorry white ass to the beach. Further, since you are such a snob, you would leave it to some black-boy valet to park your car. There's only three or four such places."

"I'm beginning to hate uppity blacks."

"I believe you mean uppity *niggers*."

"Maybe. But I've never quite understood the difference except to note that Nigger belongs with Kike, Hunky, Polack, Wop, Chink, Mick, Spick and Limey, all those sharp stick-in-the-eye words. And besides, thanks, James, I appreciate you coming out here."

"What the hell, Spunky, you be my pseudo daddy."

From the point of view of a casual onlooker from Ohio it might have looked a little unusual. Two grown men sitting atop a picnic bench on a nearly deserted stretch of Florida beach watching the waves chasing the Curlews on an overcast, windy, thoroughly gloomy day. One man, well dressed, black, with expressive motions, the other, older, white, dressed in jeans, an open collar and a rumpled sport jacket.

We talked for more than an hour without mentioning Jake or Donna.

The vulnerability range of the human body is enormous. We can die from a scratch or survive a plane crash. Sometimes I think I know why. Other times I'm sure I don't know anything. Donna was released and Alan Barber said it was okay for her to come to the office, half days for a while, then full days would be okay. She chose mornings then stayed all day, from the beginning.

She didn't speak of it but I never saw anyone so obviously content to be in a particular place. Under locksmith Winkler's supervision I hired a contractor to clear sufficient room to do some minor alterations. That enabled us to drive directly inside the building, after opening the overhead door by remote control. Donna would drive her battered little hatchback inside before stationing herself at the front desk where a peep hole enabled her to see who rang our bell. We also had a black and white TV camera which viewed the entire front area in case someone tried to hide.

She clearly felt safe, but it was far more than that. She was often alone during the mornings when I did my workouts and checked in at Mark's office. She had privacy for whatever she cared to do.

I began to skip breakfast in favor of inviting her to lunch. She agreed to it a couple of times but, despite my taking her to the best places around, she said she preferred fixing lunch at the office. We had a refrigerator, a microwave oven and a small table in the back where she soon took charge. The lunches kept getting better and soon they became a highlight of my day. It was just her and me, a man and a happy young woman. I couldn't decide whether it was yesterday's Donna or today's who was playing house. I knew I enjoyed it, probably way too much for either of us.

Donna lit the place like Christmas and she made it her own. There were comfortable couches in the event she overdid it and needed rest. There was privacy for her therapy and exercise, even showers and bathrooms. The place became a model of cleanliness and order. Except for the bathrooms, where good smells and beauty products were mated with attractive shower curtains, mats and larger than life towels to convey a sense of feminine abandon.

She had TV, phones and friends. My people were actually her people after all. She was always happy they came and they were always delighted to see her. She soon scheduled in two female acquaintances who referred to themselves as models, as indeed they were, at least on occasion. Each of these women were surviving as best they could with what they had. One had been sexually abused as a child, to the point that she could find no support and ran from home at far too early an age.

The other was a refuge from an incredibly abusive marriage who was unable to face the events which finally forced her to escape. No amount of protest on my part mattered. I constantly reminded Donna and each of my clients, that I was not a qualified counselor, that I was little more than a reader of books, someone who could reference what Thomas Aquinas or Jean-Francois Lyotard might have said about some shade of existence and pass it along.

Despite these facts, Donna was a believer. "You do help these people, Stone, I know them and I know you do. Maybe it's because you listen and never criticize."

"Maybe," I pointed out, "it's because they hear themselves, and in doing so they begin to understand, and once they understand, they're able to adjust and heal."

"Okay," she said, "who needs to know how aspirin or penicillin works? The point, I think, is that it does."

My cell phone rang from inside my gym bag as I was pulling the toilet kit off the top shelf of my locker, preparing to head in for a shave.

"Stone?"

"Yeah, Mark, what's up?"

"Are you coming by here this morning? They found Alicia Bates' body near Jacksonville."

"The sonofabitch is headed our way."

"Maybe, maybe not. Interstate ten goes from J-town to Los Angeles."

"How did you hear?"

"Our local boys. They're still plenty interested you know."

"I'll be right over."

"Stone?"

"Yes?"

"Don't tell Donna, okay?"

"Did you take some stupid pills this morning?"

"Sorry, it's just I know you two are close now."

"Bad turn, Mark, back off. Nothing's changed."

"Hey, pal, I can get fucked up too. I'm entitled."

"Probably more so than anyone except Donna, and she's clear as a bell."

"I hope so. See you."

I couldn't get up off the bench. Everything I didn't want to think about was pursuing me like a rabid dog in a bad dream. I've read somewhere how it's possible for some people to become so distraught they actually throw away their life just to be rid of their pain. I felt that way. I wanted to face Saint Jake, to fight him. To kill or be killed. Either way the pain would be over, and I needed the pain to be over. But I was just being self-centered, my pain was nothing compared to Donna's. At least it was over for Alicia Bates, no one could help her now. No one could hurt her either. She had closed the door on her pain.

I didn't want to hear the raw data so I just asked, "Same stuff, Mark?"

He must have understood, he didn't describe her condition. "She was found in a marshy area off the causeway leading to Amelia Island, just north of Jacksonville. From that point Jake has three choices: south or north on I-95, or west on I-10."

"He was moving south from Savannah. He's on his way here."

"Maybe."

"Maybe's ass. Mark, I'm going to Jacksonville and look around. I've got to. He won't expect me."

Mark walked across to his littered desk, cleared a corner and sat before lighting one of the silly little cigars with the wooden mouthpiece he favored.

"Good idea, Stone. You go ahead, run up the interstate and watch for southbound vans. Jake will no doubt paint large white stripes around it. Perhaps he'll put his name on the side. Maybe with stars between the letters, like in MASH. If you miss him it's okay, just turn left at I-10 and repeat the process until you get to LA. Don't forget to send cards."

I stood there looking at him, feeling stupid, not knowing what to say.

"It'll be better for everyone, Stone. The last thing we need is a nervous Nit picking up his skirts, running around the room shouting scare words."

I still didn't say anything.

"Sorry, Stone, but it's not your ass Jake is after. It's the woman I love and running up and down highways isn't much help."

"Got any coffee at this ranch? Maybe with a stiff shot of brain power and backbone to go with it?"

"You got the coffee, pal. As far as the booze, I don't know if I ever told you but I'm a recovering alcoholic. I don't keep the stuff around."

"Then how about a punch in the mouth? I don't like me much all of a sudden, maybe that would make me feel better."

"Save it, Stone. Stow all that self-centered hate and confusion until Jake shows up, then use it, you might need it."

Donna had steamed vegetables covered with a ton of melted cheese, set up for lunch when I arrived.

"Oh, oh, a favorite dish, what's going down? Am I being ungrateful or presentient?"

"Both. I do have someone coming at two to meet you."

"What have you found for me now, sweetheart?"

Usually Donna never looked directly at me. She always averted her eyes and I often wondered why she did so. Now I suddenly knew, even though I didn't understand. When I spoke she raised her eyes to mine and our gaze locked as firmly and with more intensity than I would have thought possible. My ears pounded and my breath failed.

"Oh, Stone." It was a whisper than rose from some naked depth, from past lives, complete, perfect and full of all that could be.

She turned away, walked to the reception area door and closed it behind her. I stared at the door for a long lost lifetime.

Donald Simms was a pretty young man, there was no more accurate way to describe him. He was seventeen, very thin and very wary. Donna buzzed me at two to say she was sending him back. That was the sum total of my knowledge. So I stuck out my hand, "Pleased to meet you, Donald, I'm Locke Stone. Have a seat, would you like coffee, or a soda?"

"No thank you, Mr. Stone."

"Have you known Donna very long, Donald?"

"Almost a year. Ever since I came to Lauderdale."

"Well then, that makes me odd man out. You know Donna, she knows you and I have no idea of why you are here, can you help me out Donald?"

God, I thought, *I sound like a pompous ass.*

"I'm not sure…I think it's because Donna worries about me. I think she thinks I'll get hurt.

"Fair enough, Donald, now I will stop trying to sound like some high school teacher. Please accept my apologies."

"For what, Mr. Stone, I'm a little confused."

"So am I, Donald. Maybe I can't picture you having a real problem. When I was your age I was hoping to become a college All American, I had the idea it would get me a lot of girls and that's all I really wanted."

A hint of something passed behind his eyes, defiance?

"I don't."

"Does that mean you're gay? Or am I placing too much emphasis on your comment?

"No. You're right. I'm Gay."

"Okay, does being Gay complicate your life?"

Donald sat up a bit straighter, looked around as if to see whether anyone else was present, "Are you for real for Christ's sake? Of course being Gay complicates my life. In fact, it's got it all fucked up."

"Is that a pun, Donald?"

"A what?"

"A pun, you know, a bad joke."

"Oh, yeah, that is, no, it's not a joke."

"Look, Donald, I will ask you some stupid questions simply because there are lots of things I don't know anything about. Being Gay is one of them. Why does being Gay fuck up your life more than being Albanian, or having one arm or, I don't know, being black?

"Because being Gay is worse."

"Then why be Gay? I'm sorry, I think that's another stupid question."

He actually smiled, "Yeah. Like why be black?"

"Okay, pal, you smiled, I caught you. Now, let's talk a little, that's what I do you know. Did Donna explain I'm no kind of doctor, that I can't treat you, all you and I can do is talk and tell each other the truth?"

"No. She said you were the king of France and you were looking for a Prime Minister."

"She was absolutely right, so, please, tell me your qualifications. Why should you get this important job?"

"What do you mean?"

"You're applying for the very important job as Prime Minister, tell me about yourself, tell me why I should hire you."

"You're weird, Mr. Stone."

"Believe it, fella, believe it, but maybe you are too. Go ahead."

"Well…I'm kind of smart about some things."

"Tell me."

"Like shapes. I see things by how they fit together, how they work. Take clothes, for example, most people don't realize how their clothes make them look."

"I like where this is going, Donald, tell me more."

"We all know about the old men with their dress socks, wing tips and walking shorts, it's a big joke. Worse yet, socks with sandals, aack! Or what about women with those baggy sweaters. They think they're hiding their belly. The sweaters come down below their ass and make it look like a Mack truck."

We went on for a hour and never mentioned Donald's problem. But his observations about clothing, styles, fit, color and shape impressed me. His descriptions created crystal clear images in my mind. I didn't know how to label it but this young man was one extremely smart and talented person.

I was actually eager to meet with him again so I asked Donna to work him in twice a week.

"You did it again, Stone."

"Did what?"

"Donald walked out of here just a tiny bit taller than when he walked in."

"Thank you, Miss-missing-at-lunch, and when shall *we* talk?"

"Never, Stone, never."

"You're telling me our feelings for each other are off limits?"

"Totally, eternally off limits."

"It may not actually matter you know, not talking about something doesn't make that something disappear."

"One of the few absolutes in my life, Stone, is that you are in my corner. I don't know when or how it happened but I know you are there for me. You can't possibly know what that means to me, it may be the most important thing in my life right now. It's also very easy for such feelings to be misunderstood. Stone, I'm afraid I couldn't survive without your support and I don't understand why, but the idea of messing that up terrifies me.

"Please, keep accepting me on my terms, just as you have been doing. I'm aware that Mark believes he loves me and I know there are others who like me, but my mind is trapped in a maze you wouldn't believe. I'm at least two people. I'm a child. I'm a woman. I've lived through death. You've made me feel the first feminine arousal in my entire life. I'm crazy as a tick. I was planning to become the bride of God and instead I became the whore-trash of the devil. I hate. I hurt. I can't bear to look in a mirror because all I see is wormy, rotting, stinking flesh. Oh, God, Stone, I'm so afraid I'm not going to make it."

"Donna, I can only promise that you and me, and Mark, are together and we're one hell of a team. We will either all live through this or none of us will. And when it is done you will be everything you wish to be. Everything that has happened until this moment has no meaning, it is all nothing more than electrical impulses which form a variable memory-tree upon demand. Living today in a manner based on fallible input from yesterday is to do a great disservice to the creator. Think about that."

Our first suspicious reports from New Orleans were confirmed when a Tulane student was rescued from an attempted assault. Her boyfriend, a football player coming to meet her, knocked one man to the ground enabling her to break free and run to safety. Both students made a clear identification of a second man who was reported as huge, naked to the waist, with painted stripes on his body. The assailants escaped in a dark blue or black van. The New Orleans police said they expected to make arrests within twenty four hours.

"We're right back where we were when he was in Savannah and Jacksonville, Stone, we're at his mercy as far as where he's going next."

"Mark, do you suppose it's possible that Jake is cunning enough to be laying a false trail?"

"No way."

"Okay. But it spooks me. Usually, we can't get any information on this guy until he's long gone. But ever since Savannah it's as if he's holding up big, *Jake is here now*, signs. If he starts making noise in Baton Rouge, or around the Texas border, during the next few days then I'm going on full alert about two days later."

This time it was Mark who was silent.

Malka Yelick was our resident cookie monster, a title she won hands down. Always a warm person, trying so hard to be happy, Malka took special pleasure from my employment of Donna. She would arrive early for appointments and stay as long as she could. She chatted with Donna at a level she could never reach with me. Her every contact with a man, any man, was sexual. Her response appeared to be Pavlovian. Anytime a male entered her sphere, she would be stimulated at once and try to achieve sexual contact.

Conservative by nature, I try to avoid extremes of all kinds: actions, language, commitment, eating, drinking, and especially social and sexual intercourse. Malka was a test. Regardless of how our discussions began they always resolved into sexual matters, for that was her problem. Theoretically, I should have been able to talk about such things with her as objectively and dispassionately as if we were discussing any other addiction. My absence of formal training for counseling might account for my discomfort but, if that were the case, then what accounted for her total lack of discomfort, I wondered. She would tell me about unbelievable liaisons in the same tone she used when telling me about her cookies.

Our cookie monster spent her waking hours seeking gratification and she found it in remarkable ways, in ridiculous places, with an amazing variety of men. From bank presidents to plumbers, men ranging from age fourteen to age eighty, from doorways to golf course greens. Malka pursued her quest with singular devotion. Once in a while, she cracked me up;

"You made the other security guard stand and wait?"

"What could she do? He wasn't finished. Me neither."

Or amazed me:

"Right there in the car, with three other people?"

"Well, he had his blazer jacket on his lap and everyone thought I put my head down because I didn't feel so good."

And sometimes impressed me:

"How many men are on a bowling team, Malka?"

"Five, but one man couldn't do it."

I spoke the usual platitudes which I related to addictions.

"You will want to make a thorough study of the downside of indulgence. We know that anyone who overindulges in food gets fat and probably shortens their life. Those who overindulge in distillates injure their brain, risk insanity and premature death. What do you believe is the downside of overindulgence in sex, Malka?"

"Too much smiles?" Said with accompanying giggles. It was sometimes hard to achieve sober discussion with Malka.

"Seriously, Mr. Stone, you don't smile enough. I would like to help *you* for a change."

"Downsides, Malka. We're talking downsides resulting from overindulgence, please."

"Okay. There is more chance of disease because there are so many different men. I know that, so I try most to fuck with married men, very young men, older men and, most of all, I like shy men."

"So it is your idea that such men have fewer sexual contacts thereby offsetting your extravagance. Is that correct?"

"Yes. And sometimes I use even rubber, but I don't like them. Mostly I like to give a good scrubbing, but mostly I can't do that."

"Okay, Malka, that's enough for today. Tell me about these new cookies you brought. I'll make the coffee while you ask Donna if she would like to join us. Instead of a happy hour we'll declare a cookie hour."

After Malka left I spoke with Donna, "I usually have some idea about the root cause of most people's problems, at least I think I do. I often think I know what's blocking their recovery, but Malka throws me. I realize the source of it goes back to her being the family gang-bang, but why can't she get around in front of it now?"

"I have an idea about that, well, actually more of a suspicion."

"Care to share?"

"C'mon, Stone, I have no knowledge about such things. I wouldn't presume to suggest that I—"

"What a crock. You're not only wise beyond your years but you've experienced more of life's challenges than most people will face in three lifetimes. You insist that I help people despite my lack of training. So, c'mon, tell me your ideas about Malka."

"Back off, sailor. What about patient confidentiality?"

"They're not my patients. I'm not a physician and, besides, you're my partner, partner."

A very strange look. Silence, then, "Stone, I'm a whore on temporary leave. Collecting two or three hundred dollars for a few minutes of compliance doesn't qualify me for much. I'd like you to remember that."

"I'd like you to forget it. I once broke a leg while skiing, but I don't continue limping."

"Please don't tweak me, I can't handle it yet."

I was forced to look away, to clench my fists and to tense every muscle in my body in order to stop myself. I never wanted more desperately to take someone in my arms. I so wanted to just hold her, to shield her from harm, to protect this fragile and delicate creature whose trust and regard meant so much to me.

XI

Marilee wanted to kill Saint Jake. More, she wanted him to never have existed, she wanted to erase his filth from herself. The slime of his being disgusted her vision of herself and would do so forever. His existence made a return to the world of Father Wood, to the sisters of the Immaculate Heart of Mary, and absolution impossible. Knowing these things enabled her to swing the large, heavy, open-end wrench with both hands even as a flood of anguished tears washed her cheeks. Down upon his despicable, striped head, down with every ounce of disgust and hate that had sustained her for so long. She wanted to beat all physical existence out of his crushed skull. She raised the wrench again and sobbed as she smashed as hard as she could.

She was physically weakened, or it might have been that her genes were those of civilized, gentle people, but something within her withheld an ounce of force. Something too small to comprehend left a tiny spark alive in her personal demon. The measure of her tempering was yet to be.

Despite his apparent death, Jake's accomplices feared him. Instead of rolling him into a watery Florida ditch they parked the stolen van, with him inside, on a driveway leading to the emergency entrance of the hospital in Fort Meyers. They believed he was either dead or would shortly die and they wanted no part of a murder charge. They also didn't want to carry him. Compared to that chore, stealing another vehicle was no big deal. In a matter of minutes they took one from the hospital parking lot.

Shortly after, they exchanged that one for a different vehicle in the parking lot of a Fort Meyers theater.

Against all odds, Jake survived his injuries. Despite disinterested surgery and the resentful nursing that he deserved. He was, after all, in police custody as a car thief and a suspected armed robber. He was eventually released to police custody then plea-bargained to a sentence of eight years. The overcrowded Florida penal system spat him out in thirty months, just enough time to fully recover and hone his hatred.

Jake immediately headed to Tampa where he robbed a small time drug dealer, brutalized a street whore and stole a van. After a few days of such rest and recovery fun, he was ready for business. He headed back to the rural crossroads near Fort Meyers where everything had gone wrong for him. At this point he felt more determination and focus than he had for years.

His mere presence was enough to produce answers and when he exerted his brutality, Jake got results. When he questioned the folks at the ramshackle back country Texaco station they remembered him all too well. They remembered the silent, deep black Florida night and the bloodstains on his pants. The oil stained ticket for eighteen dollars and forty cents worth of gas was still pinned above the cash register. Old Mrs. Caldwell had scrawled across the bottom in pencil, "twenty two dollars beer and gas."

He learned from Mrs. Caldwell's retarded grandson, Brocky, that Roland Pell had stopped for gas that same night. That Pell was on his way to deliver a load of turnips to his uncle's place in Naples, just as he still did during season. Just as he did last Wednesday evening.

Brocky knew those things because everybody still talked about that night. The stories had grown around Jake, Muff and some older guy arriving all stoned. They were drinking beer and bragging how they had traded their "blonde cunt" for cocaine and cash to a bunch of Venezuelan sailors in Tampa. They still talked about how Muff staggered out after Jake had been gone too long that night. How he came running back to drag the older guy out into the night, all the while hollering about Jake's bloody head and how somebody had grabbed the girl.

They had raced away without paying. Mom Caldwell stuck the bill on the wall so nobody'd forget, in case any of them showed up again. But nobody asked Jake for money this time either.

Jake used his big, dirty, Bowie knife like a cleaver when he took off all four fingers of Roland Pell's right hand. The cut was at an angle with all of the little finger gone but part of the index finger remaining intact. Jake raised his knee off Roland's back and pulled the arm with the bleeding hand to roll him over. Then as he knelt on his chest he amused himself with a joke, "Well, you can't jack off no more, so, unless you tell me, I'll cut off your cock. It's up to you, nigger."

Young, heroic, Roland Pell actually thought about it for a minute before deciding Jake was right, he would have no reason to cut him anymore after he told how he had taken the girl across to Fort Lauderdale. It was years ago, she must be long gone by now. So he told. And he was right, Jake had no more reason to cut him. He did it because he liked it. Roland felt sorry and confused as he bled out. Laying there, staring at the full moon from alongside his Uncle's storage shed, he imagined he could still see her face as she collapsed into his arms, and he was glad.

In unique ways the habitat of Randall Comsworth Preston, near where the vertical railroad bridge magically lowered itself across the New River to accommodate approaching trains, was perfect for Jake. It was very near the center of downtown Fort Lauderdale. The exotic Riverwalk weaved nearby. Outdoor cafes and bars crowded the water's edge at every chance. The multi-million dollar high rise jail provided pleasant views of multi-million dollar boats, multi-millionaires living just alongside, crowds walking along exclusive Las Olas Boulevard, dining in multi-million dollar restaurants and squeezing Rolls Royce's, Jaguars and Mercedes through crowds of tourists from every exotic or hum-drum place in the world. The

County courthouse, reached by upturning bridges and an under-river tunnel, was nearby. Vacant lots were constantly being prepared for new structures, each was packed full of construction equipment, with workers pick up trucks and vans jammed into every available inch of space.

Incredible numbers of derelicts, addicts, drunks, people homeless by preference or by lack of ability, wandered about, serving to please the party crowds by enabling them to revel in their imagined superiority. There were hundreds of places to park, to sleep, to be lost in a blaze of exotica wherein only those flying the symbols and decor of the moment were visible to all the others displaying the same mating sights and scents.

It was the rare, unlikely, yet likely place where Marilee Cutter would be seen one early afternoon. She appeared as if by magic. Her little hatchback pulled to the curb and deposited Randall Comsworth Preston. He was off to collect his monthly check, she was en route to pick up Aleena Wakins for her first ever visit to a Gynecologist.

Earlier, Donna/Marilee had tried to help Preston sober up by having him spend the night on her couch. She failed to convince him to bathe but she did get some soup into him and she gave him as good a wash as she could manage.

The rest was too easy. Jake, wearing his warm-up, cover-up, along with a watch cap pulled low on his forehead, shared the first of two bottles of passable rye with Randall that same afternoon. By five o'clock, the hour Randall promised to bring part of his money to Donna for safekeeping, he was passed out among the TV boxes and lean-to's spattering the scrub growth, near the rust colored vertical bridge.

Donna/Marilee was smiling when she opened her door expecting to see Randall Comsworth Preston, her trusted friend.

XII

Jacob Chimoro, Saint Jake, earned the reputation of being cunning by exhibiting strong survival instincts on occasion, much as any other animal might. Jake left the north bound freight train as it slowed when passing near downtown Boca Raton. He boosted a Buick station wagon from behind a small, trackside strip center, used it to reach a large mall with a movie theater where he traded it for a GMC van with tinted glass, one of his favorites.

As he drove north he slid into the usual state of numbness he preferred whenever he was alone. Jake did not like to think about anything except his next act.

He was always frightened as he peeked out from behind the old trunk when his mother had men. He was afraid of the pushing fire as he sneaked out to rifle their rumpled pockets for loose change. The Lizard God sat on the trunk and watched everything and no one would touch him or look behind the trunk but she would scream when he found no coins or when she couldn't sell him to the men for extra coins. Many men had beaten him after he made a noise, he didn't care, but sometimes they beat his mother too, and he worried she would die or worse, she would scream all night until the man came and hit her. One night, a few years later, she did. As Jake killed her, he knew he had to do it, she was making too much noise anymore, all the time, too much noise.

Long before he neared the Georgia-Florida border he remembered he had heard that Smother Tipton was living in Savannah with an old whore they had both known in Santa Fe. Jake figured Smother couldn't be satisfied with such an arrangement for very long. Old Sally probably couldn't bring in enough to keep him in cheap beer.

While Jake worked the downtown Savannah dealers, just West of Bay street, trying to get a line on Smother, he noticed a lot of young women. They were passing in and out of the downtown art school, small-stepping through the tidy park-like squares nearby. He felt the familiar warmth in his crotch, the pleasant thoughts, and knew he'd come back soon. But right now he was without money or help and he needed both, broke was okay but he couldn't stand being alone. Men like Smother gave Jake courage, a sexual outlet when they had no female around and most important, mobility. Jake was too big to move fast but with a helper or two he could arrange like chess pieces, he could direct victims into his grasp. He could never have approached the cop on duty outside Donna's hospital room in Fort Lauderdale, for instance, anymore than he could have found hospital clothing that would fit him.

Smother ran off after Jake killed Bushy Willis for straight fucking Marilee after he had forbidden anyone to dilute his juices. Smother worried that Jake was getting too weird, but Jake knew he could reassure his old pal.

Jake was right, Smother wanted to get back to the West. He hated the dampness and smell of Savannah. When Jake showed up he was eager to team up, grab some cash, get back on the road and have some real fun again.

During the hold up, Jake ordered Smother to bring up the van while he stayed behind to keep everyone face down and quiet. That was far safer, he reasoned, than trying to run to the van. He worried that he had shouted Smother's name when he ordered him to leave the kid alone. He also worried that the van had been spotted, so he had Smother drive to a covered parking garage to steal a different one. The garage was also near the art school and Jake was eager to make a score.

Nothing worked right that day. Smother wanted to bugger the kid in the store and the resulting argument wasted too much time. When they tossed their belongings into the only van they could find, it was junky and partially full of cardboard boxes stuffed with old clothes. Then, when Smother stopped and slid over to the passenger side to ask Alicia for directions, more things went wrong, Jake slipped when he slid the side door open. The sound of the door startled the friendly, smiling girl who froze when she saw Jake. He managed to grab her, but as he pulled her inside, her flailing arms scattered everything she was carrying. Books, sketch pads and loose sheets of work in progress fell across the grass. Jake was sure they had been seen. That meant another vehicle switch which would be risky, especially with this young girl in tow. He was dangerously pissed off about everything.

He rapidly pummeled Alicia into submission as he ordered Smother to head out I-16 to route I-95 then south toward Jacksonville.

They had only ten miles to go to reach the North or South choice at I-95, but Alicia was dead before they got there. Jake had quickly smashed out her front teeth with his wooden piston. Then he hauled her, in a stupor, up on her knees, facing him, in the prayerful posture he favored. But then he screwed up again, he was so full of anger and frustration. As he rammed his bulk against her face he simultaneously put his huge hands and great weight on her small upper back. The combination snapped the vertebrae in her neck and she frustrated him still more by falling limp in grotesque death.

Jake was silenced. Smother was enraged and began to develop a bad feeling about his decision to join up with Jake again.

It was coming dusk in a full and glorious display when they turned East at the first road in Florida in order to rid themselves of their burden.

Alicia's eulogy was brief. As they dragged her toward the marsh grass Smother complained, "I didn't even get to fuck her once."

Jake looked across at his old friend and made another Jake-joke, "Go ahead, she won't care."

This time they both laughed.

When Jake and Smother argued as they approached Interstate ten, Smother said something that caused Jake to have one of his flashes of cunning.

"I'm not going to Lauderdale with you, no fucking way, they'll be waiting for you, cops and all. They probably hear stuff about where we go, them fuckin cops is got everything wired up, you know. You said we was going to San Antone or Santa Fe, so let's do it. Fuck her anyway, we'll get another broad, one that's not beat up. Just take it easy next time, okay?"

Jake remained quiet and when the turn off arrived, Smother said, "Okay, I'm takin Ten West, okay, buddy?"

"Take it. I feel ready for makin some noise in New Orleans."

XIII

Nothing could be golden with the threat of Jake hanging over our heads, but everything combined to try. The Gods of nice do meet with some frequency among the flowering trees, sweet breezes and high blue skies of south Florida. One need only remember to look upward while stuck in traffic or frozen at the third bridge of the morning. For those of us who learn where the tourists do *not* hang and then learn the back streets and devious ways of getting around, it's a nice place to be. Most locals only wish is that a few million winter people who stop at Disney World would then turn around and go home.

Such were my thoughts as I swam my goal laps in the eighty four degree water of the yacht club pool. I was usually alone except during those mornings when a group of club ladies would meet to do water exercises. Nice ladies, affluent, educated, accomplished ladies who cared about all the right things, including themselves. I knew, and liked most of them and their bouncing, chirping voice-songs added to the ambiance of the place, the time and my sense of well-being.

How is it possible, I wondered, for this world to co-exist alongside that of Saint Jake's? Is there some marvelous secret hidden in the answer to that question, do we require the bad in order to appreciate the good? In the face of so much bad why do we fail to deal with it? Why, for instance, do we cling to the absurdities of racial, religious and ethnic differences instead of realizing that we need to practice the prejudice of good against bad? It all seems so damn obvious while I am swimming in the warm protected waters of a safe facility located in the midst of a well-protected mini-section of a problem-plagued state in a diminishing nation.

Donna was eager to see me when I arrived at the office. "Stone, you have to level with me because I'm trying to make a terribly hard decision."

"I always level with you."

"No, you don't. But now you have to. Promise?"

"Yes. But I don't think I want to hear this."

"Look, I know you and Mark are working very hard to track him."

I knew at once that she didn't want to say the name.

"But, for obvious reason, I guess, you don't mention any of this stuff to me. Both of you guys are so protective."

"Go on."

"We all pretend, we act as if these injuries I'm recovering from came from a fall, or an auto accident. I even understand that. I'm so lucky to have you and Mark who really care about me. No matter what. But I'm getting better now and I can't stand the risk anymore. I can't actually talk about things and I don't know how much you and Mark know, but I know dying is not a bad thing. It's better than…better than…being caught and…I think…you know. I'm going away, Stone. I've got to go away."

"Donna, I think I understand. The police say he'll never come back here because we're on to him. We know he went from Jacksonville to New Orleans. Everyone thinks he's going back toward Santa Fe."

"Who's with him? I know some of his rotten friends."

"Last we heard he had a guy named Smother with him."

I lost her. At the mention of the man's name I swear I actually saw her disappear deep inside herself as she fell into my arms. I carried her to the couch and put her gently down before rushing into the bathroom to return with a damp face cloth to put across her forehead. I was frightened as I checked her racing pulse and listened to her regular, easy breathing. I decided to call Alan Barber at the hospital, but first I went to the refrigerator for ice. I wanted to call Mark, instead I just held the improvised ice-bag to her head and the sides of her neck.

"I'm sorry," she whispered, "but he was there...too much rushed back...he was there when it happened...it was the first minute again...I couldn't..."

She was awake but her eyes remained closed.

"I suggest we hold off on any more talk. I don't think you're ready."

"Yes. But, I'll never be ready."

"So, who needs to talk anyway? How about those Panther's? Let's go to the hockey game tomorrow night. What d'ya say? We'll get a burger and beer afterwards."

She looked at me and smiled a small, Donna type smile.

When I told Mark about Donna's remarks, he said, "She's a hundred percent right. I don't think he'll ever come back either, but that's not enough. Right now she's a sitting duck. I want to marry her and go live in Seattle, or Bangor, Maine, anywhere. Anywhere Jake will never find her."

"But, he'll live in every shadow, Mark."

"So, what are you saying, Stone."

"Right now I'm saying I want the three of us to have dinner tomorrow night. I think we have some serious talking to do and this time she needs to be in on it."

"What about spooking her? The whole thing scares her to death."

"I don't know, but let's try to stay away from names and references to anything that happened in her past.

"That's tough."

"So is she, she knows it's bad. But she told me something when she came out of it yesterday that I think might be important."

"What'd she say?"

"She said she never expected her reaction. That it was as if a giant wave suddenly rose up and crashed into her face. Did you ever learn any of the details of her escape?"

"Not so much as a word. I've made a million guesses but I don't know a damned thing about it. Why?"

"As she was coming around, she said, I wanted to kill him, I needed to kill him but I failed. Then she said, now he'll kill me, like the others. I don't know any more and I didn't think I should ask. But it sure as hell conjures up some wild thought-pictures."

"You've got to keep your goddamn curbstone psychiatry to yourself, Stone, I don't want to lose her. I don't want her to run off or go nuts."

"I couldn't agree more, Mark, I walk on eggs all the time. But I'm afraid she might be suffering a need to expurgate some of this stuff. I mean, Christ, how much crap can anyone hold back?"

The dinner was tough and Donna was beautiful. The white glove service at Le Dome was perfect and our table in the sheltered window booth of Le Cave was silent as a whisper. We three were so compatible that I couldn't remember being with people I enjoyed more. I loved Ben and Sharon Stern as much, perhaps, but the sexual tension between Sharon and myself was a bit like biting down on a peppercorn fragment, after a fine dinner. With coffee and brandy served, I spoke up, "Shall we talk about leaving town?"

Donna beamed a full power smile at me, "Just me, Stone, just me."

Mark spoke up, "I want to marry you and move to Thailand, or Rifle, Colorado. You name it and we're gone. You know I mean it and you know I mean tomorrow."

"Don't make me cry, Mark, I don't deserve so much. I don't understand how I found either of you guys."

"Unless you two agree to knock off this *I don't deserve* stuff, I'm going home. Enough is too damn much, we're sitting here talking like a bunch of ninnies. So, forgive me, but we have serious stuff to talk about."

"Okay, Stone, it's been a nice evening and I love the lady."

"Everybody loves the lady, but she thinks she's better off leaving Dodge on the next stage. You're the smart guy, ex-cop here, should she?"

It was as bad as a condominium meeting. The bottom line is we like and trust each other and we believe we can protect ourselves. We have the police turned on and they are doing a good information job, our mail-out hot line is working well and we are holding our street troops together; each one talks with Donna no less than once each day. Even Randall Preston is alert more of the time than I would have thought possible. Donna is in a safe environment with minimal exposure, to the extent that Mark or James or myself even joins her for shopping. So far, she has agreed to all these measures and has totally complied. Her position, regarding a move, was that she couldn't live like this forever and she is endangering her friends by staying around.

Neither Mark nor I mentioned the latest police information. There was no way to do that without mentioning Jake and this conversation didn't need to be derailed.

"There is a common failing," I said, "that we should not overlook here. People always tend to believe nothing will change unless they do something. Basically we're all programmed to believe things will stay as they presently are and that simply is not true. More so in this case. We're in sort of a circle of wagons and we believe the Indians are getting ready to attack at any moment, and the tension bugs us. We can't do this forever, we say. Well our situation will *not* remain as is, it can *not* do so. Our Indians are messing with the cavalry every day and the troops don't like that, they might just blow them away tomorrow. Or they may run away, or get hit by a train, or come back here, in which case we'll nail their asses. But things will not, cannot, stay the same. Not for long. That, I can promise you."

"And one more thing," Mark said, "nobody rides away from the circled wagons. It's just too easy to pick us off if we let the Indians play divide and conquer."

"You're dead right, Mark. Donna, you're the key. No one can tell you what to do, but if you have the guts to stick it out, and we both know you do, then Mark and I will swear to keep you safe until the Indians are gone."

"You two sure mess with a girl's eye makeup. If you will escort me back to the fort, I promise to provide a nightcap and then to bar the door when you leave. I have a new client to write up for my boss to meet tomorrow."

I phoned James at mid-morning when I figured he would still be unraveling his day. "James? Stone here, let's get together."

"Everything okay, you hear something 'bout the freak?"

"Nothing new. I just want to meet and greet."

"Don't be tryin, Stone, you can't talk the talk anymore'n you can walk the walk."

"I know, James, I know, but it always sounds like fun."

"That's what it is, a fun feeling. So what're we talking about?"

"I want to bring you up to speed on everything."

"I haven't had my coffee yet, how about Shuster's in twenty minutes."

"You're on."

"I'm gone."

This part of town was just getting it together. Around here early breakfast was something you did elsewhere. James was sitting against his front fender reading the paper as I pulled up.

"I don't know why I keep trying to find *somebody* who ain't lying. I sure won't find anything straight in the paper. Let me ask you, Stone, when did omission stop being a sin?"

"Before my time, James."

"Man, I didn't think anything went back that far. By the way, how *does* it feel to be standing so close to the finish line?"

"I may piss on your grave, James. I don't smoke."

"Touché brother Stone, I expect you just might, smoking or no. How's my pal, Donna, holding up?"

"She has decided to stay. Mark and I talked it over with her at dinner last night. By the way, I couldn't reach you, tried all afternoon, you missed out on a fine dinner. My treat."

"Well, I'll just tag you for breakfast. I was busy. I got your messages but I knew you guys could handle it."

"Everything okay?"

"Tits, man, everything is tits."

"That's good, isn't it?"

"The best, Stone, the best. What made her decide to stay?"

"I'm not sure. We talked about friends, sticking together, circling the wagons and stuff like that. I think she really feels safe with all of us looking out for her."

"Yeah, she's covered and all, it's the unexpected shit we got to watch. Like opening her door, she won't do that again."

"That bothers hell out of me, James, I've never understood why she did it."

James stopped his coffee cup in mid-air, "Old Randall was due at that exact time. She took my sister to the doctor that day after dropping the old man off at the bank. He made her promise to wait for him so he could bring his money *exactly* at five o'clock."

"Why the hell wouldn't she tell us that?"

"She loves that old man, Stone. She wouldn't want you guys getting in his face, she's everybody's protector."

"But she told you?"

"Only because I'm brave, clean and reverent. Truth is, she didn't tell me, Randall did, he's been feeling like shit ever since. Saint Jake fed him booze to—"

"Randall actually saw the sonofabitch?"

"Oh yeah. Jake pumped him to get the time and address. Hey, now, he's suffering enough, don't you get in his ass and don't be giving me up, either. I just didn't realize you didn't know, and I think you need to."

"James, you know I won't say anything. Can you convince him to tell me, or Mark?"

"Maybe, but why?"

"I'm not sure. I'm no investigator but maybe it can help, we'll get a police sketch artist or something."

"Right on, brother, then we'll shine the Bat-light in the sky and make Robin buy some real pants. I'll talk to him, Stone, he's an okay old guy, he can't help the booze."

"Thanks. Is it okay with you if I tell Mark?"

"Do it. I want anything that *can* help, to help."

"You okay with Aleena, now?"

"Got to be. She's getting to be a boss mare all too fast. It's like she went from child to woman in a blink with that baby in her belly. She's dead set on school, then college or special education and now I'm seeing something new. Used to be, when I would talk to her about improving *her* life, she wouldn't give me much back. Now, if I suggest she don't want her baby to be loaded down with no stupid Momma, she makes it clear she wants that more'n I do."

"How does she want more."

"Right now, she don't mess with the boys cause she don't want her baby to come from some trashy Momma. I'm not sure that'll last but, I don't know, she's a mule. If I talk about a high school diploma, she talks about a college degree. If I say be a nurse, she says, why not a doctor. Some of that talk is your fault, she's always telling me how she can become *anything* she's willing to work for."

"You know it's true, James."

"What I know is, it's scary, too damn scary. Go for too much and you'll be on your ass, getting stomped."

"Maybe you ought to think about setting an example for Aleena. You know, leading the way through higher education."

James stood up, reached in his pocket and threw down ten dollars, more than enough to cover the check we hadn't received yet.

"I got places to be, Stone, and you ain't makin no damn sense."

"James, you have a fast head. You're already ahead of me and you don't like where I'm going."

"Sit on it, Stone. I ain't interested in nothin you're peddling."

Going ahead, he waited just outside the door as I finished up then joined him out on the sidewalk."

"I can help, James."

"Right now you best worry about helping Donna. This Saint Jake is bad shit. He's maybe gonna watch both of us die. Aleena's baby ain't made it yet and she's only a high school freshman. We got time to think about tomorrow, if we get one."

XIV

After angling up to the front of the building I stopped and looked at it in a way I hadn't done before. I tried to think of myself as someone who wanted to break in. Trying to think as I imagined Jake might. The metal front door with its obvious dead-bolts and the adjacent windows with their equally obvious electrical contact plates, were the only places large enough for entry. I walked around to the north side which, except for two small ventilating fan grills, had no openings at all. The back wall, like the front, admitted light through narrow horizontal windows running atop high brick walls, just under the overhang. Nothing there. The overhead door on the south side looked to be the weakest point. Winkler had done some clever things however: when closed, the door had a substantial vertical metal bar attached to a strong metal cross bar. The arrangement enabled the vertical bar to drop into a reinforced slot in the floor. The whole thing wound up giving me the feeling someone would have to move against tons of concrete in order to force the door inward and yet it offered little resistance to anyone seeking to crash out.

All bushes and landscaping were cleared away to eliminate hiding places. Someone would have to sprint a considerable distance, at high speed, to be able to reach the closing door in time to drop down and roll under. In that unlikely event, Donna, who had been carefully instructed in safe entry procedures, knew how to back out, smashing through the door, in order to get away safely. I felt good about all that and the fact that the floor and roof were solid cement.

"Good morning, Mr. Stone. You look pretty smug for someone who's a bit late."

Donna understood I felt it was extremely important to be timely with my scheduled meetings with our wounded birds. I was afraid any action which could be interpreted as a put-down, would be immediately regarded as such and might undo hours of progress.

"I was checking the perimeter of the building."

"What are you looking for, rats?"

"Exactly."

Heading through the reception area door I sang out, "Yo, Raymond, is the coffee hot? I was hung up doing a safety check, please forgive me for being late."

"That's okay, I understand."

"Have I ever shown you everything that's been done here, Raymond, would you like to inspect the place?"

"Me?"

"Sure, why not?"

With coffee cups in hand, Raymond and I repeated the same inspection made a few minutes before. I reasoned that even such a relatively minor display of shared confidence was better therapy than anything I could tell him. He took it all quite seriously, measuring possible openings and such, then I realized he was a thorough person. Of course, he was a bookkeeper, probably a damn good one.

"What do you think?" I asked.

"I think I'd rather try *any* other way to make a grab. Even right off the street rather than trying to break into this place. Did you think about how safe it could be when you bought it?"

"No. I just liked all the interior wall space for book shelves."

Back inside, Raymond poured himself another cup of coffee. I noticed because, although it was a small thing, it was something he'd not done before.

"Something happened and I need some help, real bad, Doc."

My heart began a slow Tango as I immediately assumed he had advanced from flashing to something worse. I drank some coffee before answering.

"Call me Stone, Raymond. Everybody else does. Do mean you did something real bad, or you need help real bad?" I forced a smile.

When he looked at me I realized it was a stupid thing to have said, the intimation could be shattering to such a fragile personality.

"C'mon, Stone, for Christ's sake. I'm talking about something nice here."

"No offense intended, Raymond. I'm sure you know that."

"Yeah, I do. But I want you to know I'm taking to this computer stuff like a duck to water. I can't believe I've been scared to death all this time, I'm such a putz. But I tell you, I not only understand it I can even see what's coming next. I can't believe it."

"I'll bet you were a pretty good student when you were a kid first studying accounting."

"I was good, but I figured it was all simple stuff anybody could do, but computers, forget it. By the time they came in I was too goddam scared."

"What were you frightened about?"

"I don't exactly know. I was this skinny, mousy little shit and by the time I got to the eleventh grade I was scared. Like I had dreams of becoming a CPA. I heard how much money those guys make and I knew I could make it too. Until I started getting scared.

"My old man was a stupid guy always looking for a big hit on the horses. My Mom was, she just had a bad time…she was, anyway, I decided I couldn't do a fucking thing. I quit school in the eleventh grade and started keeping books, I was always scared.

"But now this woman is coming over asking me to help her all the time and telling me how good I am. She's really nice, you know? Maybe I'm nuts but I think she likes me. I mean, I know she already knows some of the stuff she asks me about."

"She sounds nice, Raymond."

"Oh yeah, she's nice, she's kinda classy and I get the feeling she's lonely. She told me she had to look after her mother and now the old lady is dead.

She's about my age I think. I'm scared, Stone, I've never been with any woman except for some whores. I never had one regular date, even in school. I'm so scared I want to run away."

"Well, maybe that's the best bet, Raymond, just drop out of class until next term."

"Are you fuckin nuts? No, you're puttin me on. Why're you doing that?"

"That is one of your options, isn't it? All I'm doing is what I always do. I'm pointing out that you have options, your life is your own. So damn it to hell, tell me what *you* want."

"I'd like to get to know her better."

"Do you feel you need my permission? Do you want me to write you a note saying it's okay to ask her out?"

"No, I just want some help for Christ's sake. Tell me what to say."

"Okay. Tomorrow night, what's her name?"

"Margaret, Margaret Horn."

When she comes over to see you tomorrow night just say, Hey Margaret, let's go to the movies to celebrate my birthday."

"It ain't my birthday, Stone."

"Do as I say, Raymond, and it might just become your birthday."

"Has anybody called in, do we have anything scheduled this afternoon, Donna?"

I wanted to meet with Mark to decide whether we could use Randall's sighting in any practical way.

"Donald Simms and Bunny Brewster both confirmed for tomorrow afternoon. Malka called to check in, everything else is quiet. Do you want to see Mark before or after lunch? I'll call him and set it up."

"You've gotten me hung up on our lunch sessions. Call and see if I can get with him afterwards. I'm going back to make some fresh coffee"

I was sitting at our small, Italian folding table thinking unsorted thoughts, half listening to the classical musical background sounds. Donna appeared in the doorway a few minutes later. She stopped for a moment, fully back-lit, the bright light of the front window softening her outline. The effect was numbing; not many angels had entered my life.

The spell continued as she began her happy house-playing. She hummed a little tune while she nuked some New England Chowder and pulled a fresh, crisp green salad from the refrigerator. She wore a cream colored, short sleeve sweater, not the baggy sort, a fitted style that was well suited to her small frame. Her slacks were a tailored off-white and the overall result was, to me at least, absolutely perfect; clean, feminine and classy. That she should be the center of such a raging, insane storm was incomprehensible.

"What's your problem, Stone? Are you holding back something bad?"

"Nothing like that. I was just thinking about you—"

"I guessed as much and I think I owe you some sort of explanation about where I stand. I owe so much to Mark, and lately to you, I am awed by it all. I feel humble and I realize I owe you both more than I can repay right now, maybe ever. I know I don't deserve the care and love you two give me but it's wonderful. I've never felt more protected, secure and happy in my life and it is healing me.

"You are still my perfect date, my perfect guy. But, please try to understand, I have to fight every minute to keep focused on today. I can't look at tomorrow or permit myself to think about anything that's past. I'm too afraid. I feel if I don't hold myself in a rigid, right this minute time frame, I will spin off and never find my way back. The nights are unbelievable. But you're making it possible for me to hang on because I can concentrate on your clients, *our* clients. I can focus on them and their problems. It's working, I'm crawling back, but it's slow, Stone, so painfully slow.

"I know you and Mark know far more than I can face. I know it's unfair, but I can't cope, not yet."

I reached out to her and she came into my arms, not as a woman but as a child. It was the first time we had ever embraced. Holding her in my arms with her face buried against the terrors of her world, I experienced a sense of tenderness beyond anything I'd known. I also understood, for the first time, that until the worm was unalterably excommunicated from her soul she could never become who she had been.

My voice was forced back into my throat as I tried to speak, "I don't have all that much to offer but whatever I have is yours. A lot of people love you. This nightmare will pass, I swear it will. In the meantime, I won't push you about anything. It'll keep, and we'll both know when you are ready."

I held her away at arms length and smiled. "So now, want to brief me on Dottie Brewster?"

"It's Bunny Brewster. Give me a minute," she walked off to the washroom while I poured myself another cup of coffee and wished for the hundredth time I knew what the hell I was doing.

I heard Donna return as she walked up behind me.

"Bunny Brewster is a waitress at Daisy's Deli, my favorite breakfast spot. I would guess she's thirty four or so. Average looking, thin, bright, great sense of humor, has two little girls at home and a husband who periodically beats her to a pulp. She loves him, she thinks. She also thinks she's at fault. The only reason I was able to convince her to come and talk to you, well actually there are two reasons: secrecy, she's afraid of what might happen if her husband found out. No, three reasons, she's worried about her little girls and I told her a small lie."

"Sounds to me like you told her a couple of lies; you know I'm not qualified to deal with her kind of problem. In my secret opinion she should either shoot the bastard or get the hell out of town. What kind of nutty advice would that make. I'm always worried I might actually make someone's situation worse, such as in this case. What's the lie?"

"She has no money and if her husband caught her spending any this way he might break something, like her fingers, or her head. If I told her I was charging her on my account, she wouldn't come either. So I told her you had a government grant for battered wives."

"Do you have any idea…never mind, I'll see her tomorrow. Is Mark expecting me at two?"

She smiled as she nodded.

After I stepped out of the front door I stopped to await the sounds of Donna locking up behind me and to scan the area. My building had a small porch area from which I could check out a swath of about a hundred and eighty degrees. Running from left to right was an intersection with a large empty lot spanning a full block. Then a city block of park area containing a basketball court, tennis courts, playground equipment and benches spaced around green areas. The street passing in front of the building also afforded a clear view. The only places out of my line of sight were the street alongside, which I could cover by taking three steps to the edge of the porch, and the parking area north of the structure. To visually examine that area I had to walk past my parked car to the end of the building. In all, I felt we were very secure. I heard the door locks click, then heard the sounds of Donna rattling the plastic vertical blinds as she peeked out to watch me leave. I considered each vehicle in sight as well as each person in the park before I walked over to check the small northern parking area. Everything was clear.

Getting into my car, I drove north to the corner, then east for three blocks, two more rights which brought me back to the building then a final right before I actually left the area.

Too cautious? I wondered, or is that another perfect oxymoron.

"I'm sorry to say this, Stone, but Randall Preston really bugs me. It is totally irrational, considering I'm a recovering alcoholic, but that bastard wallows in his addiction. He's not stupid, well maybe he is, but he's educated, and yet he makes no effort to admit his problem, face it and deal with it. I suppose my feeling that he's the *real* reason Donna damn near got killed is what pisses me off. That, and the fact he still hasn't learned anything, he's going around wailing, *Oh poor me, I feel so bad about almost getting that lovely child murdered.* What bullshit. He doesn't feel bad enough to admit he's got shit for brains, from years of hiding in the bottle.

Or maybe it's only because I want a drink so goddam bad every fucking day of the world."

There was no appropriate way to respond to Mark's comments. His feelings were a problem he would handle…or he wouldn't.

"What about a sketch artist, Mark."

"From a description by someone too drunk to keep an appointment? Or are you just changing the subject?"

"You tell me. As far as the sketch, I might be able to help. I've studied so many reports and written descriptions, I think I can picture Jake in my head. I also think I saw him from the bus that day. Of course, I could be totally wrong, too."

"I'm just edgy because we haven't heard a word about Jake in too long. Christ, he could be sitting outside your building, watching for a chance."

"Mark, you're the expert but how could that be? Donna's living in a new place and she's not on the streets anymore. Jake's been inside my place but he doesn't . . .never mind, I just answered my own question"

"He could also turn Randall over, shove a bottle of booze up his ass and he'd tell him everything. I know you trust Randall more than I do but I know more about drunks, I am one."

"There's also the possibility that Jake is in a dormant period. In study-ing those reports I noted he would occasionally sink into the muck. He apparently goes on prolonged bouts of drugs, booze and broads. A couple of his pals reported that when things "got right," which for Jake means getting a string of street whores under his protection, he would sometimes stay down until he messed with the wrong people."

"Okay, let's see if you can get something better out of Randall than the few lousy descriptions we've got. We'll crank up our mail-outs around New Orleans. Maybe we'll get lucky and if he's standing still somewhere, I *will* nail that sonofabitch, hopefully in his sleep."

I called James to find out whether he had convinced Randall to tell me about meeting Jake. Answering service. Later that night James called back,

"Randall tells me he is scheduled to see you day after tomorrow and he *will* tell you the story. He promised."

"James, Randall is a drunk. His promises are soluble, he's missed his last two appointments."

"I can't promise he'll be sober, but I promise his skinny ass'll be there, Stone. I'm bringing him in."

When I walked into Calahan's it was late for the dinner crowd, early for the party people. Laurie slipped an arm around my waist as she guided me to my favorite booth then slid in alongside me.

"Do you have something to tell me, Smooth? Been way too long."

"Tell you, like what?"

"Some poetic or philosophical way of dumping my winsome butt?"

"You're my pal, Laurie. You never complain and you never bug me. I may take advantage of your good nature, like recently, when I'm honestly busy and I'm sorry about that. But you have no idea how much I appreciate you."

"Okay then, enough silly talk. I prefer what we whisper when I'm at your place. And, oh, my, what a good idea that is."

I watched her walk away, as she knew I would so she gave it an extra swish. Despite the constant, nagging worry about Jake, I had a sense of well being. I decided some good grilled fish, followed by ice cold beer, then sweet, warm Laurie, were all overdue.

"Seems every time I see you, you're eating. I don't understand how you keep from tubbin out, Stone."

"James, you rascal, come join me. I could use some good company on such a fine night."

"Rascal? I don't know why I waste my time with somebody who uses words like rascal. Just what the hell is a rascal?"

"One who is playfully mischievous. Or, in your case, one who is supercritical, often short of patience."

"Moi? I am nothing if not patient. I will, in fact, lay an excellent example upon you. Most every day I go to my favorite stool, in my favorite place to break the fast, usually between eleven and noon. Now for the past sixteen consecutive days some, usually chubby, broad arrives just as my food does. She will invariably sit within two stools of me and start lighting up an endless series of those goddam filter tip, extra long, weed fires, blowing smoke all over me and my food. Now, you wanna know what makes me so patient? I ain't killed one of the bitches yet, and God, how I want to. You explain why they do that kind of shit and I'll buy you a set of tires."

"Chubby women think smoking controls weight?"

"Can't be, it's just like diet soda, all them fat smokers order diet soda. I never see a good looking, slim woman smoking or sucking on diet soda, so that stuff must be what makes 'em fat."

"Don't male smokers bother you just as much?"

"It's weird, but men are less pushy about their smoking, they look around first and sometimes they'll even step outside."

"Get out. Sounds like you're being prejudiced."

"I have news, Stone, I am *very* prejudiced against slobs and bad asses."

"Are there ash trays at the counter?"

"Got nothing to do with it."

"Is there a no smoking section?"

"I like sitting at the counter."

"No doubt about it, you *are* a sweet person."

Laurie arrived, "My favorite guys, together again. How you doing James, how's Aleena?"

"She's satisfied. Smug and showing."

"Tell her I said pretty soon we'll be able to babysit for each other."

"Is this poor man's Cary Grant treating you right? He *is* strange, and so damn square. I know some nice guys be happy to push him out the way."

"Oh no, James, old Smooth promised if I am extra nice this evening we can have an actual date, when I get off."

"I'm ain't touchin *that* line, darlin."

She pointed her finger under her chin, made a slight curtsey and moved away.

"I stopped off to see Randall again, told him if he wasn't reasonably sober when I came to pick him up I would chuck his ass into the river. But he worries me. The man is a mess. I hope you don't let him in on anything important. He's a weak spot. He pissed and moaned for twenty minutes about not knowing where Donna's new apartment is. I can't believe you've been able to keep her from telling him. Any chance we could send him on a world cruise or into an old drunks home for a couple of months?"

"You and Mark are sure hard-ass on the old guy."

"Stone, he nearly got Donna killed. How many chances you want to give him?"

XV

Donald Simms strutted in looking like a male model. He wore a double breasted jacket that fit as the designer intended but seldom does, a collarless shirt unlike anything I had seen, with tailored slacks that were born with the jacket in mind.

"Great looking outfit, Donald. Looks really expensive."

"Thanks, and thanks. I like for threads to look like big bucks."

"Yours do, and then some. I've been thinking about you and your obvious creative design talent. Have you ever done anything about enhancing that, about a career in one of the related fields?"

"Well, I meet a lot of guys who talk big, and I figure I'll eventually meet somebody who really does have the right connections."

"Get over it, Donald. There is only one person in the whole world you can rely on, only one who will do you any good. Don't buy off on the connections baloney. If you want to make it, then pick your field, learn to maximize your talent and go all out for it."

"Everybody else says it's who you know," then, with a twisted smile, "or, in the arts, who you blow."

"You ever hear any top level guys say that?"

"I've never met any top guys."

"Well, Donald, I have. I was in the advertising agency business. I dealt directly with lot's of top guys and none of them ever bought into that trick-bag. But before we get too far into the road to success stuff, let's talk about the specific field of design which you think you are best suited for. I should point out to you that I was deeply involved with graphic design during my ad agency years and I made enough money to become independent at what is generally considered a very early age, although maybe not to you. In short, I may be able to offer some suggestions that have proven to be successful, after we have our talk.

I had rubbed the genie's bottle, Donald Simms was still going strong when I pulled his chain an hour later.

Sharon Stern's phone call arrived on the silver threads of chance as most such critical points of change do. "Locke," Sharon was one of the few people alive who called me by my middle name, "Ben is dead."

Big Ben Stern took a very long time to die. That he did so was good because he was a thoughtful man and the delay enabled him to accomplish things important to himself and others. In the eighteen years following the pronouncement of his "any-minute" death sentence, he managed to both increase and rearrange his assets in order that his much younger wife would have a full range of options. He was a good man who was unique as well. When I first met him it was as a new advertising client who took a position no other client had taken with me; he asked whether I could make his business successful. No clever approaches or bending of beliefs, he simply asked, "Mr. Stone, now you know my goals. Can you cause me to attain them with the percentage of operating income I can, and will, turn over to you for advertising and marketing?"

He never second guessed me nor backed away from commitment. I came to love him as an example of what a man should be. I came to love his wife, Sharon, as a woman. First because he couldn't, then because she and I became so close, so comfortable and so compatible. To the extent one can ever be certain of unspoken things, Sharon and I understood our times of intimacy had Ben's blessing. It never changed the fact that I felt shamed and diminished by feelings of betrayal, regardless of Sharon's assurances of Ben's love and appreciation. Each time reminded me that I was an imperfect man, a flawed creature. Now Ben was dead and I had to say something to Sharon, holding herself silent while I dodged and scrambled trying to avoid my overpowering thoughts.

"Sharon, I just don't know what to say. It's been coming for so long I came to believe Ben would always be there. Are you okay? What are the arrangements?"

"No arrangements, Locke, he had clear instructions which I followed. Everything is over…I would like to come and see you."

"Of course."

Sharon took three days to drive from Atlanta to Fort Lauderdale. Finally she called and spoke to Donna regarding my schedule then arrived late on a rainy, overcast afternoon. Slipping off her raincoat she came into my arms without a word. We held each other for a long time until she backed away, looked at me, then at Donna.

"I'm sorry to be so rude," she smiled at Donna, "but my husband and I both loved this man for many years. I'm Sharon Stern, a long time friend."

"I'm Donna Delgado, a recent friend and temporary employee. I am so happy to finally meet you. Perhaps now I'll be able to learn more about Stone's mysterious past."

"I will pass along all his carefully protected secrets. I'm staying at the New Roney Plaza, perhaps we can lunch tomorrow. I'm in desperate need of female company and some inside information on shopping. I just threw rags in a bag before I left. I was in rather a state."

"I would love it, it's a date." Donna beamed in a way I had not seen before.

I felt as if I had my nose pressed against a glass as Sharon followed me to my office. I was distracted by my lack of ideas for how to keep Donna from an exposed shopping trip tomorrow. But I turned back to Sharon.

"I expected you would stay with me," I said.

"Locke, my lover, my pal, I swarmed all over you every time I had a chance for so many years. Now that Ben is dead, I realize I can't do that anymore. I'm nutty as a Georgia pecan pie but somehow I feel it's no longer okay. I guess because…maybe because Ben isn't around to say it's okay. I know it'll pass, I hope. But is that crazy, or what?"

"What scares me, Sharon, is that I understand."

"One of the last things he said was, "Go to Locke, you'll help each other.""

"Is that why you came," I asked.

"I think so. I have a thousand other reasons, but I think that's it. I can come with Ben's blessing. I think perhaps I'm crazy. At best, I'm confused as hell."

"How about a couple of drinks and an early dinner?" I asked.

"Not tonight. I'm tired, feeling ugly and without proper clothing. I just wanted to see you then I'm going to the hotel, take a massage, some steam, a salad and an early bed. But I would like to see you tomorrow. In fact I'd love a rain check on dinner and drinks. By the way, she is adorable. I have the feeling Donna is special in lots and lots of ways. So, c'mon, don't kid a kidder, do you love that young woman out there?"

"I sure do," I said, "In a very special way."

"What on earth does that mean?"

"I wish I knew, Sharon."

"Does she know?"

"I have no idea. We're standing on opposite sides of a great chasm."

"Are you telling me she's married?" she asked.

"No, but she was once about to become a bride."

Sharon kept her lunch date with Donna while I agonized over this worrisome new wrinkle. I had to preserve Donna's protective environment and it was clear that Sharon's presence could compromise her safety. I had no right to discuss Donna's situation with Sharon yet there was the greater duty to protect Donna's life. Unsure of which way to turn, I decided to speak with Donna after today's lunch in order to gain her permission to include Sharon in our little group of insiders. I had some strange feeling Donna might refuse, it didn't make sense but my gut told me she might. Then what? I trusted Sharon, I would tell her regardless of whether or not

Donna okayed it. I would just have to risk Donna's alienation, something I didn't want to do.

The situation looked worse after lunch when Donna returned flush with pleasure and excitement. It was the first time I thought about the vast scope of experiences she missed out on during her years of imprisonment in Jake's vans.

I'd always thought about the brutality and torture, now I began to think about the deprivation. It was staggering.

Donna was literally bubbling over with excitement over her new friend, "Stone, you'll never believe what she said."

"Try me."

"She said, well first she asked me about you, you know, about how I felt, and I said, as I always do: Oh, he's my perfect guy, my perfect friend, my perfect date. You know, like we kid around. Then she said she was so glad. She said it was about time somebody leveled your snobby ass. That's what she said, then she said, one look and she could see you were a dead bird. Isn't she just too much?"

"Donna, you and I need—"

"I'm sorry, Stone, but your three o'clock's due any minute. Do you need anything? You started to say something?"

"It'll have to keep until after this appointment. It will take a few minutes, and it's important. We'll talk then."

Bunny Brewster turned out to be one of those women who disappear from the world's screen for a time. One minute they are young, vital, at the peak of their looks, playful and sexually attractive. Then some mysterious cell division takes place. When we notice them next they have become "older" ladies and there seems to be no actual, gradual conversion time. Yesterday, they *are* a happening, today they *were* one. Somehow, in the changing of the tense-guard some molecular shift takes place and the myth that "men age better" gains another vote.

It was painful to sense her fears as she edged into my office. I knew I had to handle her sensitized nerve endings as if they were exposed and raw. I stood and extended my hand.

"Hi there, Mrs. Brewster, I'm Locke Stone and I'm pleased to meet you. Donna has told me how often you help her get her day started on the right track."

"Oh that girl is so special. I've never heard her say the first nasty thing about anyone, no matter what and, oh, it's nice to meet you, too, Mister, ah Doctor—"

"It's just Mister, and please, have a seat."

"Okay, Mister Stone. Donna has told me a lot about you, too."

"I'd like to ask you an offbeat question, Mrs. Brew—"

"Bunny, please, I'd feel more comfortable if you call me Bunny. Everybody does. I mean it's my name, well, since I was a little girl. My other name don't matter, you know."

"I understand. Have you ever seen the movie, "The Wizard Of Oz"? The Judy Garland version?"

"Lord Mr. Stone, that was made twenty years before I was born."

"Yes. Of course, I realize that. But it *is* a classic and they show it frequently and, if you've seen it, it helps me make a point."

"Well, sure. I guess everybody's seen it, probably lots of times."

"You remember the girl was helping everyone find the wizard to get their problems solved? The Lion wanted courage, the Scarecrow needed a heart and I always forget what the Tin Man wanted."

"The Tin Man wanted the heart, the Scarecrow needed a brain."

"Ah, yes. Good. Now, this is just a fun question, but if you met the Wizard and he could give you anything you want, what would you ask for, Bunny?"

"Well, that's easy enough. I'm like the scarecrow, sometimes I think I need a new brain. I'm an awful screw-up."

"Does screwing up get you in trouble?"

"Lord, yes. I'm forever makin my husband mad." Then, following a painfully long, silent pause, "I guess Donna told you."

"Donna doesn't tell me much. The rule around here is that it's best to hear things right from the horse's mouth. It's the only way anything gets accomplished."

"Do people always tell you how things really are?"

"I don't know. Besides, how things actually are usually isn't as important as how people think things are. That's what we have to live with and what we have to improve."

"I don't understand."

"Okay. Let's picture two people. One is rich, has a big car and a big house and a big job. He's a big shot, used to running everything. He even knows what is best for his wife and children. But they don't feel the same way about things, his kids run off and his wife takes to popping too much white wine.

The other man is just a working guy, never has a dime to spare, his car is falling apart, his roof leaks and he can't afford to send his kids to a decent school. But his wife is happy to see him when he comes home from work and his kids think he's a great Dad.

"The first guy is absolutely certain his life is crappy, and the second guy believes he's the luckiest man in town. The *facts* would indicate otherwise but the *feelings*, the *beliefs* are what really matter. Does that make sense?"

"So you're saying it's what people *believe* that's important, not necessarily what really is?"

"I think that's how we live our lives. Don't you?

"Yeah, I guess. I have to think about all that."

"Terrific, that's exactly what I want you to do. In the meantime how about you telling me how you think everything in your life is going?"

Bunny Brewster, unclenched her grip on her purse for the first time, sat back in her chair and proceeded to tell me how she screwed up so often. Before her first hour was up she had begun to explain how it was that her husband sometimes lost his temper and had to straighten her out.

As I walked Bunny to the front door and set up her next appointment with Donna I stayed put until they finished and Bunny was gone. Then Donna beat me to it.

"I know, Stone, I know. But I was careful when we went shopping, I really was. You know I don't want to take any chances. But Sharon is so nice. I haven't been able to be with someone like her, hardly ever. God, it was like a different world, a different life, one I've never had."

"This is so damn tough. Because you're so right. But I'm going to hit you right where you live; it's not just you, but when you let down you risk everybody. You didn't just take a chance on yourself today, you risked Sharon, other times you could risk Mark, or James, or—"

"Okay. All right. That *is* a low blow. But you're right, I didn't exactly think of it that way."

I reached out to her, held both her upper arms and made her look me in the eye. "There is no right or wrong. This whole thing will pass. I swear to you it's true, it will pass because it has to pass. Events have no choice, they have to happen. I promise you with all my heart and on everything I believe that you will be released from this nightmare. You are surrounded by people who love you and that makes you fortunate and special. Please, hold us all together and you will be fine and your life will be good. I know it, I swear it, I promise."

One corner of her mouth raised in what required imagination to be judged a smile, "Goodness, Mr. Stone, can't you ever manage to be serious?"

Then, "Tell me, oh great Philosopher, what shall we do?"

"Oh, I dunno," as I crouched into a Groucho walk and flicked an imaginary cigar, "Ah yes, I could tell she was a jockey's daughter cause all the horse-men knew 'er."

"I didn't mean *that* serious," she said with a laugh.

"We're going to bring Sharon into our little club, that's what we're gonna do. Let's call and take her to dinner."

"No! I don't want to hear it. I can't hear it. I like Sharon, I want to be with her and I understand what you are saying, but I can't be there. I can't hear what you have to tell her, okay?"

"I understand."

"And, Stone, you have to promise me you'll tell her not to get involved, that maybe she's taking a chance and she should come back later, when everything's okay. *Before* you tell her about…about it. Only tell her if she *wants* to stay, all right? Promise?"

"Promise."

"Will you take her to dinner?"

"Yes, I'll call now."

"Call me later?"

"Sure."

It was four hours later when I called Donna. "May I come by for a minute, please?

"Sure, want to tell me anything?"

"I'll be there in a few minutes, okay?"

"Okay."

When Donna looked through her view-port she saw both of us and her unlocking procedures moved fast yet seemed to take forever. She looked very small when she finally swung the door wide.

Sharon spoke first, "I'm moving in, if you'll have me, honey."

The "toughest" street hooker in town reverted to a seventeen-year old virgin as she fell into Sharon's arms and released the most heart-wrenching, sobbing, crying tears I'd ever seen. She had years of agony to express and despite my certainty that this was the healthiest thing which could possibly happen, I had to leave. My own tears threatened to bust loose, and I didn't belong here at this critical, healing moment.

I woke early the next morning, nervous as a cat. I couldn't lay still even though it was too early to go to the club. I hopped out of bed, made a cup of instant coffee and began jumping an exercise pattern, moving my feet through the changes a Broadway dancer had shown me years ago. It was a good thing to do because it called upon a slight bit of awareness to stay in the pattern and it also burned off excess nervous energy.

I wanted to call Donna but it was too early. Then I realized not one of my new pals was an early riser. Then I re-realized that wasn't true at all, they were most all up by seven thirty or so, except James, of course. But here I was, bouncing around like some silly pogo-stick creature at six thirty. I carried my coffee outside onto the balcony where another gorgeous Florida day threatened.

After what seemed hours, I finally called my office a few minutes after nine and Donna came on strong, "Hey Mr. Perfect date, do you know I love ya?"

Donna was bubbling over, "Having Sharon move in is the greatest. I had begun talking back to the TV and pacing a path in the carpet, it's a wonderful idea. I love it, I can *not* begin to tell you how *much* I love it, thank you, thank you."

I didn't know what to say, "Well it was her idea, don't give me the credit."

"Right, Stone. I'm only beginning to understand what a master manipulator you are."

I didn't think so, but it sounded kind of neat, "I'm headed over to Mark's office in case you need me, I'll be back for lunch. We still on for lunch?"

"You bet. See you then."

Mark was as edgy at mid-morning as I had been at six. He kept moving things on his desk, his right leg was jiggling at high speed and he sat down and got back up four times for one cup of coffee.

"Something must be going around, Mark, you're as jumpy as I was earlier today. Have you heard something?

"I think Jake was picked up and released on a minor beef in Baton Rouge. I'm trying to get more information, everything's pretty vague so far, but I've got somebody on it. I'm mostly hung up on what you said the other day, about Jake having extended periods of laying low. I keep thinking about it."

"Sounds like you might be fighting the obvious."

A couple of pounds of tension blew. "What the fuck does that mean? Don't give me your psycho-babble bullshit, Stone, I'm not one of your goddam cripples."

"Sorry, Mark, sometimes I take the wrong tack. All I mean is it sounds to me as if you have an idea that fits the situation, sounds right, even makes sense but for some reason you don't want to do it."

"Kind of like the way you talk?"

"Exactly. Now, can we get on with it?"

"It makes sense that even a wacko like Jake can occasionally fall into a situation that works for him and so he goes, as you said, goes dormant until he screws things up. I can't pretend to understand the motives at work, hell, I don't care about the why's and wherefore's, I just want that sonofabitch. That's what's bugging me."

"How about you telling me what you're not saying?"

"I want to take him while he's down. I want to take it to him. If he's quiet for a spell then let's go end it. That's what's bothering me. One, is he sitting still and two, exactly what do I mean? Am I talking about murder? That's the only sure way to stop this crazy bastard, is it him or Donna? Someone has to die? Jesus, Stone, it sounds crazy when I say it, am I missing something here? Can you see any other real solution?"

"You have fingered a basic problem, my friend. The absolute solution will only occur after one of the participants is dead, it's that simple. But we can't deal with that truth. Jake can, we can't. So we, like most people in the world, hope for some sort of miracle, we hope someone else kills him, cops, another psychotic, anybody but us. Most everyone faces problems the same way. We blame anyone we can and we beg for help from anyone who might take up our cause: church, government, schools, police, you name it. We run, we scream, we point fingers, we do almost anything to avoid the hard choices."

"You make people sound damn near as bad as they are."

"Some people are good, my personal estimation is about ten percent. How else do we account for someone like Donna…and yourself?"

"Whoa, Preacher man, before you start to pass the collection plate, let's get back to it. Say we find Jake in hibernation and we get the drop on him, could you pull the trigger?"

"No. Could you?"

"Intellectually, yes. I can put any one of several pictures in my mind during his kidnapping of Donna and there is no question, he needs to be dead."

"Granted. Can you do it?"

"What do you want from me, Stone? The answer is yes, no and I don't know."

"The next question is, if we find out he is dormant, do we try?"

"Not we, me. No sense you going, somebody has to stay here to protect Donna if I fail. By the way, I spoke to her this morning and she sounds like a different person. Getting Sharon Stern to move in with her is the greatest thing, almost the greatest thing, I can imagine. She feels so much better. I have to thank you for that one."

"I appreciate the thanks I'm getting from you both but it was Sharon's idea, she's the one who moved on it the minute I told her the story. And yeah, it's great. I had no idea how important female companionship is to a young woman, it must be some important part of growing up.

"Mark, on the other matter, we have to know about Jake. If we find out he's dormant we'll have to move fast. Let's think about strategy after we know for sure. I know I couldn't do it alone and I suspect you can't either. Our only chance is together…I think."

"Done. Now, I'm having another problem, Stone. Let's do lunch, I need to talk."

When I phoned Donna to cancel lunch she reminded me Randall was due in at three, "Is everything okay with you and Mark," she asked.

"Everything's fine, you know Mark, straight arrow right down the line. I feel so damn lucky to have him as well as James in our corner that—"

"Then try to imagine how I feel about all three of you. Stone, promise you won't do anything foolish. I have a strange feeling now that things are going well."

"Oh yeah, well remember, relax and keep your guard up. Try *that* while you're chewing gum. Nothing to fret about, Mark just wants to talk at lunch. See you before three."

Mark ordered a steak for lunch, preceded it with a cup of soup and a large salad. "Sometimes when it gets bad I try to bury it by eating. Eating is sort of a self reward, too, you know."

"You're talking about alcohol?"

"I told you I'm a recovering lush."

"I don't mean to trivialize, Mark, but I believe few, if any of us, are symptom-free. Some things are more obvious, more obnoxious, more easily hidden, but they exist just the same."

"What are yours?"

"I'm acrophobic, scared to death of spiders and wary of exposed vulnerability. But I don't go around calling myself names, that smacks of "poor me" stuff."

"You're also kind of a hard ass."

"I wish. What do you do about the booze, do you go to AA meetings?"

"No. The bar association has an office in every state which handles us."

"I don't understand. Handles? How?"

"Attorneys, Judges, anyone who is a member of the bar, an officer of the court, can't just go to public places for treatment or follow-up help. It wouldn't look right. We're afraid the general public would lose even more respect for us. Our association arranges things so that we work it out in a sort of closed society."

"A secret gang of legal drunks? There's something to shudder about."

"That's the point, that and the fact that we have no choice."

"Oh?"

"Once another attorney, a judge, or anyone for that matter, reports us to the bar association, we face losing our license if we don't show up and clean up."

"Wow. I'm impressed. That's a great idea. Too bad we can't pull everyone's license the same way."

"For Acrophobic's or drunks?"

"Whoops, caught with my prejudices down. One more example of "my problems are okay, but yours are bad. " Seriously, Mark, I'd like to help. Tell me what to do."

"You've already done it. Besides, I don't want to hang out with some Yutz who's afraid of spiders, for Christ's sake."

"Your black boy, sidekick, drove me here today, Stone, just how do you propose to return me to my villa?"

"Your refrigerator-box villa is only two blocks away, Randall. We all assumed you would enjoy the walk. James helped you get here today because you haven't shown up for your last three appointments.

"There are great demands on my time. I have better things to do than waste my counsel on a Visigoth, such as you."

"Is that why you showed up today, to impress me that you could remember what a Visigoth was?"

"Hardly. I made a promise to James, who is a fine young man, a credit to his race."

"That why you just called him a black boy?"

"Are you trying to fence with me, Stone? You are outclassed."

"I never duel with an unarmed man, Randall. Do you have something to say that I can deal with or did you just show up to trade insults?"

"From what I hear I am the only one who has been sufficiently alert to catch a look at the foul perpetrator whom no one else has seen. What do you think of that, you twit?"

"Of what? You haven't said much."

"Stone, you are too dense to live. Don't you understand? I saw the man who attacked that darling child you now have toiling at your front desk. I actually spoke with the striped-ass gorilla, I know his secrets."

"If Mark Todd arranged for you to meet with a police sketch artist, could you provide a working description?"

"I studied the man with an eagle eye and a photographic memory."

"That's very good, Randall, this matter is far too important to ignore any possibilities. Is there something else you want to tell about that evening when Donna opened the door to her assailant."

"When she what? She did what? Did she tell you why she did that?"

"No. She's protecting someone. Actually she's risking her life to protect someone who was willing to sacrifice hers."

"Pity. Poor confused child. I don't so much as have her new address you know. I have serious business with her and she tells me she has promised to tell no one, not even me, her dearest and best friend, her protector. I'm the only one astute enough to spot the man, you know. That's very important, that's worth a great deal in fact."

"Randall, you have time left on your appointment. Is there anything you want to talk about? Anything you're not satisfied with, anything you want to get off your chest?

He wanted to do the right thing, wanted to do so all his life but it was so much easier to listen to the song of the bottle. It sang of his undiscovered greatness, of his incredible latent talents. Others would never understand. So Randall Comsworth Preston stared at his shoes, sniffed a couple of times then wiped his nose with the back of his hand, "I attended The Wharton School, you know. I spotted the bastard, that's worth a lot, you know."

I walked Randall to the front door in order to keep him from badgering Donna about her address.

"Do you want me to drive you, Randall?"

"Huh?…It's only a couple of blocks. I'll enjoy the walk, you know."

XVI

"Stone? Looks like we don't have to decide yet, Jake took off on I-10 like a scalded dog. A report came in from the Louisiana State Police that he ran off from a self-serve gas pump in Lake Charles two hours after he got out. He's headed for Beaumont, Texas. Looks like he didn't want to wait around 'til the Baton Rouge boys discovered their mistake."

"Did the Louisiana people mention whether anyone was with him? Do we know anything about the arrest?

"Jake threw some guy across a bar and the bartender called the cops. The odd thing is that Jake wasn't out of control, not really busting up the place or anything and when the cops showed up, he went along quietly. Nobody filed any charges and they turned him out in the morning without bothering to run him. There were a lot of people in the bar so no one knows whether he was alone."

"Sounds wrong, Mark, and you know it. The hair on my neck is standing up, this whole thing smells."

"You still think this Bozo is smart enough to lay a false trail then double back and catch us off guard, don't you?"

"This morning you and I were discussing whether or not we'd have the guts to kill him if we could take *him* by surprise. And the one thing we agreed on was if he could take *us* off guard, he wouldn't waste a second wondering whether he could knock us off. You said he was headed for Beaumont, just across the border, how do you know that?"

"I don't. It's just what he told the guy at the gas station…before he smacked him. Shit! I know what your next question's gonna be, why the hell does a running felon tell a witness where he's going?"

"I would have said it better."

"No sense taking chances, you talk to your telephone gang and I'll see if I can turn on the police. It would take him two or three days to get back here."

"Speaking of phones, Mark, suppose we do some calling. Jake likes to ride the Interstates, what if we calculate a day's travel, what, three, four hundred miles, along I-10? Then we call Sheriff's offices and the city and state cops to tell them about Jake and ask that any sightings be fired back to us."

"Can't hurt. Both directions?"

"Good idea."

"Hey there, Aleena, you're looking well, and, James, I'm glad to see you, I don't know whether it's your charm or your pretty face." I was concentrating on keeping the parts of my split-brain attention from spilling over. James and Aleena deserved my focus, regardless of how full of Jake-fear I felt.

James slid into a swagger-walk as he sang, "Wherever I go they call out my name and that, in itself, is some sort of fame."

"From obscure books to obscure songs, you *do* amaze me, James."

"I remind you it was Nat King Cole, a brother, who did the best version and made the song popular. I think some Frog wrote it."

"The song, the writer and the singer were *all* before your time, James, so it's hard for you to deny your wide-ranging intellect, m'friend."

"It's the black man's burden, Stone. What're you looking to talk about?"

"I don't wish to intrude on Aleena's time but I want to update you on the latest input from Mark, stuff like that."

Aleena, who impressed me each time we met with her apparent race toward maturity, spoke up, "You can talk about the bad-ass all you want,

Stone, James and I do. We figure it's important for me to know what's out there."

"Makes sense. The record on this guy indicates he has grabbed girls your age.

"This latest input is not necessarily a big deal but Saint Jake is acting strange. He's making too much noise, telling people where he's going, causing the kind of trouble that calls attention, things such as that. It worries me because I have this weird idea he may be laying a false trail, making us think he's heading West, causing us to relax, then catching us with our guard down."

"Does Mark think he's that tricky," James asked, appearing sprawled and casual but looking deadly alert.

"He didn't at first. I've been studying the Jake information Mark has gathered and I began to worry that Jake sometimes shows a kind of animal cunning. Now, Mark at least considers it a possibility. Earlier today he suggested I alert our troops while he tried to spin up the cops. Jake is lately around Beaumont Texas, just across the Louisiana border. If he turned, it would take him two or three days to get here. As far as I can tell he's never been on an airplane in his life so I think we can rule out everything except driving."

"What else we doin? Donna told me about Sharon, that's a winner. Should we be tightening up with them?"

"Yes. And how about helping Mark and me call all the towns along the Interstate?"

"Sounds skinny, but worth it. First I want to pump up my own crew, I've put a few people on the high ground. After that I'm there."

"Stone," Aleena spoke up, sensing James and I had finished our update, "you keep telling us how we can run our own lives and make 'em as fine as we want, but what about all these crazies running around messing everybody up?"

"You know I don't know anything for sure, Honey, what I do is make reasoned guesses. My guess is this; because TV, radio and newspapers come at us around the clock, twenty four hours everyday, we get nothing but bad news. Even the news that's good is presented as bad. That's what we like, that's what we buy, so that's what they sell. That makes bad news bigger than reality. It's like looking through binoculars, everything's gathered from far away, squeezed together and brought up close.

"Less than a lifetime ago we had nothing except newspapers and neighborhood gossip, our news was local and outside stuff was old news by the time we heard it. Today, every bad thing that happens in the entire world is scrunched up and shoved right in our face. If someone does something rotten in Cairo or Perth Amboy, we know all about it in two minutes. We used to hear only about the doings of local folks, now we hear every bad thing six billion people do.

"Sure, there are people around whose wires are crossed. And bees sting and dogs bite and you need to know these things, but you also need to know they are rare, really rare. Chances are you will be able to live your whole life without coming face to face with anyone who actually wants to hurt you. Even if you do come across someone dangerous you can almost always avoid trouble by stepping aside, getting out of their way. That's what they mean when they teach you in Sunday school to "turn the other cheek," like, don't fight, just walk away if you possibly can."

"Sometimes you have to fight back, don't you?"

"Yes. But not unless the danger is real. If somebody threatens you for your money or your car, give it up. Your one precious possession is your life and it's precious to you, not some stranger. I think that's the dividing line, fight for your life but give up your stuff."

Now James spoke up, "How's she supposed to know, Stone, for that matter how's anybody supposed to know when the money or the car won't be enough? Tell us how we know, beforehand, when it's gone too far and we better start fighting."

"Now you two are ganging up on me and either one of you is tough enough by yourself. You guys ask harder questions than other people, usually I can just chat along and make an easy buck. You two make me earn it."

"Poor baby. But I 'spect you have an answer, even if it's wrong."

"As a matter of fact I do. It happens I've thought about this question before and I *do* have an answer. But remember, it's my answer, I expect we all have to decide for ourselves when it's time to fight.

"Years ago when I read Truman Capote's book, *In Cold Blood*, I decided I would never let anyone disable me. There was a scene when the father, hoping to appease the killers, allowed them to tie him up before they proceeded to kill his family right in front of his eyes. Right then I swore I would fight to the death before I would allow anyone to disable me. No exceptions. If someone wants to tie me up or force me into their vehicle, that's it, right or wrong, I'm fighting. I'd sure as hell rather die out in plain sight than on some country road. I'm not going to make it easy for someone to take me out, or worse yet, make me watch while they do someone else first."

James put his arm around his baby sister's shoulder, "Lena, honey, for the first time since I've known him, Stone has said it right. I know you heard every word and I want you to know every word is right. Remember what he said."

During the evening I had cause to remember James' comments about right and wrong. I've never been more wrong about possible solutions than I turned out to be about Malka Yelick. I had consulted Augustine, Descartes, Spinoza, Hume, Kant and Bergson, each of whom drove me further into confusion. Donna, on the other hand, spoke with her a couple of times, observed how she dressed, moved and spoke. Then, she considered the wide world of possibilities, without the limitations imposed by my random bits of knowledge.

"Malka, I'd like you to meet a special lady I know. She plays piano in

The Pirates Den lounge in the Roney Hotel. Come to my place for dinner then the three of us will drive over there for a drink, Dusty comes on about nine."

None of this was mentioned to me, of course. Donna said later I would have sent an armored car and a pair of bodyguards along, she was right. It wasn't that Donna wanted to take risks, she just felt she and Sharon would be less likely to do something foolish if they were able to exercise their own judgment now and again. She understood that her self-appointed guardians, were overly cautious, but with good reason.

Mark had located a sub-let deal on the apartment that we moved Donna into following her release from the hospital. Her name didn't show up anywhere, the phone was in the primary tenant's name and Donna's mail was sent and received at my office. We understood these precautions weren't foolproof but we were determined not to make anything easy. The location was in an expensive section of costly homes and townhouses near the Yacht Club—not the sort of neighborhood Jake would be likely to cruise, too many lights, cops and eyes.

Sharon drove a conservative, dark blue Cadillac with automatic door locks and, despite their contrary assurances, she and Donna would occasionally go to a carefully selected restaurant or shopping center together. They also knew one of us would drop everything, anytime, to accompany them. James and I had obtained our permits to carry concealed weapons and Mark had hustled us out to the local firing range to insure we understood the basics of weapon handling.

It was during an island of safety that Sharon drove Donna and Malka to meet Dusty Moran, the red-headed, lusty voiced, singer, comedian and darling of the beach crowd. The result was love at first intermission. Malka stayed until closing, hardly noticing when Donna and Sharon left.

Malka literally ran into my office the following afternoon. She had been in the reception area sharing her miracle with Donna. When her allotted hour arrived she rushed at me like a linebacker in the clear. "Mister Stone, Malka is a bird from the cage. Donna knew, she took me to wonderful woman and I fell in love for first time. First time ever. I never felt so good, now everything is right, I can see everything in world. Everything you told me about life is right. Please sit, sit down, I can't wait, I have so many questions, I have—"

"Malka, stop, please."

For the first time I felt free to approach her, I took her arm and held her hand, "I am very happy for your happiness and I am anxious for you to tell me about it. But I don't know the first thing about Lesbian love. I would never have guessed that your eagerness for men was all wrong. Also remember, Donna is the one who gets the credit. Now it is you and she who will have to teach me, is that okay?"

"Please, Mister Stone, we will learn together."

"Donna, how in God's name did you decide what Malka needed was to meet a woman?"

"I didn't really. But you're always talking about our human need. To belong, to be connected -although you don't always act as if you believe it- you know, to be part of life, to have someone to do for, to suffer for, if necessary. I was just standing, talking with Malka one day and her life seemed to weigh so heavily upon her. It was as if she was saddled with a thousand pounds of non-stop troubles.

"All that connecting talk was going through my mind when I suddenly thought about Dusty. It was like a revelation. Dusty lost her lover five months ago and she's been drinking and using and she's so lonely. She visited me in the hospital often and we talked, I've known her a long time. She's very sweet, very vulnerable. She told me a lot about her own childhood, maybe that's why I thought of her and Malka.

"I just stopped talking that first day, I had to think about whether what I was thinking made any sense. I thought about what you said. I could see being with men wasn't doing it for Malka and that left women. Like, if she couldn't connect to the world through men, why not try women?"

"Why not, indeed? I didn't have to say six words just now, Malka told me in exquisite detail how she and Dusty spent the night in each other's arms and both awoke to a bright new world."

"Does it confuse you, Stone?"

"Yes. No. Actually it opens a whole new line of thought. For me, at least, it's a whole new thing that will take me a long time to figure out. I find myself anxious to learn more about all this from Malka."

"Are you talking about the sexual part?"

"I don't think so. What has me spinning is this whole idea of connecting to the species by connecting with one other individual. This is too much, too complex, too coincidental: a single particle of DNA can't connect, can't be part of the structure, part of the cell structure, unless it finds and joins with it's proper mate. That's a silly bit of over-simplification but it'll do. Only then can it become part of the cell, part of the creature, part of life, part of the universe. Somehow, that's us, Donna, it doesn't matter so much with whom we connect, as long as we do. Then we become part of everything. But without such a connection, we're an outsider, a renegade, a lost soul."

Bent over now, imitating Igor's famous side-step, foot-dragging walk, Donna carried her coffee cup toward the doorway.

"Okay, Herr professor, okay, I'll go look for another brain, I think maybe you're going to need it. Sounds like you're speaking about reproduction, and it's my guess that Malka and Dusty may not accomplish that."

XVII

Day two of ignorance. Thirty hours into the fear and frustration. The second day of not knowing Saint Jake's whereabouts came up too windy for most beach goers. The white water breaking a hundred yards from the shore served as a foreground for the whitecaps lashing the deep green water beyond. This would be a blow-boat day, the pejorative name the power boat crowd applied to sail boats in retaliation for their craft being referred to as stink-pots.

The sun-star was huge, deepest red, spilling sideways into the gulf-stream as it cleared the horizon and it's guardian haze-pile of lifting clouds. I walked the firm, wet sand which felt so good against the bottom of my feet as I tried to decide whether Jake would arrive today or tomorrow. The beach was practically deserted at this hour and the rhythm of the water produced a calming effect.

I thought about the forthcoming test, how it has ever been thus, always a test, a wall to climb, an obstacle to overcome. A young, defenseless woman is stolen from the world by a demon. She is locked in a foul prison and constantly tortured to the edge of death until one night the angels arrange her escape. Now a band of misfits has somehow come together sharing only their common determination to protect this true Princess. The demon will pursue her unto death because in his attempts to capture her soul, she captured his, and now one of them must die.

Could a reader of books, an alcoholic ex-cop, a young uncertain black man, a middle-aged flasher and a sot who played Barrymore, amidst the detritus of a weed lot, capture and destroy the demon?

The Princess or the Demon, only one could survive. And, unskilled as we were, unless we prevailed, the demon would be forced to destroy us too, lest we dog his track forever.

The early walkers were beginning to show up as I left the beach and headed for the club. The wonderful character in Helprin's, *A Soldier Of The Great War*, plunged into the ocean each morning and swam through waves and tides. I wondered, *Helprin's swim was heroic why couldn't I do that, instead of swimming in a heated pool?* By the time I reached the car I decided Helprin's man swam in the surf because he didn't have a club with a heated pool.

Following the swim and gym I went directly to Mark's office and phoned Donna.

"Everything's fine here, young doctor Barber wants you to call him this morning and you're scheduled to see Bunny Brewster after lunch."

I phoned Alan Barber at once, expecting he wanted to talk about Donna. "No, Stone, Donna's recovery is remarkable in every way. That girl has magic genes. I called about something else. I work with another physician here who is badly in need of your help, his name is Ron Joshua, when can he phone you?"

"What's it about, Alan, how can I help this fellow?"

"It's too complicated and I don't have time to go into it now but it has to do with Philosophy and a flock of things he's trying to organize. I'd rather have him explain even though I'm the one who told him you could help. What's a good time?"

"Three naked women and a bicycle."

"You been hanging with James too much."

"Ask him to call me right after lunch. At my office. Did you say Ron, Ron Joshua?"

"You got it."

The entire list of calls to every police operation for three hundred miles along I-10, East and West from the Texas border, was completed and we had not received a whisper of response. Of course Jake could have taken any of numerous routes. He could be calmly laying up in Beaumont, or any one of a dozen other towns. But, I didn't think so.

I began to plot the probable distance a van travels on a tank of gas. I decided it was three hundred miles. Next I traced the most likely route from Beaumont to Fort Lauderdale: I-10 East to I-75 then South to the Florida Turnpike, would Jake use a toll road? I decided he wouldn't, a decision reached by the scientific method of listening to my gut. No, he'd stay with I-75, even though it was longer. Would he drive more than three hundred miles a day? More science; yes. I figured him to be more of a four to five hundred miler, especially when he had a destination in mind. I began to mark likely gas stops and overnights with some sort of vague plan in mind for making more phone inquiries when Mark asked, "What the hell are you doing?"

"I'm not sure, Mark. I feel like I'm playing auto club. I'm trying to divine Jake's route and timetable."

"Any worthwhile conclusion?"

"Only that it can either be a two-day push or a three-day drive."

"Or a never-never. Wouldn't it be a pisser if somebody planted Jake in a swamp, or a desert, and we spent the rest of our days wondering—"

"Paint your mouth black, Mark."

Donna was quiet as we shared lunch. It was a standing joke with us that we two could fill up the whole building with words during a single lunch break, especially if we had wine. Today was different.

"You're expecting him aren't you, Stone?"

I held my amazement in check. This was real breakthrough stuff. Donna never permitted the slightest reference to any aspect of her personal nightmare. I wanted to acknowledge the achievement but I felt it was the sheerest of bubbles, breathe too hard and it would be gone.

"Every day. I think you know that."

"Thanks for not lying. But today is different, isn't it."

"Only to me. There's no real reason. Two days ago he was in Beaumont, Texas, he might be in San Antonio, or back in Santa Fe."

"Or parked across the street."

"The police think he'll never come back because he knows they want him here, they think he'll just write us off. They also think it was probably a fluke that he was here at all, that he was surprised to discover you here."

"You and I both know better. He has to come."

"Donna—"

"Shhh, Stone. It's okay." She stood up and walked around to my side of the small table then she held my head against her waist, "Everything's okay. Do you want cream in your coffee today?"

Ron Joshua's voice was crisp, clear and his words came fast. He sounded like a man with far more to say than one lifetime would permit.

"Alan Barber told me you knew how to organize things and I sure don't. I don't have the first idea about what to do, I mean I know *what* to do, I just don't know how to go about it, I don't know *how* to get it done. I've set up, at least I've applied for, a non-profit set up. There's a ton of damn paperwork just to take a baby step, you know?"

"Ron, I don't have the foggiest, suppose you start from way back."

"Sorry, I do that all the time. My business is medicine but my love is Philosophy, does that make sense?"

"All too familiar, please go on."

"I read it, write it, even study it. I'm been taking Philosophy courses forever. I'm always the oldest guy in some professor's class, in fact, some of the professors are my age and they've become my buddies. I've had this dream for a long time, I want to rescue Philosophy from the classroom and bring it into the real world, where real problems can be discussed and debated. Now I have this patient, a very rich, extremely nice guy who is dying and wants to do some good. He's been my patient for a long time, he and I have talked a lot and now he wants to do some things."

"What does he want to do?" I asked, feeling this was one very strange conversation.

"He wants help in order to set up a million dollar chair so the local university can hire a good, top-grade man to run their Philosophy department. The chair would be in his name, and after we get that done he wants to finance my program, he wants to put up a hundred thousand to get it started. What do you think?"

"Sounds good. What's your program?"

"Well, that's it…I don't actually have one. I have an idea and a goal but I've never set up n organization and I can't afford to waste time doing the wrong sort of things. It's like I said, Stone, I know what I want but I don't have the foggiest notion of how to organize it, to set it up. I don't know how to make it happen. Alan told me you've been involved with the Aspen Institute and things like that. He said you knew how a philosophical organization should be run."

"It's true I was quite deeply involved with The Aspen Institute—"

"God, man, that's the biggest and best program in the world. How soon can we get together, we'll be co-founders and—"

"Hold on, Ron, we haven't even met. What you have in mind sounds like candy to me but I'm right in the middle of a major, around-the-clock problem. It requires every ounce of attention I can summon for the next few days."

"As in how long?"

"Give me a week. I'll either have resolution or respite by then. We'll have lunch and you can tell me exactly what you want to accomplish. I'll tell you whether I can help and if I'm interested."

"That'll work, I just want to be sure my patient is still alive. I don't want to use his money unless he gets to first see something worthwhile happening. In the meantime I'm working with the University President and Board to work out the details of funding the chair in his name."

"I like that, it sounds like your man deserves special attention."

"He's does and he's getting it. I've promised him we'll keep him alive long enough to attend the presentation *and* the first meeting of the new whatever it is."

After hanging up, it hit me. One week, I said, without thinking. Something has to happen, everything's focusing on *now*. God, it has to, none of us could stand much more uncertainty, it's too brutal.

Bunny Brewster waited up front while Donna walked back to my office, "Bunny's here and we have a problem."

"She's injured?"

"Yes, she's been beaten and she doesn't want to see you cold turkey.

And Stone, I have a problem, too."

"Please sit down, you look as if you're about to fall down."

"I am. I don't understand these things that pop up out of nowhere and tear me up. The minute I saw her bruises, the swollen face, the walk, I felt it all. That giant wave that washed over me before, started coming at me again, I had to get out of there. I'm feeling every kick and punch, what is all this?"

"I think it's fear. Totally understandable fear in your case. You know exactly how every hurt feels, as it happens and afterwards. Let's try a small story that my Psyche. Professor used to use. Are you in the mood?"

"Yes, anything to get me over this, otherwise I'm…never mind. Tell me a story, Daddy," she managed a small smile.

"Okay, picture yourself walking along in the center of a vast plain. It is dead-flat and crystal clear, you can see for many miles in every direction and it is deserted out to every horizon. You are fine, you are neither tired nor thirsty and you are quite content to be walking along when you notice a far distant cloud of dust. Something is approaching. You stop and take notice because it's coming directly toward you.

"After a bit you are able to make out that it's a broad reach of creatures approaching pretty fast. There's an entire band of them. Soon you can make out that it's a war party of well-armed, fierce savages running steadily in double time. They are your worst fears and they're coming directly at you. What shall you do? You look around and quickly realize you have just two options: you can try to run away, which you realize is silly. If you try they will just speed up and quickly overtake you or, you can charge at them and put up a fight. That's even more foolish because they are many and well-armed.

"But then you realize you have one other option. You notice a two foot high boulder nearby. After a moment to consider, you walk over to the large stone and sit down. You just sit there and watch. In effect, you welcome all your worst fears. You sit comfortably and say to yourself, okay, let's just see how bad these guys really are, let 'em come.

"Now, no self respecting warrior is going to attack a friendly, unarmed person sitting on a rock, smiling and waving. Oh, they may look fierce and shake their weapons as they close on you but they have no real choice, no choice at all. They can do only one thing, they can just keep on running and pass you by.

"The idea is that fears exist only in your mind and if you just relax, let your fears come rushing at you instead of fighting or running away, they have no choice, they have to just keep running."

Donna said nothing. She sat across from me, looking down at her hands, folded in her lap.

"It's gotten me across a couple of bridges, if they weren't *too* high."

"All I want to do is start fresh, Stone."

"Every morning you are resurrected from the previous life which ended the night before. The baggage wants to be carried forward, but it's your option."

"There's something else, Bunny's bruises are fresh and real. Re-living mine feels a lot like a lack of gratitude. I mean, I'm here, with friends and I'm healing. Thanks for the dumb story, I'll bring Bunny in."

"Hi, Bunny. You look as though it must hurt just to sit down. Can I help you."

"Thanks, I'm okay, I just took a bad fall."

"If we're going to spend our time lying to each other then let me tell you how I was an incredible fighter pilot hero who saved the world during the Viet Nam war. I also have some terrific tales about being a secret agent after I was an astronaut. Can I go first?

"I don't want to be mean, Bunny, but all we can accomplish with lies is to waste each other's time."

Silence. A hurt look.

"Bunny, please repeat after me, just say the words, don't think about them, just say them; I am married to a bully."

"I can't."

"Being married to a bully is a bad thing but there are lots of ways to be a bully. I know men who are bullied everyday of the world by their wives, I'll bet you do, too. They all survive. There are worse things, Bunny. So please, just say the words so we can begin to speak honestly. I'm not a cop, you know."

"I'm sorry."

"You can take one hell of a beating and come up smiling but you can't say, I'm married to a bully?

"We're not married."

I smiled, put out both hands as I repeatedly curled my fingers toward me in the universal, *c'mon, tell me* sign, "and so…"

This nice woman, suffering what had to be painful bruises across her lumpy swollen face managed a weak return smile,

"I'm living…with a bully."

"You're also halfway home, Bunny."

"How do you figure that? I sure don't feel like I'm getting anywhere. Unless it's up off the floor," another smile.

Having finally admitted her problem to another person, presumably for the first time, Bunny began to show signs of relief. It was as if the admission pulled the cork from a vintage bottle of regrets whose time had come.

"Lord, Mr. Stone, I just don't know. I try so hard not to upset Harry, but I never can be sure what's right and what's wrong. I seem to forget a lot or else I get confused. This time it was corn beef. I was sure he liked it before. He said it stunk up the house and tasted like shit, he threw the whole thing in the sink. I should have just shut up but I was so surprised I just blurted out about him liking it before and that made him mad. He said nobody called him a liar so he punched me in the chest. It really hurt. I cried and that always makes him mad, real mad so he punched my face then I told the babies to run. Everything I do keeps making him madder. I just can't learn to shut up. I just got a big mouth, ma used to always say so."

"Bunny, I'm not here to argue with you so I'll just accept what you say. You want to blame yourself for Harry punching you out so, okay. Let's agree that you are the sort of person who says and does things that make him so mad he has to beat you. Let's say you can't help doing the wrong things and he can't help getting mad and beating you up. So nobody's in the wrong and nobody can help what they do. Do I have that right? Is that the position you want me to accept?"

"Well, I don't know. I don't know if that's the right way to say it."

"But isn't that what you just told me? Where did I get it wrong?"

"Are you mocking me, Mr. Stone?"

"No. But I *am* trying to get a foundation for us to build on. We need one factual statement we can agree on so we can work from there. I was just trying to repeat what you told me. It's *your* statement that matters, Bunny. Do I have it wrong?"

"You know damn well you do, you made me say it before, Harry's a bully. He shouldn't be punching me out all the time." Bunny's mouth was trembling and twisting as she tried to hold back the tears,

"I've got everything screwed up."

"We slipped off the track there, Bunny, let's stay with our statement. How about this; Harry's a bully."

"Back where we started from."

"I guess that must be the basic problem, right?"

"There're some complications but yep, I guess that's it, that's the basic problem all right."

"Tell me about the complications, Bunny."

"I didn't mean nothing, just about me screwing up and all, I mean, I do some dumb stuff and Harry's got a right, sort of…"

"Let's put it on the table, Bunny."

Another small smile, "I already did. It's just silly stuff. One time I had a black eye and stuff and Mack, he owns the diner, was consoling me after the lunch shift, just before I was going home. He got a little excited and I guess I wanted to get even, maybe—"

"Hold on, please. I try never to know about anything that could cause someone to get hurt if word got out. And besides, I'm not sure this has anything to do with your situation."

Bunny stood up, hurt pride was flashing from her eyes, "I think you're being hypocritical, Mr. Stone, and now you're embarrassing me. I'm supposed to face up to things so we can tell the truth and the minute I mention something you don't want to hear, you shush me and say it's not important. Well, I think it's important. I let Mack bend me over his big office chair and raise my skirt every day and it's nice, he likes it, and I feel better. I'm not very smart but even I know that has to be part of my whole problem. You can't just fit everything in a nice little box you know."

"Before you decide to walk out of here, Bunny, let me say you are absolutely right. Your act of compensation is a part of the whole picture and I was just being chicken-hearted. Please accept my apology. I need to think about all this and so do you, you came a long, long way today and I don't want to waste that. You're on the right track and you obviously are thinking very clearly, more so than me. I'm sorry. You're doing very well, please come back for your next appointment. I will have done some research and some thinking by then, okay?"

"Sure. I'm sorry I kind of blew up but I'm hurting, you know? I'm sorry if I shocked you."

"I promise it wasn't shock, Bunny. I used to work in a large office where…never mind, not important. We'll talk about all this stuff next time."

I walked her to the front office to blunt any surprise our short session might cause.

"Bunny and I have some things to check on before our next visit so we're stopping short today. Put this one down as a no charge, Donna."

"Miss Bunny had a happier hop on the way out, Doctor Dolittle."

"I swear, everbody gettin smart-ass round these parts. But I'll tell you Bunny Brewster made several giant steps today, she even told me off. I'm just going to have to go for a higher class of trade. How about I bring Chinese over tonight and join you and Sharon for dinner? Maybe we'll call Mark and James and get up a poker game."

"Sounds like fun except I've never played poker in my life."

"Well just loosen your purse strings. I have a hunch James and Mark are both good, and me, well I'm just a wonderment."

XVIII

Day three. Even the morning air feels wrong. Southeastern Florida is made livable by the ocean breezes and when the wind turns bad -comes from the West- it brings Everglades bugs and legions of pursuing Dragonflies.

Despite our late poker game at Donna's place, I couldn't sleep worth a damn. I tried to blame it on Sharon; turns out she's a great player and after coaching Donna, she, Donna and James took Mark and myself to the cleaners. The humiliation was painful but we managed to get a return match promised within a week. During much of the night I wondered whether we would all still be alive after a week. In my fevered mind today was J day, I convinced myself he was back and would strike quickly. I was up and pacing around before sunrise, cursing myself for not knowing the exact route of Donna's early morning runs.

The tension was unbearable. I broke my usual routine because I couldn't help myself. I drove to Donna's neighborhood determined to watch for her to leave so I could follow. I wasn't parked for more than three minutes before I spotted Mark's car rounding the corner. He saw me as he passed then circled and pulled in behind me. He slid out of the driver's seat and walked up to my window much as he must have done hundreds, maybe thousands, of times when he was a cop.

"Should we let her know we're here?" I asked as I lowered my window, then I followed his gaze. Donna and Sharon were coming out of the building across the way and they spotted us at once.

Mark said, "Nah, we'll keep it a secret, Sherlock, or should I call you Moe?"

"I'm not too sure, Curly."

These two wise and understanding women smiled and waved, much as if Mark and I were stationed outside their apartment every morning when they came out to begin a brisk walk before starting to jog.

We, somewhat self consciously, trailed them across a nearby bridge to highway A1A where they had miles of nearly deserted beachfront sidewalk for running. In less than half an hour they were returning and they signaled us to join them at a Dunkin Donuts shop.

"Is this an event we can look forward to each morning?" Sharon asked, or is there something special going on today?"

Mark ordered two apple fritters before he responded, "Hell, we were still outside discussing last night's game, trying to figure out how you guys did it to us."

Following the coffee break I told Mark I was going to stop at the office this morning before I did anything else. I said I might go to the gym then stop by his place after that.

He understood at once, "I'll drive Sharon and Donna back to the apartment then I may come by your place, too. I've got a couple of things to show you."

Donna had grown progressively more quiet. She and Sharon understood at once that Mark and I were on full alert, she had already spoken to me concerning my paranoia about today. Neither woman said anything. Donna accepted Mark's implied promise to escort her to the office where she knew she could question me once we were alone. But, later, she said she wasn't sure she wanted to talk about it anymore. Neither was I.

My little office-retreat was as quiet as a church this early in the day. I felt a resolute calmness wash over me. I walked through the stillness, flicking on lights, thinking about the unfolding events since that day a beautiful young, play-acting, devastated woman entered my life. That was it, play-acting was one of the keys. She offered herself as a common street-whore yet conveyed the essence of an angel. She was doing penance, cleansing herself as she sought to cleanse others. Her own life-script had been invaded and destroyed until now she was creating a new one, finding her way back to justification of herself, to herself and for herself. Her brilliance was in understanding what needed to be done, in knowing she had to satisfy herself, with her new self.

How interesting, I thought, that those of us who chose to join with her during this transmogrification were enhanced by the effort. Once again, I was struck by the sense that the more I knew, the less I understood.

Those who find something, some myth, some system, maybe some drug, anything that enables them to say, "That's it, now I have all the answers," are fortunate in a way. They can stop reaching, learning and wondering. They can close the door on new knowledge and happily go along sifting, sorting and comforting themselves with the opinions and beliefs of those who came before.

My epiphany settled me with the realization that whatever had to be done was best done from the vantage point of calmness and control.

The overhead door ground upward as I walked past and for some reason I ducked aside and reached behind my back for the solace of the revolver. It wasn't there. I remembered I left it in the car after I removed it earlier this morning so it would be handy. As the worm gear pulled the door up Donna's little hatchback was revealed, immediately followed by her smiling, reassuring face shining through the windshield. That made my day, despite the realization that, as a protector, I was a Doofus.

It was satisfying when the overhead door was fully closed with Donna securely inside. The steel rod slid firmly into its sloped trench and we were safe.

"Good morning for what, the third time?" I smiled.

"If you include leaving my place after the game then three is right. You look as if you're feeling better, Stone, anything that needs to be said?"

"I do feel better and I want you to know why. Whether or not today happens and whenever it does happen, if it *ever* happens, we're going to handle it just fine. I know it, I promise."

"How about I make us some coffee," she said, "I could use some."

Before I could punch in the answering service numbers on the cordless phone I picked up, it rang in my hand.

"Stone? Mark. New Orleans police have a positive ID on Jake as of ten o'clock last night. Captain Slater called and said he has one of Jake's guys in lockup. Jake is hanging out in the French Quarter trying to take over a couple of street girls. They haven't nailed him yet but they're looking. The guy they've got, Pauley Herman, is a two-bit hood they caught boosting a van from behind the Royal Orleans Hotel. Herman had been with Jake and he was supposed to meet him later with the van. Says he doesn't know where Jake is staying. Stone?"

"Yeah, just thinking, Mark."

"Me too. This may be the shot, we know where he is but the cops don't have him yet."

"Do you personally know this Captain Slater."

"Met him at a Perp-handling seminar, I was thinking of leaving Florida at the time. Slater's a big dog, good man."

"Ummm, good."

"Stone? He's getting back to me before three, he expects to have Jake in custody by then. I'll keep you posted."

A time-freeze made itself known, this news was too much, too flat, too something I couldn't define. As if none of us should take a breath until something was certain. Donna was staring at me as I hung up. Nothing to do but tell her straight.

"New Orleans Police spotted him last night but they didn't catch him yet. They expect to bring him in today."

"They won't," she said, "he uses his pals like cat's paws, they get caught, he stays in the shadows. It's always that way, they're all so frightened of his craziness that sometimes they want to get caught, just to get away."

"How crafty can he be?"

"Which man? There are lots of demons in that one bag. Sometimes he's the reincarnated Lizard God from Mexico, that's why the stripes, that's big with him. Then he'll be crazy and say he can't be hurt or killed. He's killed a lot of people, Stone. The authorities don't know this man. Other times he's so lethargic and stupid it's sickening. When he's clean he can be incredibly crafty, it's as if he knows what people will do before they do it."

"That's a big help."

I was afraid to say more, this was the most direct admission of Jake's existence Donna had made, she actually came close to saying his name. She had to know this monster better than anyone alive and yet we didn't dare plumb those depths. It had to come from her. The poison was still in her system and it could destroy her yet, unless we drew it forth gently, with great skill.

"Let's call Donald Simms and see if he can come in this morning instead of after lunch. It's too late for the gym and I have no reason to go to Mark's place."

Donna gave me one of her strange, "I know what you're up to," looks and walked to the front to make the call.

I felt strange as Donald Simms walked in. It was as if I was some sort of empty shell. I looked at him, I extended my hand, I heard words but my receptors were turned off. Simms could have been another of those mindless meetings we all have at cocktail parties, a name and face forgotten before the release of the handshake. *Maybe he is too young to be worthy of thought, hell, nobody thought about me when I was his age. Maybe he's too good looking. Maybe I don't like Gays or maybe the buildup and anticipation of the Jake violence which has to come, must come, will come by God, maybe that's it. It's probably the news that Jake's in New Orleans. No.... it's none of that. Mark will want to force the solution. It's been too long, it has to be done and what will I do?*

"I'm sorry Donald, what did you just say?"

"Are you okay, Stone? You look pretty grim, man. I was just saying that I've been thinking about everything you said last time, it really got to me."

"Do you feel you have genuine design talent, Donald?"

"That's the strange part. I think I do. I don't know whether it's enough but I think I do. Nobody in my family has done more than whatever came their way. I mean we're just not the kind of people who go after anything. It's like, don't stick your neck out cause it'll just get cut off. All I ever heard was how big shots controlled everything and if you weren't one of them there was no chance."

"Well, Donald, all that, in a word, is just pure bullshit. You can go and read a flock of Sociology books or Psychological treatises which dredge up tons of manufactured phrases to explain that sort of conditioning, but bullshit does it very nicely."

"I don't understand."

"Then let me explain. You see, Donald, I think you're smart enough to understand a simple, straight truth. For example, there is no one, nor any force, devoted to blocking your way. There are no barriers between you and what you want to accomplish for yourself except those you may wish to construct or those you accept from other people who are anxious to share their phony beliefs with you.

"Another example; before World War Two virtually every young man in the United States read Horatio Alger books and they believed what they read. Later his stuff was totally discredited as far too naive, but a couple of generations of young men had managed to get the message. The Alger books were simple: figure out what you want to do, find a way to do it, do it better and more earnestly and honestly than others and you will become a great success. Period. Whole story.

"What happened to the kids who read and believed? They won their big war and became successful and wealthy. Those who followed, who were far too hip to read anything like Alger? They lost their war and whined about success, they reasoned that the earlier guys had just benefited from dumb luck."

"So you're saying, despite the fact I quit school, I'm Gay, that I have no experience, or training or help from family or connections, I can still be successful?"

"Is that what you heard me say?"

"Yes."

"Do you believe me?"

Donald got up and paced up and down alongside the far side of the conference table, "God, I sure want to, Stone."

"So it comes, as it always does, down to choices. Other people have told you that success is impossible for you to gain on your own. You have chosen to believe that until now.

"Now, I come along and tell you none of that is true. I tell you getting into the design business consists of nothing more than getting into the design business. You go there, you open the door, you walk in. After that it's up to you to determine your degree of success.

"You have a choice. You can continue to believe as you have or you can choose to believe your life is your own. It's up to you. It's always up to you. It's such a simple truth that ninety percent of the people refuse to believe it. They spend their lives sitting on their ass bitching about bad luck."

"What exactly do I do?"

"Hell, I don't know. Yes I do. You go to the library and get the Manhattan yellow pages and you look up and copy every page that has anything to do with design, garment manufacturing and whatever cross references they show. Then you get on the phone and you call every Marketing Director and every Vice President who will speak to you and you tell them what you want. Be honest, be truthful and never try to be clever or cute. Tell them you simply want in, you'll work in the mail room, be a gopher, do anything at any price. Then be prepared to go there, live there and work there. I can't say what responses you'll get but I want to see you back here in one week with complete notes on no less than forty phone calls. Will you do that?"

Donald dropped his wise and bored affectations, "Yes, yeah, I will, I'll do that."

"Good. Then here's a present for you." I pulled open my top left hand drawer and handed him a worn, but totally readable copy of Alger's, *Cash Boy*.

When Mark called at mid-afternoon I felt sure I was mentally prepared.

"Slater reports his people have missed Jake by inches a couple of times but so far, nada. I'm gonna fly over this afternoon, Slater says he'll arrange for me to talk with this Herman guy."

"Does that mean you've decided to take it to him?"

"You know it does, I can't live like this."

"You can't do it, Mark."

"Hide and watch, Pal."

"I'm going with you."

"I know."

"I'll call to alert James, what time you picking me up?"

It all moved so fast I didn't have time to think. I tried, without much success, to avoid the look in Donna's eyes.

James said he would cover Donna "Like a sheet of Swedish, bullet-proof steel," before he said, "just for the record, this is a dumb move, Stone."

I countered with, "Are you saying I should let Mark go alone?"

"I'm saying what I'm saying, it's a dumb move."

Donna simply said, "Give it to me down and dirty, Stone, I need to know what to do."

Still avoiding the Jake word with her I said, "The report is his buddy was caught last night and they are right now trying to dig him out of the French Quarter. Mark feels it's too good a chance to miss, he knows a police Captain there and he wants to make sure nothing goes wrong."

"There's more, Stone, there has to be."

"Only fantasy stuff that'll never happen. We squeeze the guy they have in jail, get a lead and catch him before the police do, he attacks and we nail him. Then we team up with John Wayne and ride off together."

"Promise me you'll look after each other. I couldn't survive losing either of you. When will you be back?"

"Two days, max."

XIX

We landed at New Orleans International after the rush hour which enabled us to rent a car and drive into the city in just over an hour. Captain Slater arranged for us to stay at the Cornstalk Hotel on Chartres street in the French Quarter. He explained that this converted old southern mansion with its huge rocking chair filled verandah, was the best information center in New Orleans.

"For a price, you can discover or fix anything hereabouts," he told us, "it's a class place where everybody who's in the game passes by."

While Mark drove directly to the jail I phoned the hotel to notify the desk of our arrival and to advise that we had business to attend to before we would be checking in.

I was told, "No problem, Sir, we're ready whenever you arrive," such courtesy, I assumed, was helped along by Captain Slater's authority.

The two hundred and fifty year-old central jail house is at the intersection of Tulane and Broad. It's only twenty minutes from the hotel and we made it with time to spare. Slater cleared the way for our visit and we were ushered into a room usually used for attorney conferences. Mark was familiar with such places and he sprawled into a totally uncomfortable wooden chair. He was silent, preoccupied, planning his questions for Pauley Herman. I stood, sat down, then got up and walked around. I hated this place, I felt trapped, claustrophobic. I was never big on dirty green and ammonia gray wall paint combinations. I forgot all that when Pauley Herman was brought in. The buttoned collar of his faded blue denim shirt was loose around his scrawny neck. He was chinless with large brown teeth and stray tufts of facial hair. A large pointed nose barely fit between close-set beady eyes which flicked back and forth. I wanted to smack him. It makes no damn sense except to say he was that sort of creature. You see a cockroach and you have an impulse to step on it, see a hairy brown rat and you want to whack it. The man was a goddam spider with a strange, irritating way of tilting and lowering his head which made him appear to look up at you as he spoke.

"What can I do for you gents?"

Mark moved directly to the point, "I hear if you steal a car around here and take it out of town they give you a medal cause they're so glad you didn't strip it and leave the junk on the street."

"Yeah, they do say that, the niggers strip em and leave em."

"So you were going to take the van out of town?"

"Nah, we wuz meetin down at Elysian Fields Park, Jake gave me an ace and he had a couple more for me."

"You were with Jake at ten o'clock, right?"

"Right. We'd been runnin the streets, havin some fun when Jake said to get him a van, a nice one he could sleep in."

"How did you get caught, Pauley?"

"Somebody must'a seen me, I heard one of the cops talkin about somebody made a phone tip."

"Mark," I said.

"I know, Stone hold on till I—"

"You guys are the guard dogs from Fort Lauderdale, right?"

"I turned, tried to pull open the door but the guard was just outside. He flipped the lock and I took off down the hall. I had the car keys and I was punching James' number into my cell phone as Mark came running after me.

"Stone, hold up."

"This is a fucking set up, Mark!"

"I know," he replied.

James answered, "The man is on."

"James, we've been mouse-trapped, Jake is in Lauderdale, lock down right now! Is Donna okay?"

"She's fine, we're cool here, but hurry home."

"Mark, that smart miserable sonofabitch called in the car theft and headed for Florida, he's got twenty four hours on us."

"Plus our flying time, Stone, and he had to be bragging for that pus-bag to know about pulling us out of town. You drive, I have to contact Slater."

Captain Slater came through for us once again, I decided if he ever ran for office, he had my vote. When he heard our theory he didn't waste a moment on second guessing.

"I'll keep pushing here in case you fellows are wrong and meantime I'll get you a jet out of Moisant. Go right to General aviation. What about your luggage?

"We still have it but the Cornstalk needs to know."

"We'll handle it. Keep it below the limits boys, better to get there a couple of minutes later than never."

I love the way a jet plane floats down out of the sky. When the pilot cuts the air speed for descent I always feel as if I'm riding a leaf. I think I've heard it called flaring. But whatever it's called it feels like floating to me. It's like heading toward shore on a following sea, there's the same sense of support, of buoyant forward sliding movement. I am no more a seaman than an airman but I like both sensations.

The whole flying, floating magic is enhanced when it happens at night over an area such as south Florida. From Palm Beach south for more than fifty miles, a carpet of lights shines from the stark black of the surrounding everglades, the Atlantic ocean and the countless miles of connecting waterways. Regardless of how you feel about flying, religion or Laurel and Hardy movies, a night landing in south Florida is one hell of a show.

As Mark and I walked to his car in silence we must have shared a similar feeling. We called Donna's apartment, she and Sharon were locked in for the night and she told us how James was rotating a half dozen friends outside her place. Mark and I were empty sacks, men without purpose. We had jumped and danced a jig to another man's tune. We didn't know whether we were right or wrong, about Jake, about New Orleans, about anything.

"I wish you weren't a drunk, Mark."

"Me too, why?"

"I think I'd like us to go get drunk."

"Me too, and because I'm hungry I wish you weren't such a turkey, it just makes it worse."

My big Jake day turned out to be a big mess. Now that it had passed we were back in the trick bag of trying to stay alert. So I held a coffee meeting.

By ten thirty the following morning we were all together at the conference table in my office: James, Mark, Malka, Sharon, Raymond, Donna and me, those of us who were involved in fighting the strange battle of Saint Jake. On an intellectual level I was satisfied this was a smart way to make certain we were operating as a team with all preparations and planning in good order. On some deeper primal fear level I knew this was for reassurance, a comforting security huddle. In California it might be called a "group hug."

"I wanted us to get together this morning because I think we need a coordinated, cohesive plan. We need a strategy for how to proceed, what to do next and how to keep our little network working as smoothly as it has until now.

"Our problem exists because of one deadly man. He is usually helped by temporary followers but he is essentially alone. We number seven here plus at least a half dozen who have helped us before and are eager to do more. We also have the police and Sheriff's departments helping us because they want this guy too."

Mark spoke up, "I think we need to recognize an important difference between the police and ourselves. They are basically a reactionary force, they are neither structured nor sufficiently manned to do much in terms of prevention. In other words; they act *after* something has happened. In our case we damn well have to act before something happens."

James added, "I think we're pretty good on defense. I thought about Donna's movements and tried to imagine myself in the freak's place and I have to tell you, he's not about to find easy pickings. Personally, I worry a lot more about the unexpected, he only got to Donna the last time because old Randall promised he would knock on her door at five and she was caught off guard. That particular thing won't happen again in a thousand years, but a different set of circumstances could occur and give him another chance."

"Jake," Donna said quietly, "his name is Jake and I appreciate how each of you avoids saying it in front of me. But you are the people who saved me from him last time and who have given me the strength and confidence to get past him and everything else that happened. Thanks to you I can stand to hear his name. I'm not denying his existence so please, just go ahead and speak out. I promise I won't fall apart, at least not right away."

I felt my old teary-eyed nemesis returning. "It's true. We've avoided using Jake's name in front of Donna because thinking about him, let alone hearing his name has been traumatic for her. We all know she survived a brutal attack by this demented bastard just a few weeks ago and recently she's been able to face some of her memories. She is this man's target. She is the reason we believe he has no choice except to try again. I believe all of that is true because he has been beaten. He was originally defeated by Donna and again, a second time, by her with the help of her friends.

"Mark has done a great job of collecting information over a period of several years and I have carefully studied it. Those studies convinced me that during the past few weeks Jake has been laying a false trail in an attempt to convince us that he didn't present an immanent danger. He was doing so, in my opinion, to cause us to relax. If he can get us to relax that could bring on exactly the sort of mistake James is concerned about.

"Jake can't strike without surprise, that's his primary weapon and while it's a good one it is very limited. In fact, if we can somehow stay alert it won't exist at all. During the last few days I convinced myself that Jake went even further. I believed he was smart enough to pay some clown in New Orleans a hundred bucks to swipe a van at a specific time after which he promised to meet the guy and pay him a couple of hundred more. Then Jake phoned the cops telling them where and when they could nab this guy. Jake immediately headed for Florida expecting that this event coupled with all his carefully planted talk would cause us to rush to Louisiana, leaving Donna unguarded. I actually convinced myself he is that smart. And, as you all know, I bought my own baloney. Mark and I rushed off to New Orleans. Because Mark was smart enough to ask the right questions we were able to see the risk and head back here. Fortunately, Jake is not as smart as I make him out to be."

Everyone looked toward Donna as she quietly spoke again, "You're wrong, Stone, he can be plenty smart. I understood what you and Mark were up to and if I didn't know for certain Jake could be that smart, I would have stopped you from going to New Orleans."

Not knowing what else to do, I continued," In any case, his attack has not materialized despite all my jumpy conclusions and now we don't know what he's up to. We only know that as long as he's alive and on the loose, the danger remains incredibly high. I appreciate what Donna just said and it makes sense. Mark and James have doubted some of my strange conclusions but they have gone along because it is better to be safe than sorry. And that is still true.

"The point of all this is to admit I don't have a sure sense of what to do next. All I know is Saint Jake has no limitations, he can do whatever he wants, whenever he wishes. Despite the fact that he is one against our dozen it's still an unfair fight because we're operating in the dark, we have no way of knowing what's next. Jake doesn't have to deal with all of that, he's free to act according to his own notions, he doesn't need to worry about ours."

Mark cleared his throat, "I'm not sure why, but I have to say something I'm not anxious to bring up."

"I hope this isn't gonna turn into some damn confessional thing, that shit gets downright embarrassing."

Mark smiled at James, "I'll try not to make you cry, pal. The thing is I can't get past the bottom line here. As long as Jake is alive he will be a threat to Donna. I didn't go to New Orleans on some half-baked whim of Stone's, I went there hoping to kill the man."

An "Oh, my God," escaped Sharon. "Mark, Locke, what about jail? Won't it solve things if he is caught and sent to jail?"

"Only if somebody stiffs him on the inside," James volunteered.

"At most, it's a second best solution," Mark said, "considering prison dumping, early release, escapes, and so on."

I added, "In any event, it's out of our hands because the acts are his, we're limited to reactions. That's why I hope we can construct a good strategy this morning. We need one we can live with and yet is foolproof. Mark, James, what do you guys suggest?"

It was Donna who spoke up.

"This man we call Saint Jake destroyed me six years ago when he crashed into my life and scattered the torn pieces of my existence over thousands of miles and millions of years. Finally, I was given one chance to destroy him. I failed. Now he is returning to destroy me. In a way, that's okay, because we are somehow bound together in the sense that we cannot both exist. I don't pretend to understand why that is so, but I know it is.

"I can't explain what I mean when I say I had angels who protected and preserved me through those terrible times. That may not be such a mystery but the fact that I still have my angels, is. They are you. Please don't try to makes sense of what I'm saying or try to apply logic, we are well beyond both here. It's not a matter of names or faces, it's something inside. I feel the same connections I've felt in the past. I know this is true and while we may not be permitted to understand, I think we all know it's true and that we will make it. We'll make it because we're together.

"I love you all and I thank you. Now, anyone for more coffee?" She was smiling even as tears rolled down her smooth cheeks.

Even James remained silent. Donna got up and carried the coffee pot to the table, offering refills as she moved.

In the end we decided that maintaining our impregnability was best accomplished by going about our business. We also decided to draw straws once each week in order to select one member of the group for whom we would take special responsibility. The idea was that, despite our belief Jake was out to attack Donna, he would have to attack through one of us first. We reasoned if we looked out for each other we would keep our defensive line in peak condition.

Donna drew James' name, "I guess that shows who the top angel is around here," he crowed.

Mark drew Sharon's name, James pulled Mark's. Sharon drew mine, I pulled Donna's name and Malka and Raymond drew each others.

"Since you're looking out for me I'm about to take you dancing over in my part of town every night this week, Donna. Ain't no Saint Jake gonna mess with nothin over there."

"And I suppose you expect me to go along?" Mark asked.

"Me too?," I added, "you're Mark's protector and I'm Donna's."

"Malka, you and Raymond come on and we'll have us a scrum."

Malka leaned forward, "Thank you, James, but what is a scrum, please?"

"It means to engage in a scrummage, Malka, like a very small, tight party, but forget it, Mark's already messed up a good idea."

Malka shrugged and sat back.

Just after twelve the front doorbell rang and Mark followed Donna who moved to answer. He watched carefully as she looked through the view port then checked the wide-angle TV screen before turning the opaque verticals so she had a full wide view of the front area all the way to the street. She opened the door to the extent the heavy duty, Winkler installed, bolt-through chain permitted and accepted the boxes of food.

"How much, please," she asked.

"Thirty six eighty."

"One moment, please." She closed the door, threw the dead bolt and walked to her desk for money from petty cash.

Returning, she once again checked the view port and the TV before turning the dead bolt and opening the door, "Here you are and thank you very much."

"How much of that was for my benefit," Mark asked.

"All of it, I usually just throw open the door and holler, come and get it."

Ignoring her sarcasm, "Do you recognize the mailman and people like that?"

"When I don't, if it's not a regular or if they just have an odd look that day, it's as you just saw, Mark. I don't want this to go wrong anymore than you. I love how you worry over me but I promise I worry just as much."

Always the cop, Mark replied, "Yeah, well I'm going to have Winkler do something else to that door. Our man tops three hundred pounds and I'm not sure about that chain rig he has on there."

I had my mouth full of Chinese when Donna told me about Camille. "I'm sorry, Stone, I didn't know about your special meeting and I set up an early afternoon appointment for you. She's a lovely lady and her problem can't wait. I mean I didn't mean to push this on to you without checking first but you didn't have any conflict today and I figured—"

"Hold on, Speed. Suppose you back up a foot or so as in, where, when, why and how? You know, the usual basics, instead of zooming these fast balls over the plate."

"I met her at breakfast and she's very nice, probably about your age and she just needs someone to listen and you do that so well. I know you can help her and I know you'll like her, she's very bright. Excuse me for a second, Sharon needs some help. Back in a sec."

It was half an hour before I caught Donna's arm, "Since I'm being so manipulated and managed, may I at least know the time? I have something to do this afternoon and it's almost one."

Donna's smile always flattened me and now she slipped me one of her best, "I wouldn't dare make a one o'clock for you. Camille Emerson won't be here until one thirty."

Camille Emerson was going to be difficult for a flock of reasons. Foremost was my feeling that her problem was so far beyond my understanding that, search as I might, I wouldn't find any philosophical answers. Just as intrusive was my confusion and concern about exactly how she found her way to me. Donna dodged the question which succeeded in planting it more firmly in my mind. Yet I knew Camille, like everyone else, deserved careful attention. My solution was to propose a get acquainted session.

I barely reached the back office after seeing the last of our lunch crowd out when Donna rang and said Camille had arrived.

"Please bring her back."

For reasons I hadn't yet come to understand, I liked having Donna escort people back to my office. They appeared to like it, too.

Camille was beautiful, well groomed, expensively and conservatively dressed, great figure and good legs. In all, she presented a commanding feminine presence. My thought as I stood to welcome her was, *this is a walking powerhouse who is obviously in the wrong place.*

Donna took her leave after decorating my thoughts with a knowing smile.

"You make quite a first impression, Mrs. Emerson."

"Camille, please. So do you Mr. Stone. I would feel less discomfort if you were older, as I expected you to be."

"Well then, that's a good way to begin. We'll just talk for a bit about impersonal things in order to decide whether or not you can reach a conclusion concerning my suitability. Once that decision is made we can schedule get-togethers if you feel they are warranted."

She leaned back into the corner of the blue couch, crossed her long legs and said, "I like that. Suppose you go first."

I took the opportunity to present my full compliment of disclaimers; how I was unable to treat anything and all the rest of the chatter that went along with that. It always sounded so dull and repetitious to me but I tried to keep in mind clients were hearing it for the first time and how important it was that they completely understood my limitations. I had come to realize it put the relationship on a more level plane. Unlike that of Physicians, Attorneys or Priests, who generally believe they must appear superior in order to be most helpful. My posture of being sort of an advocate for a higher level of self-regard, rang most true when delivered at eye level.

"I sense you are not especially interested in my situation, Mr. Stone, and perhaps I can't blame you. You see in me a supercilious, middle aged woman wearing expensive clothes and some jewelry I haven't hocked yet. A circumstance I will correct upon leaving here because I have no money, no valid credit cards, I'm terribly hungry and I am living in my car. I prepared to come here today by cleaning up as well as possible in the lobby washroom of the Holiday Inn, whose parking lot accommodated me, in the back seat of my car last night."

"You win, Camille. We may both have difficult days going but I can't even come close to matching yours. However, what you take as disinterest is actually total fear. I meet people like yourself, people with genuine problems, and all I can offer is to act as a sort of agent. We can speak objectively about your circumstances until we reach a point where I understand things reasonably well. From there I can call upon my years of philosophical study in order to save you the trouble of doing so yourself. I can either recall, or research, whatever the great philosophers say about your problem and hope their advice might do you some good. But that always seems to be such a small weapon to use against such massive problems. Thus, the fear."

"I am an overly proud and extremely stupid woman who brought on her own problems. Your angel-assistant spotted me sleeping in my Mercedes during her sunrise jogging session. She insisted on buying breakfast two days in a row and talked me into seeing you. She believes you hung the moon, so here I am, and trust me, I am more frightened at this stage of my life than you could possibly be. My attorney husband of nearly twenty years took on a young hard-bodied playmate. I "fixed" him by leaving town. He claimed desertion, tied up every dime, for years, I'm sure. I'm ready to sell drugs or something, except I don't know how to go about it."

I didn't hear much after Camille jarred me by revealing that Donna sometimes jogged alone in the mornings. I wasn't aware of that exposure and now I understood her reluctance to explain more about meeting Camille. I would deal with this new problem just as quickly as possible. Meanwhile Camille was looking at me in a way that made it clear she was awaiting an answer.

"I think you are obviously right. Following the principle of clearing the forest one tree at a time, I think you have only one tree to chop at this point; you need a job so you can move out of your car."

"That's it, it's that damn simple? Those are your great words of advice?"

"Yep, that's it. For now. What can you do?"

"What you see is what there is. I have no formal, commercial training."

"Okay. However, I have an idea. You just sit there and relax. If you would like some coffee, soft drink or whatever, you'll find a little kitchen-lunch area right through there. I'm going to make a couple of calls."

It occurred to me while we were talking that Camille Emerson looked incredibly impressive and would, in my opinion, be worth her weight as a hostess in a fine up-scale restaurant. I called and reached Mark who had just returned to his office. I described her and the circumstances to him, he made a call and in a matter of minutes an interview was arranged. If my hunch was correct, Camille might be employed by sundown. She wasn't thrilled with the prospect but she did see the wisdom of it. I offered her a cash advance to cover shelter and food until she began to get paid. Her pride preferred pawn. I think she made the right choice. We agreed we would talk about the rest of her "trees" in upcoming visits.

"Please, Stone, don't be silly. The man we're worried about never takes a deep breath before noon. I am absolutely safe running at sunrise and Sharon is usually with me. You know I try not to worry you, I drive directly into the building from home and otherwise I never leave my apartment without you, or Mark or James. Sharon and I practically live like monks, if she hadn't moved in I'd be stir crazy by now."

"This thing is tough to live with, Donna, I know that. You're doing a good job of it and you know, better than anyone, we can't let down."

"Of course I do, I'm determined to take no chances. Just so you know, my protective pal, I'm meeting Sharon at Neiman's right after work . I *will* park right at the elevator and we'll be at your place by six thirty. Okay?

"By the way, I think your idea of getting Camille Emerson on her feet before doing anything else is one of your better moves."

"Thanks, I hope we hear whether she managed to get hired by the time we go to dinner tonight. Mark thinks he'll know by then."

"I have a hunch the beautiful Camille will do just fine, at least on the surface."

"I may find myself learning things from her before we're through. In any case, I have to take my car in for service and pick up a rental this afternoon. Please watch yourself, even at Neiman's, and I'll see you later, at the apartment."

XX

Among the many minor irritants in my life is having to take my car into an auto dealership for service. It's a chore I detest, to the point that, except for warranty work, I avoid dealerships at all costs. It has become common practice, one which I believe is a petty exercise of power, to waste the time of customers who find themselves caught in any sort of service trap. Perhaps it all began with physicians when, during the fifties and sixties, specialized medical practice consultants developed the concept of stacking customers, first in the waiting room, then in treatment rooms. By victimizing customers and eliminating house calls, income averages zoomed by two or three thousand percent. Following that success a lot of other businesses, including car dealers, banks, department stores, you name it, found they too, could grow profits by inconveniencing customers. Or, on the other hand, perhaps I'm just becoming a grouch.

By the time I wasted a couple of hours watching incompetent people doing ineffective things in an indifferent manner, it was after five. I called Mark and received no answer. I decided to head for my apartment to grab a shower and shave before Donna and Sharon showed up. Waffling and brake-pumping my way through Federal Highway traffic I was startled when James phoned.

"Stone, the freak is back. I came looking for Randall. Stone, man…shit, Randall is dead. He's got an ugly, foot long, square-shank screw driver stuck right through his throat, pinned him to a goddam board. Looks like it wasn't very long ago. Paramedics are on the way but it won't matter. This is sorry shit, Stone, really sorry. This fucked up old man didn't hurt nobody. We have *got* to take that sonofabitch down. Is Donna with you?"

"She and Sharon are at the Galleria. I'm on my way to pick them up and take them to my place. You talk to Mark?"

"No, not yet."

"How do you know it was Jake?"

"Do you want to think it wasn't? And, Stone?"

"Yes?"

"Nobody drew Randall's name."

"I'm sorry about that, James."

"Yeah man, me too…we got work to do now."

I had reached Sunrise boulevard, just a few minutes away from the Neiman parking lot elevator. "James, find out what you can, call me, I'll call you, you know. And, James, I'm sorry about Randall, I really am."

"I know. Go get her, Stone."

Donna's little hatchback was parked less than twenty steps from the elevator. *All right!*

I pulled into a non-parking spot, jumped out of the car and stopped dead. *What now? Do I go up and search for her? No, she's reasonably safe in the middle of Neiman-Marcus, she'll have to come down the elevator. I'll stay right here.*

I reached behind my back seeking what comfort I could find from feeling the gun stuck in its small, belt-holster while I visually examined every vehicle in sight. Nothing. The elevator was down and a legal parking spot opened near Donna's car. I rushed to my car and successfully completed the change before the elevator car made one more round trip. It felt like a silly thing to be doing. Donna and Sharon were not among the disembarking passengers. *God, what if they went to other stores, would they come back to this elevator?*

Each time the elevator lifted back up into the store above I tensed until it returned, crouched, ready for action. Trying to look everywhere. Time seemed to stretch out unbearably as I kept redialing Mark, between elevator trips. When Donna's legs finally appeared through the glass walls of the descending car I was surprised at how easily and surely I recognized them and, seconds later, how thankfully glad I felt. I elbowed other people out of the way in order to put my arms around both women as I led them directly toward my car.

Sharon spoke first, "Hey, what's up, Locke?"

Donna was totally silent, she actually appeared to grow smaller. It wasn't necessary for her to speak, she knew from the moment she saw my face.

"Why're we going to this car, what about Donna's? Tell me what's happening, please."

"Just stick together, Sharon, it's possible we might run into a problem. We're not taking any chances, that's all."

I put them both in the back seat and took one more look around before getting behind the wheel. In order to avoid bridge openings across the Intracoastal Waterway, I headed left out of the parking area, then left again after we crossed the north fork of the New River. South to Las Olas boulevard, left a mile, then right for one short block.

I was on full alert as I drove under the twelve story building and into the parking area. Thankfully, the parking garage is an open area paved all the way to the waterside docks with an exit I could use if I so much as saw a van or anything else which looked suspicious.

I thought briefly about stopping alongside the garage entrance to the lobby and hustling the women inside but I was sure everything was okay. Everything looked normal, no vans, no suspicious people lurking about. *He wouldn't come here.*

My parking spot was no more than thirty yards from the rear entrance. I helped the women out of the car and headed for the double doors. I heard a small scuffling sound when we were less than ten yards from the door, just before I saw Sharon suddenly pitch forward. I saw her arms reach out to break her fall as I bent at the waist and spun. Then I saw the huge form of Saint Jake reach a meaty arm from behind Donna's head and jerked her backwards.

My irrational thoughts were, *They can't, it's daylight, there's no van!*

As I spun and crouched, Smother's knife missed my gut but slashed across my right arm which was coming around into the blade with great force. I dropped and rolled, trying to get some distance.

I watched, as if I had time to do so, as Jake lifted Donna completely off the ground. *I'm finally seeing him!* Smother brought me back to reality by smashing a kick into the same arm he had cut. I had the illusion my arm was nearly cut off.

I reached up and was able to grab Smother's belt with my left hand. I pulled him down as I tried to swing my right arm but I couldn't, it wouldn't move.

Sharon was scrambling to her feet and scrabbling toward the door of the building. As I pulled Smother down with full forced I slammed my forehead up and into his face. Raising my knee as he pulled back I got a lucky kick into his throat. He fell backwards as I got to my feet and screamed for Sharon to get help.

I tried to get to my gun with my left hand but the holster was facing the wrong way. I saw Jake dragging Donna toward a Lincoln Town Car, *No van, no wonder.*

I managed to loosen the gun but Smother was up now and charging with his knife held out and low: *He knows how to use it.*

Jake was opening the trunk of the Lincoln.

I jumped backwards and heard the gun drop to the cement. Smother saw it and swung the knife upward to move me away as he bent to grab for it.

I faked backing away, moved forward, turned into his thrust and kicked as hard as I could manage. His knife point drove into my leg but without real force as my kick landed just below his sternum. His reaching hand swept my gun over the edge, into the water.

Jake closed the trunk with Donna inside and headed back toward me. When Smother curled, unable to breathe, Jake looked, changed his mind, quickly turned again, pulled open the door and slid under the wheel of the Lincoln. Engine racing, he backed directly toward Smother and me.

I grabbed the top of a concrete piling with my left hand, spun and jumped over the water to land around and behind it just as the Lincoln's rear tire thumped over Smother's head and rammed the rear bumper into the piling.

Jake pulled the big car into gear and headed for the exit. After a split-second freeze I ran for my car, praying simultaneously that the blood flowing from my right arm wouldn't cause me to pass out and that Sharon had found help.

As I cleared the exit I saw the Lincoln turn right through the gas station on the corner trying to head East on Las Olas Boulevard. I drove over a curb and raced for the same spot. At the corner, traffic was stopped for the flashing red lights and lowering gates of the about-to-open bridge. Jake had turned and was driving down the sidewalk, sometimes one wheel down in the curb, other times up and on the grass or close to the store fronts to miss a signpost or fireplug. He was racing to get past the stopped cars and clear the bridge before it actually opened. He bounced and swerved over the walkway, sometimes tearing up bushes and landscaping, other times banging up over the curb. When he reached the gate, the first car in line, nearest the curb was a small Geo which surrendered its right front side as Jake crashed past and through the gate just as the bridge began to raise. He was a split-second too late.

The bridge tender's elevated building was on the far side. As I raced along the path Jake had carved, I saw the far side section of the bridge had started its upward move and it was shielding the operator's view of this side. Jake's escape was blocked.

Then I realized he was too late for the bridge but he had another way out. Now that he was past the line of stopped cars he could make a U-turn and head West on the deserted far side of the boulevard

He backed sharply toward the right side of the bridge, turned his wheels left and powered his way directly at the high strip dividing the bridge right of way. Had he been able to cut his turn more to the left he might have hit the much lower street curbing divider and reach the wide-open, empty westbound lanes. Had it come to that I might have failed in a car chase.

Fortune intervened and I made it across the lower section and blocked the road. He was still on the bridge approach. The big car had straddled the higher divider, as hung up as if it were on a grease rack. His rear power wheels spinning furiously as if to echo his frustration.

I jumped out of my car hoping to catch him before he could extricate his bulk from behind the wheel. I felt I'd have a better chance if he was sitting down. I knew it didn't make much sense, but I had to keep him here somehow. No such luck, my feet hit the ground and I crumpled to my knees.

Jake was out of his car moving in my direction. I tried to accept a feeling that even if I died, Donna would be okay. *Does that make any sense? I don't want to die. Fight this sonofabitch. Donna's scared in that dark trunk. Get up!*

I heard sirens from somewhere back in the traffic. But I was terrified as I got to my feet. Deciding maybe I could move faster than Jake, I headed for the fully raised bridge. I had to pull him away, had to delay him until Mark got here. I was convinced he was bringing cops, blowing all those sirens, big, burly cops. God how I loved big burly cops right now, bigger and tougher than Jake. I was even feeling overwhelmed with love for James, a fine man, he'd handle Jake. Everyone was honking at us, my head was spinning and my thoughts were irrational.

Jake resolutely pursued me back across the bridge to the far corner of the steel grating.

Then he pulled out a Bowie knife that looked as large as a Roman short sword as he ambled, arms swinging, to where I was cornered. I turned, could I climb the vertical bridge? No, not even with two good arms. My keys were in my hand, *he's not gonna get away in my car, fight the sono-fabitch, you have to*. I threw my keys over the rail into the waterway then I backed against the railing and began pulling myself up onto it. *Ass up. That's it. I'll go into the water too, he can't get me there…*

I swung my leg up onto the flat top surface and pulled myself up with my good arm. As I reached a near-standing position, balancing on the rail, I hesitated. I saw flashing red lights racing toward us on the wrong side of the boulevard. Jake saw them too, in just that second I knew I wasn't going to chance leaving Jake up here with Donna locked in his trunk while I was swimming in the salty waterway.

Jake was lunging at me as I quickly turned back toward him and leapt directly onto his big, fat, bald head. My legs straddled his face. He was not expecting the impact and weight, he stumbled back. I tried to grab him as my momentum carried me over the top of his head but my good arm found nothing to hold except his long top shank of hair. The force of my leap bent him backwards as I landed on my knees and shoulder behind him. My face hit the pavement just as I heard the four blasts of the air horn signaling the lowering of the bridge. I still had his long topknot in my left hand. I was pulling his head back as he was falling backwards on top of me.

Still on one knee holding Jake's hair, I pulled with every bit of force I could muster. His backward, off-balance three hundred pounds fell across my shoulder and back. At that exact moment, while still pulling on his long ponytail, I pushed upward and to the side with my legs. It worked. Jake fell backwards and sideways. His gigantic body rolled off of me and dropped directly into the gap between the two steel edges of the bridge.

When a split bridge opens, the two halves are raised by a system of gears and counter weights. The two center edges are swung high into an almost vertical position creating a clear passageway for any height of boat superstructure. But the outer edges of the bridge, those sections which match the approaching roadbeds, are pivoted so they drop below the surface level of the approaching roadway. As the centers go up, the opposite ends go down. As the bridge lowers, that gap is closed as the lowering surfaces slide up, into place, as neatly as a guillotine blade fitting into the slot built into its base.

His great bulk was forced by its own weight into the breech like a fat garbage bag. He was trapped as neatly as if he *were* a garbage bag caught between the bottom of a trash truck and the hydraulically driven metal blade which squashes everything together. One arm and one leg were forced down through the opening. Jake had no way to pull himself out. We both realized that as I struggled to climb on top of him, I wanted to jump up and down on him, to use my added weight to make doubly sure he remained stuck while the steel edges of the bridge cut him neatly in half.

He clawed at my legs with his free hand. He stared into my eyes as the immense pressure began slicing him from crotch to shoulder. I worried that the resistance of the compressed body might cause a relay to switch off too soon. But gravity is the primary closing force and flesh and bone counted for little against such monster scissors.

He screamed out an agonizing extended animal sound from some great primordial depth. My thoughts were racing in a dizzy, fainting swirl as I kept trying to stand on top of Jake while he was dying.

Instead, I collapsed on top of him with my mouth next to his ear. He was silent now, panting furiously, struggling for air and staring wildly. I heard James' and Mark's voices among the other shouts.

"Jake," I growled, "Listen to me as you die. I have a message. Donna laughs at you, you ugly, rancid, sonofabitch. She laughs because you never touched her, never, not once. Hear me you putrid piece of shit. The angels came, Jake. The angels always came for her and they took her away every time. Every time you came near, she was never there, never. Not for one lousy, stinking second.

"She beat you, Jake, and the angels will never let you come back. You're done! You're nothing! You're going to feel this moment forever. You're getting ripped apart and the crabs will feed on your eyes tonight. I'm gonna keep your hair and hang it from the top of this bridge, this same bridge that's cutting your balls and your rotten body in half."

As I rolled off his shuddering body into my own restful darkness, I hoped with all my heart he heard every word before he died.

XXI

As I walked down the center aisle with Donna Marilee Anne Cutter's arm in mine I had the distinct feeling that the same angels who saved her from harm were now happily cavorting around us here in the Little Church by the Sea. Only a small number of people were in attendance. Aleena Wakins sat toward the rear in case her new baby should make a fuss. James was at her side wearing his special wise-guy grin.

Malka was there with her lady love as was Raymond Casper with his. Sharon Stern sat on the right side of the aisle, crying softly. Laurie Noble was on the left, with her three year old.

Father Wood, older now, graciously accompanied Marilee's mother on the flight to Florida, at my insistence. Marilee's father was dead and the reunion circumstances with Mother Cutter had been faced, embraced with incredible joy and were as fully resolved as complex events ever are. Cal Brisboy was there, as was August Winkler and Alan Barber, each with his lady.

Donald Simms, Bunny Brewster and Camille Emerson sat together looking as happy as people are supposed to be at weddings, even small weddings in small churches.

I felt surprisingly happy recognizing the satisfaction my most peculiar profession has brought me, knowing I had found my place. M. Locke Stone, Consulting Philosopher, was in business to stay.

Donna and I reached the tall, gangling, smiling pastor who had been a grade school chum of Mark's. He put his hand out to join Donna's hand with Mark's, who stepped in from the right as I stepped back while my two best friends spoke their vows.